THE UNITED FEDERATION MARINE CORPS

BOOK 4: REBEL

Colonel Jonathan P. Brazee
USMCR (Ret)

Semper Fi Press

A Semper Fi Press Book

January 2015

ISBN-13: 978-0692365908 (Semper Fi Press)

ISBN-10: 0692365907

Printed in the United States of America

This is a work of fiction. All of the characters, names, incidents, organizations, and dialogue in this novel are either the products of the author's imagination or are used fictitiously.

Acknowledgements:
I want to thank all those who took the time to pre-read this book, catching my mistakes in both content and typing. I want to thank Tom Rogers, my content editor, and John Baker, my copy editor, for catching my many typos and mistakes. Any remaining typos and inaccuracies are solely my fault.

Original Cover Art by Panicha Kasemsukkaphat

Chapter 1

Michiko MacCailín slowly took off her ballet shoes, grimacing at the bloody mess her feet had become. These were special order handmade Rostov's, supposedly the most comfortable *pointe* shoes available, and that had cost her almost 150 credits, but her feet had still taken a beating while she practiced her *bourrée.*

She started removing the bandages that she had wrapped around each toe and used to pad the other pressure points. With the blood, at least the bandages came off easily. Taking some wipes out of her kit, she cleaned her feet off, wincing as the solution in the wipes hit the raw flesh. She took another can out of her kit, and the cool spray of the NovaSkin was a relief. In another three hours or so, her feet would be healed, ready for the next torture session.

Michi looked up from where she was sitting along the wall of the studio. Melinda and Taro were working on their *cambrè* press lift, Melinda arching gracefully back as Taro lifted her with one hand. Taro was Michi's cousin, and the MacCailín family size was an advantage to him as he easily pressed the 38kg Melinda.

The family genes hadn't done Michi any favors, though. She looked past the two dancers to her reflection in the mirror on the far wall, subconsciously slouching as if to become smaller. It didn't do much good. At 1.85 meters and 68kg, Michi was not a small girl, and for a female ballet dancer, that was not good. As she had matured from a lithe dancing sprite into a woman, she had taken to wearing loose T-shirts to the studio, but those could not hide the swell of her breasts, the widening of her hips. She had been a budding prima ballerina at twelve years old, the best dancer among the juniors in the company. At 19, she was too big to partner with any of the boys and relegated to dancing alone in the chorus.

Michi watched the petite, breastless Melinda being pressed again and again in the air while Artair, the troupe's balletmaster observed and critiqued.

It just isn't fair, she thought for the thousandth time.

It wasn't so long ago that Artair spent a good portion of his day critiquing her. Now, he generally ignored her.

It wasn't as if Michi could no longer dance. Michi also had the MacCailín family athleticism, and she had adjusted well to her changing center of gravity as her body matured. But ballet was a traditional art, and big girls had no place in it. It had been this way for over 600 years, and it wasn't going to change on some backwater planet in the Federation.

If she weren't so stubborn, Michi would have taken Artair's advice to move on. She could have tried ballroom or synchro, two dance forms in which tall girls were accepted. She could have gone into volleyball, five, or mixed martial arts, all sports in which she had dabbled. But ballet was her passion, and she refused to give up.

The fact that her body attracted the attention of most of the men she met was lost on her. To Michi, her body, that very athletic, skilled body that allowed her to complete even the most difficult ballet move, was a traitor.

She sighed and put on her street shoes. Standing up, she gathered her kit. No one said anything as she made her way along the mirrored wall and out of the studio. With winter still hanging on, the day was brisk at about 8 degrees, and that lifted Michi's spirits. She liked it cold much better than the hot, humid summer days that could stifle Kakurega. She contemplated running home to change, but a quick glance at her PA told her she didn't have time if she was going to catch the first speech. Sniffing her armpit, she decided she wasn't too rank, and her tights and sweatshirt would not be totally out of place. She tried to call Franz, but there was no answer. Michi was not surprised. Franz would be focusing on the demonstration, and his PA would probably be refusing incoming calls.

Prosperity Square was normally only a ten minute walk from the studio, but as she got closer, the mass of people streaming in made the going slower. Michi was surprised at the turnout. Each demonstration had pulled more and more people, but this looked like a huge jump. Maybe the Workers' Rights Party was beginning to find a message that resonated. That, or maybe Propitious

Interstellar Fabrication, Inc.'s ability to cow their indentureds and other employees was finally fading.

As both a Highland Clan member and a *Kaitakusya*[1], Michiko was a free citizen. Both of her families had come to Kakurega long before the charter was granted to Propitious Interstellar. The Kaitakusya had left Tanda for a new beginning on Kakurega about at the same time as the Highlanders came to farm the lush planet, and both groups easily mixed. When the charter was granted to the company, both groups stayed, and now, most of the First Families provided services for Propitious Interstellar. They were dependent on the corporation for their livelihoods, but not under its yoke.

Michi was aware of the issues the indentured, or Class 4[2] employees, had with Propitious Interstellar. She couldn't very well be in a relationship with one of the Workers Rights Party's leading figures and not be aware. Franz Galipili was only 25, but he had quickly taken a position of leadership in the party, his ability to arouse emotions as he spoke a vital asset. Franz was an indentured, so technically, he was breaking the law by speaking out, but throughout history, all revolutionaries were criminals in the minds of their masters.

As a free citizen, Michi didn't feel oppressed. But she wanted to support Franz, so she showed up at each of his rallies.

Michi made it into the square and slowly worked her way forward to the platform that had been erected in front of the 10 meter-tall statue of the Propitious Interstellar corporate logo. This wasn't really the most logical spot from which to address the crowd

---

[1] *Kaitakusya:* essentially a pioneer or explorer.

[2] Class 4 Employees. Federation regulations classify civilian employment. Class 1 employees are free citizens who can quit as they chose. Class 2 are employees who owe time to a corporation in return for training or schooling. Class 3 employees are temporary or contract employees who work for a specific period of time. The do not get the same benefits as Class 1 employees. Class 4 are termed "indentured." They owe money for transportation or other considerations, and must work to pay off the debt. They have minimal rights, and their indentured term can be adjusted due to additional debts incurred.

in the square, but the symbolism was not lost on Michi. That had to be the work of Tamberlain Jaderon. The old man had finally worked off his indenture and was a free citizen, but his keen mind was an asset as he continued to support the party.

Tamberlain saw Michi approach the platform and gave her a smile and a nod. He nudged Franz who turned and saw her. Despite the hubbub, Franz quickly came to the edge of the platform and leaned down for a quick kiss.

"Hey, Chipper, glad you could make it," he told her, reaching out to stroke her long black hair.

Franz was the only person to call her that. The two had met at an All Hallows party, and Michi had been dressed as some sort of oversized chipmunk. She had originally intended on being a squirrel, but when Yuzuki, her little sister told her she looked like a trinocular, she added stripes to set her off. Ever since, Franz had called her "Chipper."

"Good turnout," she said, sweeping an arm to take in the still growing crowd.

"Even the jacks[3] came out to play," Franz said, tilting his head over his shoulder.

Michi hadn't seen the jacks when she walked up. There had to be close to 50 of them, blocking B Street, the main route from the square to corporate headquarters at One Propitious Interstellar. They had on riot gear and looked oppressive to her.

"Are they going to cause trouble?" she asked.

"I doubt it. What are they going to do? The people are just gathered to listen to our message. I think they just want to make sure we don't make an impromptu march up to One Propitious Interstellar."

"As if anything you do is impromptu," Michi said with a laugh.

"Well, you know how it is," Franz said. "Impromptu, planned, it all comes out in the wash. Glad you made it, Chipper. With my beautiful muse here, I will be inspired."

Franz' compliments were always over-the-top, Michi thought, but she still liked them. Franz could have his pick of fiancés. He

---

[3] Jacks: Slang for company security personnel

was handsome, charismatic, and while an indentured, he was one with his own type of power. The fact that he had picked Michi was a mystery to her, but one she appreciated. She had even broached the subject with her father about buying out Franz' contract. She didn't know if Franz would even accept, even if her father broke down and agreed, but if they ever set a date for their wedding, it would be far easier if he was a free citizen.

Someone called for Franz' attention, and with a quick kiss on the top of her head, he stood back up and went to take care of whatever emergency had arisen. Michi made her way slowly to the side of the platform where she could watch. For once, her height was an advantage. If Melinda had been there, she would need Taro to lift her if she was to see anything. The thought of Taro, lifting Melinda in a graceful *cambrè* press lift while Franz and the other speakers railed against Propitious Interstellar struck Michi as funny, and she laughed out loud. An older man standing in front of her looked around at her as she laughed, his expression disapproving. Michi stuck out her tongue at the man, who grimaced and turned away, ignoring Michi's louder laughter at his reaction.

It was another five minutes before the scratchy recording of the Propitious Interstellar anthem started blasting out over the crowd. It was Propitious Interstellar policy that for any gathering of over 20 company personnel, the anthem had to be played. Many people thought that this should be ignored at the rallies, but Tamberlain had convinced the rest to adhere to the requirement. First, it served to leave the jacks with one fewer reason to take action, and second, the way they sang the anthem was a protest itself. With a terribly scratchy recording playing, people took to trying to outdo each other in singing as off-key as possible. It was getting to be a highlight of any rally. So far, with the letter of the regulations being followed, Propitious Interstellar had chosen to ignore the farcical singing.

Michi joined in the singing. As graceful as she was physically, her singing voice left a lot to be desired, and if she sang off-key, well, who was to say that it wasn't purposeful? As a free citizen, she didn't even have to sing, but it was fun, and she got into the counter-spirit of it.

. . . for the good of all mankind, Propitious Interstellar Fabrication!

What a joke, Michi thought as the final strains died away. Propitious Interstellar was a corporation beholden to its shareholders. "For the good of all mankind" was not in their corporate policies.

Getting to be a regular revolutionary, aren't we, she thought as she caught her criticism of the company.

Her father would not approve. As a First Family, the MacCailíns made a very good living off of Propitious Interstellar. Her father had a small fitting company that repaired the nozzle valves on fabricators, and he charged the company the going rates for the work. It was enough to make the family quite comfortable. Except for her Uncle Delwyn—who imported luxury food goods for sale to other free citizens, including Propitious Interstellar management—all her many uncles and aunts worked providing services to the mighty corporate giant.

The corporation needed the free citizens other than its employees to provide goods and services, and all free citizens were not limited for their own purchases to the corporate stores. They could spend their money pretty much anywhere they pleased, and given the outrageous prices at the corporate stores, no sane person would buy anything from them.

The corporate store model was one of the major complaints of the WRP. Given the wages allotted to the indentureds, it was difficult for them to work off their indenture as long as they kept piling up debt at the stores. But people had to eat, they had to get clothed, they had to sleep somewhere. Only 31% of Propitious Interstellar's indentureds ever worked off their servitude, a rate far below that of most Federation corporations.

With the anthem over, Franz took the stage to welcome the people. This was just a quick warm-up. He would give his real speech later. But he introduced two other indentureds, "regular" people who had sad stories to tell about how they'd been treated by Propitious Interstellar. This had become part and parcel of each rally. Tamberlain said it was to personalize the issue, to remind people that this affected each and every one of them.

The first person to talk was a middle-aged lady who had been close to paying off her indenture when she contracted a respiratory condition, one that was common among the granular fabricators. The medical treatment, even though the condition was undoubtedly caused by her work, was not covered by Federation regulations, so she had to pay for the treatment, setting her freedom calendar back at least five years.

The Federation did have regulations that protected workers, including indentureds, but there always seemed to be a loophole, and indentureds didn't have the funds to hire lawyers to fight for them. Job-related injuries and illnesses were supposed to be treated at no charge to the workers, but unlike the workers, the corporations did have lawyers on staff, and in this woman's case, they argued that her disease was a precondition. The Federation advocate found for Propitious Interstellar, to no one's surprise.

While Michi could feel for her, she was not as impressed with the next guy, a young man who seemed to rail at the very concept of the indentureds. Michi was not going to bring it up, not to anyone in the crowd and not to Franz later that evening, but she wondered why the guy was complaining. No one forced him to sign on with Propitious Interstellar, after all. It was his choice, and his contract with Propitious Interstellar explicitly stated that he had to pay off his indenture. That seemed pretty cut and dry to her.

The guy finally quit complaining, and then it was time for the main speakers. Cheri Baliles was first as the party adjutant. She was a former indentured, but now a free citizen, as were most of the party hierarchy. Franz was an exception. People currently indentured usually didn't have the time to contribute to the party, and they had more restrictions on what they could do, what they could say.

Cheri announced that the noted human rights champion, Henry Jugos, had finally gotten his entry denial for Kakurega overturned. It had taken over a year in the courts, but Propitious Interstellar could not stop him from coming, and he would be holding several rallies over the coming months. This raised a big cheer from the crowd. She went over the coming schedule and other administrative issues. Michi tuned her out. She was here for Franz, and that was about it. She felt bad for some of the conditions suffered by the indentureds, but it really wasn't her fight. Instead of listening, she looked over the crowd trying to see if she could spot corporate shills. Everyone knew they were in the crowd, but knowing and identifying were two different things. Michi spotted one fervent young woman: her eyes seemed too focused, her fervor too forced.

She's got to be one, Michi thought. That or she really was dedicated to the cause.

Cheri gave way to Hokkam Franchesi, the planet chapter chairman. Hokkam had been a Class 3 employee, not quite an indentured, but not quite a free citizen, either. He had been a skilled technician who owed five years of service to Propitious Interstellar for his training. Unlike indentureds, his five years was just that: five years. After that, he converted to a Class 1 employee, a free citizen in reality instead of just theory. He'd taken the mantle of chapter chairman a year ago, and since then, the rallies and protests had become more frequent and better organized.

Unlike an indentured, Class 1 employees could be fired, but for whatever reason, Hokkam still had his job. Michi would have thought that Propitious Interstellar would have let him go the minute he took over the WRP.

She glanced at her PA. The rally would end in another 20 minutes, and Franz hadn't even started to talk yet. She knew he would be getting worked up. He seemed so in control that few knew that he still got nervous before speaking to a crowd. He was great with small groups of people, but large groups somewhat intimidated him. He focused on a few people he knew and pretended that he was speaking only to them. That was another reason Michi came to the rallies. She was happy to let Franz focus on her.

Finally, it was his turn. The crowd visibly perked up. Part of this was that Franz was such an engaging speaker. But a bigger part, Michi thought, was that he was an indentured, just like much of the crowd. He hadn't paid his debt off—wasn't even close.

Michi shifted her position to the front of the platform. Franz caught her eyes, and smiled. She knew he was getting ready to use her as his focus. He would let his eyes roam over the crowd, but in his mind, he was just having a conversation with her.

"Friends! Thank you for coming out on this brisk evening. Luckily, we've got enough hot air up here to warm everyone up."

The crowd dutifully laughed. They were used to Franz' demeanor by now. Some people thought his folksy attitude and self-depreciating style was all an act, but Michi thought that was the real Franz. He really was a humble man. Humble, but on a mission, one he would never quit until he succeeded. He wanted to serve his fellow workers, and that compassion was only one of the reasons Michi loved him. A "good" man was a term bandied about too easily, but with Franz, nothing else fit. He was a good man through and through.

"We've heard some good news today. Henry Jugos coming is a really great thing for us. The fact that the courts sided with him against Propitious Interstellar is a sign, I want to think, that the Federation is finally shifting our way, at least in upholding the law. The corporations are not the law, and they cannot pick and choose which laws they will follow and which ones they'll ignore.

"But this is just one tiny chink in the corporate armor. Propitious Interstellar Fabrication is not about to reverse its standing policies just because Henry is getting involved. We have to force Propitious Interstellar to change. We have to force the Federation to uphold the law. And if Propitious Interstellar won't listen to us, we have to take our case right to the top," Franz said, using one arm to point up past the ranks of jacks and towards One Prop Inter Fab.

As he said that, the jacks shifted in their ranks. Franz and those nearest B Street saw the movement.

"See that, the thought of us confronting the Propitious Interstellar leadership gets their hired guns nervous. Well, we are going to confront them. We will not stand by as they abuse the system, making slaves out of us. Slavery has been banned for over 300 years, so why are we slaves for Propitious Interstellar Fabrication, Incorporated today? We won't stand for it."

The crowd erupted into cheers and clapping. It kept going on, and finally, Franz had to hold up his arms to quiet them down.

"My friends, Propitious Interstellar needs us. Without us, the stream of goods flowing into the marketplace, and more importantly, the stream of credits flowing into the corporate coffers, would cease. I ask, what would happen if we just stopped working? How could Propitious Interstellar survive?"

Michi swallowed hard when she heard that. A strike was patently illegal, and Franz was skirting close to the edge. He could be arrested and jailed under Federal charges if he was convicted of instigating a strike. She wanted to catch his eye and motion for him to calm down, but he was on a roll. She looked over to Hokkam to see if he would put the brakes on Franz, but the chairman was simply smiling and nodding his head.

"What would they do?" Franz continued. "They could not survive, and they know it. And that, my friends, is our leverage. Our labor, our sweat, the very thing that puts those profits in the bank."

Franz was interrupted again as clapping filled the square. Once again, he had to hold up his hands to quiet the crowd down.

"I am not saying we should crush Propitious Interstellar or destroy it. We just need to get them to treat us according to the law at the least, and as partners at best."

There was stirring in back of the speakers' platform. Franz turned around to look behind him before turning back to the crowd.

"The PI goons evidently don't like the idea of us being valued partners with the company. But just keep calm folks. We've done nothing wrong."

The jacks? What are they doing? Michi wondered, craning her neck to see over the platform.

"Calm down, everyone. Don't interfere with them," Franz told the crowd.

Michi felt panic start to rise in her, a welling from deep in her gut that threatened to take over her body. Franz hadn't actually crossed any line, but he still was an indentured, and if the jacks wanted to take him into custody, they would. Michi was sure nothing Franz had said would hold up in even a Propitious

Interstellar admin hearing, but people had the habit of falling down a lot of stairs while in jack custody.

Cheri and a few others moved forward to stand in solidarity with Franz. Hokkam, however, actually edged further back on the platform, away from Franz.

Chicken shit chairman, Mishi thought as she moved forward, intending to join Franz on the platform. Since Michi was a free citizen and not an employee, the jacks had very little authority over her, and she had vague ideas of trying to protect her fiancé.

There was shouting in back of the platform and some screams as the jacks moved forward in lockstep, pushing aside anyone in their way.

"Don't resist!" Franz shouted out. "Let's see what they have to say."

Michi pulled herself up onto the platform. From the higher vantage point, she could see the massed jacks bulling their way forward, several people falling down in front of them to be trampled under. Other people had turned and were trying to flee, but the mass of others in the crowd worked as a barrier.

"*Officers,*" Franz shouted out, sarcasm oozing from his voice, "no one is offering any resistance. If you want to talk with me, just come on up. No one will stop you," he said, holding his hands out as if he were going to be cuffed.

Michi was walking across the platform to join Franz when the first shot rang out. She didn't know from where it was fired, or even that it was a shot at first. It registered with her, but only peripherally. The fusillade that immediately followed was different, though. The jacks had opened up and bodies were falling in front of their ranks.

"Franz!" Michi screamed as she bolted into a run to reach him.

"Stop firing! Stop firing! We are not resisting!" Franz shouted, his mic turned up high so his voice reverberated throughout the square.

He turned towards the jacks, running to the back of the platform.

Panic erupted through the crowd as people started screaming and pushing to flee. More shots rang out from the jacks, and Michi saw more bodies fall.

"Get down, Franz!" she shouted, just steps behind him.

"I surrender, I—" Franz shouted, his voice cutting off as the front of his head exploded into a gout of blood and brain matter.

Michi let out a mindless scream of terror as she closed the last few steps to her fiancé. She fell on his motionless body, pulling him up and into her lap.

No, no, no!

Franz was limp in her arms. There was a small hole in the back of his head, and as she turned him over, she slid into tunnel vision. His entire forehead was gone.

"Get an ambulance!" she shouted to no one in particular. "He needs to get into regeneration. I'll pay for it!"

She was unaware of the screaming, the firing. She was unaware when the firing stopped. All she saw was Franz, his powerful body limp and lifeless in her arms. Someone, maybe Cheri, came up and tried to talk to her, tried to take her arms from around Franz, but Michi pushed her away. She was not going to let go until Franz was in the hospital.

Somewhere in the back of her mind, she knew that no one could survive that amount of damage. There would be no regeneration. But she refused to acknowledge that.

When the jacks approached her, she screamed that she was a free citizen, that they could not take Franz. It took four jacks to pry her off of Franz. She fought them, but to no avail. They took Franz down off the platform and into a company ambulance that had driven up unnoticed bye Michi. As the doors of the ambulance closed, it was as if Michi was a marionette, with her strings cut. She collapsed into Cheri's arms.

She was unaware when her father arrived, when she was helped into his hover, when she got home. She was given a sedative and put to bed where she mercifully lost consciousness.

Chapter 2

"Are you OK?" Cheri asked as she got out of the taxi in front of the church and hurried up to Michi.

"No, but as good as can be expected," Michi responded.

The last few days had been a blur. After Franz had been killed—murdered—Michi had been briefly held and questioned until her father, with Ham Harris, the family lawyer in tow, arrived at Propitious Interstellar's holding cell and demanded her release. She had been taken to St. Graeme's for a check-up, been sedated, and then taken home.

When she woke the next day, the enormity of what had happened finally hit her, and she broke down and cried, alone in her bedroom. A couple of hours later, her mother poked her head in the room, and seeing Michi awake, convinced her to get out of bed and come out to the kitchen for coffee and a bite to eat. Only her mother and Talla, the family maid, were in the house. Her father was at work, her sister at school. It didn't seem right that they were just going about their normal routine at such a time.

When her mother told her that the company jacks would not release Franz' body, Michi almost ran out of the house to confront the bastards, but her mother held her back, telling her the union was working on it. Franz was an indentured, so the union did not officially have any capacity to be involved, but as they represented the 65% of free citizen employees of Propitious Interstellar, the company paid attention.

It still took two more days, but finally, Franz' body was released. With no family on the planet, Hokkam and Cheri had accepted custody, and the funeral had been planned for the next day.

Cheri hugged Michi, murmuring, "I know, dear. We're all devastated about this, too."

"What's going to happen now? When's the inquiry?" Michi asked.

"Hokkam's going to be working on that. He's really taking this hard, you know, considering, so it might take him awhile to get his thoughts in order."

"Considering? Considering what?"

"Oh, that's right. You wouldn't know," Cheri said, looking to where Hokkam was getting out of another taxi. "He feels personally responsible for Franz' death."

"Why?" Michi asked, momentarily confused.

"Well, it was him that told Franz to up the ante, to mention force and hint at a strike. Hokkam thought it was time to elevate the pressure, and if Franz got arrested, it would bring more attention to our cause. He never thought there would be any shooting."

"Arrested? Franz thought he was going to be arrested?"

"We thought it would be a possibility, yes. I'm so sorry, dear. If I had known what would happen, of course I would have stopped it," Cheri said, tears forming in her eyes.

"And Hokkam told him to go ahead anyway?" she asked, anger beginning to burn away some of the lassitude that had taken over her soul since Franz' death.

"It wasn't his fault," Cheri started. "Franz knew the risk, and he wanted to do it. Hokkam just—"

"Michiko, dear, I want to tell you again how sorry I am about this tragedy," Hokkam said as he came up, cutting off Cheri.

He gave Michi a perfunctory hug and a peck on each cheek as Michi recoiled ever-so-slightly. A stark vision of Hokkam, edging back from Franz just before the firing started splashed in her mind.

Not only does he tell Franz what to say, but then he hides from the consequences, Michi realized.

Still, she allowed Hokkam to kiss her cheeks and express his regrets. She was saved from listening to more of his BS by the acolyte that came out and announced that the service was about to start. She linked arms with Cheri and steeled herself to enter the nave.

As a member of The Clan, Michi was also a practicing member of The Kirk,[4] although as The Clan and the *Kaitakusya* had

---

[4] The Kirk: The Church of Scotland.

intermingled, Shinto was also observed by many. An amalgamation of religions was in the best tradition of *Shinbutsu shūgō*,[5] after all. She had never been in one of the planet's Roman Catholic cathedrals, though, and was not sure of how they did things. So she was relieved to see the closed casket in the front of the apse. She wasn't sure how she would have handled it if Franz had been in an open casket as she had heard was done elsewhere.

Cheri escorted her to the second pew where they both took a seat. Michi was annoyed when Hokkam stopped at the same pew, and the two of them had to scootch over to give him room to sit, but she tried not to let it show.

The service started, and most of it went by in a blur. The priest said some words, there was the singing of some hymns, and various prayers were made. It was actually quite similar to what took place in Kirk funeral services, which shouldn't have been surprising as the Church of Scotland was essentially formed from the evangelical Presbyterian Free Church way back in the 1800's, Old Reckoning. Presbyterian churches shared much of the same litany with Roman Catholicism.

Michi stood up, kneeled, and followed along with the gathered mourners more by rote than by intention. After Hokkam stood up to say what a great man Franz was, Michi's thoughts turned towards revenge. Not against Hokkam. He was just a cowardly ass. But revenge on Propitious Interstellar Fabrication, Inc., the ones who caused all of this. She didn't know what she would do, yet, but only that the company had to pay.

As Michi sat in a House of God, her thoughts were not on Christian forgiveness, but on vengeance.

---

[5] *Shinbutsu shūgō*: elements of various religions incorporated in a syncretic fashion

Chapter 3

Michiko pinned the red wig she'd bought at Harrelson's into place and then carefully pulled the hood of her cozy up and over her head. She checked the mirror one more time, but even with the wig, her face was deep within the hood, out of sight.

She checked the rolled tissue she has taped inside each Clodder, up against the outer heel. Both were secure, so she slid in her feet, careful not to dislodge the taped tissue. She took a hesitant step in the heavy work boots. It felt different, at least. Whether it would spoof the surveillance cameras or not by giving her a different gait, she didn't know. Super Agent Franny Justice had used the technique in "The Pullman Gambit," but flicks didn't always adhere to reality.

Michi pushed open her door a fraction and listened. The house was quiet. She slipped out, crept down the stairs, and out the kitchen door in back. She checked her PA: 11:45. She had a hike in front of her. If she drove her Sullivan, the hover's position would be recorded and could be evidence against her if things went wrong. For the same reason, she couldn't very well call up a taxi, so it was a five km hike into the entertainment district.

One thing she hadn't considered was that with two cozies on, she was getting pretty hot. The night was cool, but the exercise and extra clothing was making the hike rather uncomfortable. She slowed down her pace to keep from overheating.

Within 30 minutes, she was out of the residential area, the lights of the Slab visible ahead. She didn't head directly there, though; she turned left, instead, down G Ave, coming across the first people she had seen since she left her home. A man and a woman were staggering past, leaning together for support, clearly drunk, and both in very good moods. Michi waited until they passed, then stepped into the small garden in front of the Krishna shrine. This was an area that Michi was positive was not under routine surveillance. She gratefully pulled off her cozy and sweat pants before stashing them in back of the far right bench. Underneath, she had on another cozy, this one with the Firebird logo of Lipper University on it. She felt a little weird wearing it. Michi was not a big proponent of interscholastic rivalry, but still, the Firebirds were the "other" university in town as opposed to Michi's own University of Holcomb Diamonds.

She settled this cozy's hood around her face and then pulled out a few strands of the red wig so they were visible.

You can still quit, she told herself. *Nothing's gone too far yet.*

But she didn't turn back. Taking a deep breath, she walked around the shrine and went out on F Ave, a totally different person than the one who had entered from G Ave. Super Agent Justice would have been proud of her.

It still took her another 20 minutes before she entered the Slab. It was almost 1:00 AM, and the party animals were out in force. Consequently, the jacks were, too, keeping the peace. Michi stood taller as she wandered through the bars, restaurants, hookah dens, and music venues, trying to find a target. Two drunk frat boys hooted at her, each raising his hand in the Firebird salute, but she ignored them. Unfortunately, the jacks were ignoring her, too. She tried to catch a few of their eyes, but with the hood over her face, a fat lot of good that did.

She hadn't really thought things through. She had a burning desire to extract some payback, but she didn't really have a detailed plan. Even if she could catch the attention of a jack, what was she going to do? There were too many people out and about for Michi to do anything.

There was a place, though, where things were quieter. Michi and her schoolmates had driven through the Gut a few times for kicks but had never even got out of the hover, much less wandered about. She had to push down a little tremor that tickled at the back of her mind. The area had a reputation, and good girls didn't go there.

At that, Michi laughed out loud. Whatever she was, whatever she was about to become, a "good girl" wasn't it. She straightened her shoulders and made her way past the city's elite as they sipped their specialty drinks and listened to the latest zhoul or boxbox tunes. Michi had spent more than a few evenings herself doing the very same, but now she looked at the partygoers with more than a little disdain.

How could they party when the PI jacks could get away with murder? she wondered.

Michi walked several blocks more before turning right on Craxton. Immediately, the lights of the Slab disappeared.

Welcome to the Gut!

Several shapes stood in the shadows, rentboys and rentgirls plying their trade. They stirred as Michi made her appearance, but no one approached her. She didn't look the part, she guessed. She was not dressed as one of them, nor did she look like a party girl out for a fling. Party girls did not hide behind cozies, and they did not wear steel-toed Clodders. It was just as well. Michi wanted to quietly fade into the further recesses where she could lay her trap.

A drunk came out of the darkness, making Michi recoil, but other than a slurred, "Hiya, baby," the man was too far gone to be really interested.

One huge advantage of the Gut was that there was no surveillance there. The company put it up, but the rentboys and girls immediately took it down. The fact that PI bigwigs came into the Gut themselves probably accounted for the fact that the jacks didn't seem too dedicated to keep replacing the cameras. What happened in the Gut was not illegal, other than the inherent tax avoidance and some drug use, but still, not too many people in high places wanted their presence in the Gut widely known.

After a few minutes of wandering, Michi found her own spot: a small, alley leading back to nowhere. She positioned herself at the front of the alley, a trapdoor spider monitoring her web. If a civilian came by, she eased back until she was in the darkness, only to edge back out again as they passed. It took more than an hour, and Michi was beginning to second guess everything, when a lone jack came sauntering by.

It was common knowledge that jacks sometimes demanded freebies from the rentboys and girls. Everyone knew it was true—at least people repeated it, so it must be true. Everyone also knew that college kids were in high demand in the trade. So Michi stepped out farther in to the light, so the iridescent Firebird logo on her cozy seemed to take on a life of its own. A jack, walking alone in the Gut. A uni rentgirl. This was a no brainer.

Only the jack didn't even slow down. He walked around Michi without saying a word.

"Uh, excuse me?" she said, afraid to lose the man.

With a sigh, the man stopped, and with his body posture screaming resignation, turned around.

"Yes, miss? Is there something I can do for you?" he asked without enthusiasm.

Michi had just realized that what they all knew about the Gut may be more rumor than fact, and she immediately changed tack.

"My friend, he's, well, his dad's a VP with the company. We bought some light, but something happened. My friend's back here, and he's in trouble."

The jack immediately became alert. Light was illegal, and possession carried a stiff punishment. And if the son of a company VP had taken it, well, the ramifications could be severe. As a jack, one of his jobs was to make sure none of the higher ups were ever embarrassed in any way.

"Yes, ma'am," he quickly said. "Where is your friend?"

"Back here," Michi said, pointing to the back of the alley.

The jack brushed past Michi, hurrying to find the VP's son. He got to the end of the alley and looked around in confusion. "Where?" he asked as he started to turn around.

Michi's roundhouse kick in her steel-toed Clodder caught the unsuspecting jack right below the chin and alongside the neck. The man fell bonelessly to the trash-laden cement alleyway. Michi followed through, pouncing on the man, giving the back of his head her elbow before she realized the jack was not resisting. Warily, she got up, giving him a nudge with her foot. The jack didn't react, and it was only then that Michi saw the angle to the jack's neck. This jack would never be getting up again.

Michi jumped back, her vision narrowing as she almost lost her balance. She had to take a few deep breaths to gather herself.

How the hell did that happen?

During Michi's short foray into MMA, she had knocked out exactly one person. In her second match, she had taken down her opponent and rained hammer fists down on the poor girl's head until the ref jumped in to stop the fight. Michi's other three wins and her one loss came as a result of the judges' decisions.

Michi knew how hard it was to get a solid enough strike for a knockout. Yet here, in this unnamed alley in the Gut, she had somehow, against all probability, broken the neck of a trained jack. She couldn't believe it.

She moved back to the jack, then reached forward, only hesitating a moment before placing her fingers on the man's neck, feeling for the carotid. There was nothing. He was dead.

Michi fell back onto her butt as she stared at the jack. He looked young, only a little older than her. She wondered what his name was. She felt numb, but not sorry, and that surprised her. She was a Clan girl, a First Family girl. She was supposed to go to school, choose a profession. First Family girls did not kill people.

Yet she felt no remorse. In fact, she felt a sense of pride beginning to build up within her, an ember flaring into life. She recalled how *satisfying* it felt when her foot connected with the jack's neck, how *solid* it felt.

She reached out with one foot and gave the body a kick. It jerked under her foot's impact.

I did that, you glaikit boaby![6] I did it! I took your worthless life! You weren't worth a hair on Franz' head, and now you're less than that!

She felt a surge of righteousness at what she had done. She knew the odds of what had just happened were infinitesimally small, so she wondered if there hadn't been something else guiding her, some other higher power at work here.

Michi wanted to stand up and scream into the night, a lioness celebrating her kill. She didn't know what kind of sensors the jack had, and she knew she should get out of there before his buddies came to look for him. Despite that, she had to stare at her victim for a few more moments, drinking in the sight and cementing it in her mind.

---

[6] *Glaikit boaby*: Old Scottish slang. *Glaikit* is stupid, and *boaby* is a somewhat derogatory term for a policeman. It can also mean penis.

She stood back up and went over to the body, reaching across to slide the jack's Jamison out of its holster. The Jamison was the standard issue sidearm for the Propitious Interstellar jacks. Some companies went on the cheap for their jacks, but not PI. The Jamison was a sweet firearm, able to send out both lethal and non-lethal beams with a high degree of accuracy. It was too bad that this jack wasn't carrying a rifle, but the Jamison was certainly no slouch as a trophy. Michi slid it in her cozy pouch pocket, and without another glance at the dead jack, left the alley. There were fewer figures—service providers and customers both—still out, but she tried to walk with a purpose that might forestall anyone reaching out to her. It must have worked as no one said a word.

In a few minutes she was back in the Slab, music still wafting out from various stages. The lights seemed too bright after the dimness of the Gut.

Two jacks came walking up to her, and for a moment, she wanted to bolt. She kept walking at them, going over the various kicks and strikes she could employ.

"Evening, miss," one of the jacks said as the two passed her.

Her heart pounding, she realized that taking the Jamison had been a stupid act of bravado. The gun bulged in her pocket, and if one of the jacks had seen it and searched her, her little war on the company would be over before it even started.

She debated tossing the gun, but that might be worse. Instead, she made her way back to the shrine where she had stashed her other clothes.

Michi almost trashed the Firebird cozy, but then thought better of it. The less evidence of her passing, the better. The redhead wig came off and was thrust into the pocket with the Jamison. She pulled on the other cozy and the sweat pants, and then slowly strolled out onto G Ave.

An hour later, she slipped back into her house and up to her room. She stripped down, hiding both the Firebird cozy and the Jamison in the back of the bottom drawer of her wardrobe.

Michi didn't even shower, but simply slipped between her sheets. Within moments, she was out, and for the first time since Franz had been killed, had an uninterrupted and deep sleep.

Chapter 4

"Do you have something to tell us?" Michi's father asked as she came in the door.

"No," she responded in a surly tone as she dumped her backpack on the couch.

What do they know?

She made as if to go to the kitchen anxious to get out of her parents' piercing stares.

"I think you do," he said, stopping Michi in her tracks.

"We got a call today, from the uni, asking if you were OK. They said you haven't been to class since, well, you know since when," her mother spoke up.

Relief swept through her. This wasn't good, but at least no one knew what had happened in the Gut last week, at least as far as her participation in it.

The murder of the jack wasn't a secret. It had hit all the news feeds, and scores of women had been gathered for questioning, most from Lipper U. There hadn't been a surveillance photo released, but the fact that it was mostly Lipper girls was pretty darn indicative that there was some sort of evidence of her with the Firebird cozy out there.

The jack's name was Gerile Fountainhead. He was 23 and a Navy vet who had been working for the company for only three months. A native of RKR, he left behind parents and a fiancé. Blah, blah, blah. Michi didn't care. He was not a person to her, just a slab of cold meat.

That surprised her, when she was honest with herself. She had always considered herself to be kind and caring, a good person. But some of that inherent goodness had vanished at the rally. She wasn't even sure she felt a twinge of remorse for killing the jack. For killing Gerile, she had to remind herself. He did have a name.

She turned back towards her parents, put on a melancholy face, then said, "I . . . I just have not been able to concentrate since

Franz was killed. My mind is not working right. I think I need time."

She saw her father's face soften. Bingo! She was going to get out of this.

Then she noticed her mother's eyes narrow. "And where have you been going every day, then?"

Michi wondered if she could bluff it out, then decided it was too likely that someone would have seen her, so she decided it was better to admit to something.

"I've been down at the WRP. They knew Franz, and they are working on getting the results of the investigation. I just feel better there."

That seemed to put a stop to her father's understanding.

"Michi, I hate to put my foot down, but you are going to have to stop going there. It was bad enough when you were dating Franz . . ."

"Not dating. We were engaged," she muttered under her breath.

". . . but what with everything that's happened, you need to divorce yourself from that group."

"But—"

"But nothing! I know you were all hot and bothered when your firebrand was up there, all moral-like. But his cause is not our cause. His fight is not our fight."

"So you are going to ignore all the injustice that is going on?" she shouted at her father.

"Injustice? Is it injustice that Propitious Interstellar pays our bills? That they pay for this house? For yours and Yuzuki's education? For that Sullivan you got for your birthday last year? Is that injustice?" he thundered back.

This was an old argument. Most of the First Families made their livelihoods in service or selling to Propitious Interstellar. Some people, especially from the Yamaguchis, went on to join the company itself in the management ranks. The First Families, comfortable in their lives, liked the status quo and were afraid of anything upsetting the apple cart.

"And the indentureds? What about them?" she asked.

"What about them? They signed contracts to escape whatever *shite*-hole they came from. The company is supposed to rescue them, then let them walk? That's ridiculous, girl. And what are the Class Fours? Twenty-five percent of the workforce? Maybe 15 % of the planet's population? No lassie, this is not our fight. And with all the attention on your rabble-rousing friends, we don't need pressure being put on the family because your latest cause has you fomenting trouble."

Michi just stared at her father, trying to form a response.

"Listen to him, Michi," her mother said. "Think of the family. We do not need the attention, especially with contract renewals coming up."

"You two just don't get it, do you? All you think about is your bank accounts, and to get that, you bow down to the almighty Propitious Interstellar and let them stick it up your arses. There is such a thing as justice, as human rights, even if you're too fat and happy to realize it," she told her parents with conviction.

With that, she walked past her parents, opened the front door, and stormed off into the evening.

Chapter 5

Michi looked at Prosperity Square. This was the first time she'd been back since Franz had been killed. It looked different, peaceful, and that pissed her off. The stands were down and the trash gathered, as if the company thought they could simply clean away the fact that her fiancé had died at that spot.

People moved through the square, going about their business. Several were sitting on benches, eating their lunches or going online. Some just sat, eyes closed and faces up, enjoying the spring sun.

Was she the only person to be angry? Was she the only one who had taken any steps in revenge?

Even at the WRP, it seemed to be business as usual. Michi had just left the office. Cheri had expressed her regret, and it seemed real. Hokkam actually had tears in his eyes as he hugged her. He offered his support in anything she needed. But what he couldn't offer was answers. The chapter was waiting for the company report on the incident.

As if that would be worth anything! The company would whitewash everything. Franz' death would an "unfortunate accident" caused by the protestors themselves. No one would be held accountable.

Michi shook her head in disgust.

Her dance gear kit hung from her shoulder. She had intended to try to hit the studio, where she would normally go to work off the stress, but as she stood in the square, the mood just wasn't in her. She sighed and walked over to one of the benches close to the spot where Franz had been killed. Nodding to the elderly lady sitting there sipping a tea, she sat down on the other end of the bench, facing the spot where the stage had been set up.

Right there, ten meters away, was the last spot where she had spoken with Franz, laughed with him, held his murdered body. She didn't know if there was anything, any essence of him left there, but she closed her eyes and forgot about the world. If any part of Franz was still there, she hoped she could somehow sense him for one last goodbye.

Chapter 6

Michi had to park in the street in front of the house. She recognized Reverend Calhoun's black Hyundai in the driveway and briefly wondered if her parents were getting another of their marriage "tune-ups," as her mother called them.

As soon as she walked through the door, though, all thoughts of parental discord faded. Not only was Reverend Calhoun sitting on the couch, but the Right Reverend Duncan, the moderator for the Kakurega presbytery, was there as well. Both honored men were sitting, sipping tea, and looking straight at her. Her mother was sitting to their side, while her father was standing with his back toward her.

He slowly turned around, his face blank. Taking a step forward, he reached down to the coffee table and picked up the Jamison Michi had taken from the dead jack.

"And what is this?" he asked calmly.

Michi's heart fell, and she almost stumbled.

"It's mine. I bought it. For self protection," she babbled.

"Self protection, lassie?" he asked as the other three looked on silently.

"Yes. There have been attacks on girls at school. Just last week, a girl was assaulted on the quad. I wanted protection, so I bought it."

"And this?" he asked, using the muzzle of the Jamison to lift a piece of grey clothing.

Half of a red firebird could be seen as the cozy hung in the air.

"It's a cozy, what of it?" she tried to bluster, but her heart wasn't in it.

"A Tipper University cozy and a sidearm issued to the company security forces. You needed both of these to protect yourself?" he asked, his voice even-toned, sounding calm.

Michi tried to raise the fire of anger. "And you're searching my things? How dare you!" she shouted.

"When it's to protect the family, damn right I do, young lady. And when you endanger us all, I will!" he shouted, throwing the Jamison to the side where it crashed into the big stone fireplace.

"Now Malcom," the Right Reverend said, standing up and taking a step toward him. "We spoke about this. Let's hear what Michiko has to say, how she obtained these. It might not be as you feert. We dinnae know all the facts, either with that sad story or with your lassie here."

He turned to Michi and said, "Now Michiko, please, come sit here. Tell us what happened, child. Did this weapon belong to Mr. Fountainhead? Did he do something to you? Don't be afraid, child. You can tell us."

Michi stared at the Right Reverend. He had only just started his one-year term as moderator, but Michi knew him as a church elder. He always seemed like a nice, righteous man. For a moment, she almost gave in, almost rushed to the couch beside him to pour out her story. She had been keeping it bottled in, and now she realized it was gnawing at her, making her into something of a bitch. She wanted to get it all out in the open.

She actually took a step before her rage, her Scottish *radge*, came flowing back, filling her arteries, taking over again. The Right Reverend didn't give a flying fuck for her. He was worried about fallout on the Clan and the rest of the First Families. He was hoping that the jack had assaulted her, that she had somehow killed the jack in self-defense.

"Yes, he assaulted me. Is that what you want to hear? He assaulted me, and I fucking killed him for that. And you know what? I'd do it again, I would!"

Michi knew that the jack, that Gerile Fountainhead had personally done no such thing. She was not that lost in her rage. But the jacks had assaulted her by taking her Franz. And Gerile was a jack. He'd probably been there that day at the rally. Maybe he'd taken the shot himself. That was good enough for her.

She was not going to sit there and kowtow to her parents, to the church leaders. She was not going to apologize. At least she had the balls to do something about injustice, and she was not going to meekly try to deny the *righteousness* of her actions.

She spun around, too incensed to speak and bolted for the door.

"If you leave now, dinnae come back!" her father shouted out as she ran outside.

Michi hit the unlock for the Sullivan, but the door would not open. She tried it again, but the door remained locked. Turning back, she couldn't see anyone. But she knew they were watching, and they had disabled her hover.

She leveled a kick that did nothing to the hover's side panel, then stalked around it to head into town. One thing was now obvious: she was on her own.

Chapter 7

"Cheri," Michi whispered into her PA.

She breathed a sigh of relief as the number connected. At least her parents hadn't cut off her comms, too.

"Yeah, Michi," Cheri's voice came over the line. "What's up?"

"I'm sort of in a bind here. My folks kicked me out of the house," she told Cheri, the fact that it was she that had stormed out by choice glossed over. "Can you put me up for a few days?"

There was dead silence on the other end of the line, then a hesitant, "Oh, Michi-girl, I don't know if that's such a good idea. We're under pretty heavy surveillance now, what with all the recent troubles, and you're still pretty clean of all the dirt. I think you staying with me now could cause some complications. You're sure you were kicked out? Your dad's just not angry for the moment?"

"No, I think it's permanent. He told me never to come back."

"What did you do? I've never met him, but Franz seemed to think he was pretty even-tempered, even if a bit conservative."

"Oh, it's a long story, but really, Cheri, I need someplace. I'm willing to take any heat that comes along with it," Michi said.

"It's not just you, Michi. Me, too. I've got to keep my nose clean. Bringing in the fiancé of Franz sends a pretty powerful message, one I'm really not anxious to send right now. They are still making random arrests over the jack murder, and I don't want to draw any more attention to me."

That took Michi aback. She and Cheri had gotten close over the last few weeks, and she had fully expected being able to crash at her place until she figured things out.

"You really have no place to go?" Cheri asked her.

"No place. Nada," she answered.

"OK, wait for a few minutes. I have an idea, but I need to check first. I'll call you back in five."

Michi broke the connection, none too pleased that the call hadn't gone as expected. She was in front of a Seven, so she went in to grab a Coke. It wasn't until she started to walk out that she wondered if her credit had been cut off as well. However, no alarms sounded as she walked through the sensors. The familiar buzz of a transaction relieved her. She pulled out her PA and checked.

Well, it wasn't totally normal. Michi had been on the family line of credit, able to charge pretty much whatever she wanted. Now, she had been shunted aside to a personal line with a limit of 50 credits per month. She knew that many people managed to survive on that, but she wasn't sure how they did it.

Her PA chimed as she took a swallow of the Coke, and she snorted out a stream of the drink as she grabbed the PA and opened the call.

"Michi, I've got a place for you. Do you know the Brown Bean on Gasperson?"

"Yeah, I know it."

"OK, I want you to go there. First, let me see what you've got on," she said.

Michi held out her PA and tilted it up and down so Cheri could see her.

"OK, fine. I see what you're wearing. Go to the Brown Bean, order a latte, and sit wherever you can. Someone in an orange jumpsuit will come and sit with you. If you both hit it off, you can shack up with her for awhile."

"What's with all the secret agent stuff? You're not coming?"

"No. We've got five jacks sitting outside right now. Hell, they've probably broken the scramble on this call, but no use making it any easier for them. Better you go alone without me. Let me know what happens, though."

Michi was still a little miffed. She had expected Cheri to welcome her with open arms. Instead, she was being sent to meet someone whose name she didn't even know. But beggars not being choosers and all, as the old saying went. She drained the Coke, threw the can in the bin, and started the walk to Gasperson.

Twenty minutes later, she walked in the door of the Brown Bean, the aromas assaulting her nose. She wondered if she really had to get a latte, but taking no chances, she placed her order. She grimaced at the 1.2 credit charge. That would never have fazed her before, but now, she knew she had to make some adjustments, at least until she could get her full credit line restored.

There was no one in an orange jumpsuit, so she found an empty table by the front window and settled in to wait. It was almost another 20 minutes before Miss Jumpsuit arrived. Orange was an understatement. It had multiple shades of orange and even some reds that somehow revolved around themselves along her arms and legs, giving the impression of fire. This girl was only 1.4 or 1.5 meters tall, and she couldn't have weighed more than 40 kg, but she was obviously not afraid to make a fashion statement. She got in line and ordered her drink, then looked around as if trying to find a seat.

She slowly made her way to Michi, pointed at the empty seat, and asked, "This seat taken?"

"Please," Michi said, trying to act nonchalant.

The girl took a sip, and without looking at Michi, said, "Baggy yellow sweats, an old faded grey cozy, ratty blue jump-ups. You must be Michiko. I'm Tamara, and Cheri tells me I need to give you a place to stay. So we might as well get at it."

She stood up and stared at Michi, her brilliant blue eyes barely above Michi's sitting eye level.

"Well, you coming?"

Michi didn't know what else to do, so she got up and followed Miss Jumpsuit, Tamara, out of the Brown Bean.

Chapter 8

"That's just not good enough," Michi said in exasperation.

"Calm down, Michi," Cheri told her. "We really are working on this."

"It seems to me that you're just sitting here waiting for the company to make its final report."

"Michiko, I want to assure you that we are doing all we can," Hokkam said.

Yeah, like you told Franz to instigate a strike, she thought.

"I loved Franz as a son, and I'm devastated about what happened. Every word I said at his funeral was true, and I will not rest until we uncover the truth. But you don't know how the game is played—"

"I can assure you that this is not a game," Michi snapped.

"No, of course not. Sorry, poor choice of words. What I mean is that you don't know how we deal with the company or the city offices. We can't just bull in. It takes finesse. We've already filed a protest with the city. We had a valid permit, so technically, the jacks had to protect us, and they didn't. So we will have a legal argument, but we have to wait first for the initial report. Once we see it, Su will go over it with a fine-tooth comb so we can choose our next course of action."

Tian Su was the chapter advocate and a member of the board. By reputation alone, Michi knew that if there was a legal opening that could be exploited, Su would find it.

"So you see, we are working on it. Please have some patience. Things are heating up, and if it looks like we're addressing those other issues right now, rest assured that we have not forgotten Franz. How could we?" Cheri asked.

Michi looked over at Rosario Del Mare, the chapter security chief. He was an easy person to blame as he was in charge of keeping the protestors safe. Rosario seemed to sense her blame, and his defenses were up. He hadn't said a word during the meeting but rather glared at her.

Kuso kurae[7], *ye boaby*, she thought, combining curse words from both sides of the family tree for greater effect. *If you would've done your job, my Franz would still be here, so take your glare and up your arse with it.*

She looked at the three chapter board members. They were cowards, all of them, professing to fight for justice, but afraid of the big, bad company. She was going to get nothing done here. If she wanted vengeance—more vengeance, that is—it would be up to her.

She stood up, cutting the meeting short. She almost sat right back down when all three let their relief show on their faces, but she realized that would do absolutely nothing. Cheri and Hokkam kissed her cheek goodbye, and Michi turned and stalked out of the office.

Michi had already extracted a degree of vengeance. She really hadn't intended to kill anyone, even if she had accepted it now as an unintentional consequence. It was something she was almost totally at ease with, but she wasn't sure she wanted to kill anyone else. If she were going to take any further action, she would have to figure out what would hurt the company most, and then how she could get that done.

---

[7] *Kuso kurae*: A Japanese term for "eat shit."

Chapter 9

Michi took a sniff of the tuna casserole. It was one of Talla's recipes, a real recipe, with real cooking, not just punching something into the fabricator. Michi was far from a domestic goddess, but frankly, she was going a little stir-crazy in Tamara's apartment. She had been Tamara's guest for two weeks: she had cleaned the condo five times, and this was her third attempt at manual cooking.

It wasn't Tamara who was the problem. Her new roommate was funny, intelligent, and a great companion. It was just the being cooped up, away from school and her friends, that ate at her. She had gone to the WRP several more times, but the bustle there as the staff considered their reactions to the ever-increasing pressure being levied by the jacks pointedly bypassed her. They didn't have much time for a girl who hadn't even been a member, but was merely a girlfriend of a member.

The casserole smelled good, at least, much better than her attempt at spaghetti puttanesca the night before. Tamara had tried to dutifully eat it, but after two bites, both girls had broken out into peals of laughter before dumping the sodden mess in the recycler. They'd dialed up breaded cutlets and a salad on the fabricator and opened a bottle of malbec instead.

Michi glanced at the old-fashioned cuckoo clock above the holo. Tamara would be home in another ten or fifteen minutes. She placed the casserole on the table so it would cool, then started to rush to the shower to clean up. She had stripped off her sweat top when she had to stop.

What am I doing? she thought. *We're not married!*

She shook her head as she grabbed the dirty top and pulled it back on. She must be going crazy. Even with Franz, Michi was far from meek and submissive. She resisted giving her pits a sniff. Tamara was just going to have to accept her, rank or not.

She plopped down on the overstuffed red couch and asked the house PA to turn on the news. The lead story was the four "hoodlums" who had been arrested for "civil disobedience" the day before. The teenagers had been taunting the jacks, and while it wasn't reported on the news, several jacks had beaten them senseless.

Michi felt a slight twinge of guilt, one she quickly suppressed. She knew she had instigated the current round of unrest when she killed that jack. She hadn't really intended to kill anyone, merely administer a beating, and despite the thrill she had felt at the time, it was still gnawing at her. She wished she could confide in someone. She had almost brought it up to Cheri two days before at the WRP, but Cheri was up to her ass in alligators, so Michi just let it lie.

"Hey there, roomie!" Tamara said as she came in the door. "Um, something actually smells good. You order take out this time?"

"Very funny, haha. I made it, and this time, you're going to love it."

"You sure? Cooking doesn't seem to be your forte, girl."

Tamara Veal was a Class One employee of the company, a free citizen. She had been born on the planet to two indentureds, and her parents were still under the yoke, but that status was not something that could be inherited. The courts had upheld that for the last 70 years, and it was accepted by even the most conservative corporation now.

Tamara still worked for PI, though. She was a component engineer working on QC for the organics used in a series of Propitious Interstellar's products. The job paid adequately, enough for her to pay for the condo and make payments on her parent's debt (which was twice as large now as when they'd signed their contracts).

Michi had been surprised at how close she had become to Tamara. Michi didn't make many female friends, and in many ways, Tamara was so very different than her. Petite, hard-working, and very fashion conscious, she seemed to be a polar opposite of the large, dress-in-whatever Michi. However, they shared a warped and wicked sense of humor, and Michi thoroughly enjoyed her company.

Tamara shucked her company overalls, leaving them in a pile on the floor. Wearing only a white tank and panties, Michi could see her myriad of tattoos. These were not temporary tats. They were done the old-fashioned way with ancient tattoo guns and covered almost all of her skin that was hidden by her work clothes. Michi had been shocked the first time she saw them, but she was also fascinated and wanted to examine them in more detail, but so far, she acted as if the tattoos were nothing out of the ordinary. Someday, though, she was going to get the background on all that skin art.

The two roommates bypassed the table, instead sitting down on the couch with the casserole between them, each digging in with a spoon. They finished up the previous night's malbec while watching a game show. Michi was smart, and she knew most of the answers to the questions, but the quicker Tamara usually beat her to the punch.

When the host asked the three contestants for the name of the first cloned dinosaur, Michi launched into the attack, jumping on Tamara with a pillow, smothering the smaller girl so Michi could yell out "Annabelle!"

Tamara struggled underneath Michi, but the smaller girl had no chance. Finally Michi let her up.

"You cheated!" Tamara yelled out. "And you spilled the food!" she added, taking a small handful of the spilled tuna casserole from the seat of the couch and flicking it a Michi.

"So sue me. I got the answer right, didn't I?"

"You know what they say? Payback's a motherfucker," Tamara said, licking the tuna residue off her fingers.

Michi was brought up in the Clan, and good Clan girls just didn't curse. She was somewhat fascinated at both how easily Tamara swore as well as her prodigious library of profanity.

"Hey, pass me the wine," Tamara told Michi.

"Sorry, all out," Michi said, holding the wine bottle upside down. "You got any more?"

"We drank it all? Oh well. Have you ever had Snow Wine?" she asked.

"Snow Wine? Never heard of it," Michi said, wiping the bit of casserole Tamara had flicked at her off of her face.

"Oh, you've got to try it. Farking brills!"

She jumped up and ran to the small pantry. She reached in and brought out an opaque blue bottle.

"This is a new synth from Iverson Beverage. We're getting the license to fabricate it, so we've got cases of it for development," she said, hopping over the back of the couch, landing in a sitting position.

"And you just happened to take some home?"

"QC, my darling, QC. I've got half of the organics going into it, so I have to know what the distilled product is like, right?"

"Good enough for me," Michi said, reaching for the bottle.

She took along swig, then handed the bottle back to Tamara.

Woah! That is pretty good! she thought.

"Not bad," she said instead.

"Not bad my grandmother's hairy snatch," Tamara exclaimed. "Well, if you only think it's not bad, then I guess you don't want any more," she added, tipping the bottle up for a swig.

"No, no, I didn't say that. I think I need to taste it again," Michi protested, grabbing the bottle.

The Snow Wine had more of a kick than Michi was used to, and she was feeling pretty comfortable when the game show ended and the hourly news minute came on. It was a quick snippet of the head of PI security stating that after an investigation, the security team that arrested the four "hoodlums" had been cleared of any wrongdoing.

"Oh, suck my balls," the half-drunk Tamara said to the holo image. "Cleared my ass."

"I feel sorry for the four boys," Michi said. "Seems like overkill, but they did sort of ask for it."

"Fuck they did. A month ago, the jacks ignore them. But with that drug killing of the jack in the Gut, the rest of the jacks are all on edge."

Michi's heart faltered a beat.

"We've never talked about that. What do you make of it?" Michi asked, trying to sound nonchalant.

"What, that some jack got jacked?" she said, laughing at her own little joke.

"No, really."

"What's there to think? Some stupid jack got involved with Light, taking payments, probably to look the other way. He pissed off the wrong people and got ghosted."

Michi felt the Snow Wine cloud her head. She knew she should just shut up and change the subject.

"No, that's not what happened," she said instead.

"And how would you know that, my dear friend," Tamara said, taking another long swallow before handing the bottle back to Michi.

"Because I did it."

"Because you did what?"

"Because I killed him," Michi said, feeling the weight of the world lifting off her shoulders.

"Ha, right! And I'm the Chairman of the Federation. Bow down before me!"

"Really, I did it. I killed him. And he wasn't involved with Light or anything like that."

Something in Michi's tone must have registered through Tamara's slightly muddled brain because she stopped, took the bottle of Snow Wine out of Michi's hands, and placed it on the table.

"What are you saying?" she asked calmly.

"I didn't know he would die. I was pissed about Franz, and I just wanted to jump a jack, to pay them back. But somehow, I kicked him too hard, and I broke his neck."

The momentary sense of relief she felt by unburdening dissipated as Michi felt a dread creep over her. Why had she said that? It was her secret, and it should have gone to the grave with her.

She risked a glance up at Tamara, who sat there mouth open in shock.

"You're serious about this, right?" she asked her.

"Yeah."

"Holy frack!" she finally exclaimed, jumping up. "By St. Chuck's ass! You fucking ghosted a jack? You've got to tell me exactly what happened!"

She sat back down on the couch cross-legged, facing Michi, taking her hands in hers.

Michi turned towards her and crossed her legs as well, their knees touching. She took a deep breath, and then started from the beginning, with her vague concept of revenge and through all the events of the night. Tamara was quiet the entire time, her eyes sparkling with excitement. When she was done, she sat there, waiting for her roommate's response.

Tamara finally broke her silence with, "Well, roomie, I thought I'd heard it all. But you, you take the cake. I'm truly amazed."

"So you are OK with that? I mean, I'm a murderer."

"OK with it? Michi girl, I am freakin' impressed, and rather jealous. You struck back at the assholes when all anyone else does it pass out leaflets and jabber at rallies. You took matters into your own hands and got some revenge for your beau. But it's not over now."

"It's not?" Michi asked.

"No fucking way. You and I are going to do it again!"

Chapter 10

"You really expect to attract attention in that?" Tamara asked Michi, pointing at the baggy sweats and oversized cozy Michi had put on.

"What's the matter with what I'm wearing?"

"You look like the marshmallow man. You've got the curves, so use them," Tamara said.

"I'm not putting on rentgirl rags, if that's what you mean. I'm going to need to be able to move. And we don't want to attract too much attention anyway. Secrecy, right? In-and-out like phantoms, right? Wasn't that what you said?"

"Oh, my innocent little Michi," Tamara said sarcastically. "Look at my bammers," she told Michi, turning around and pointing at the black, molecularly-thin tights that were currently in fashion. "Shows my ass, right? But still, not flashy enough to attract attention unless some guy is right behind me. With your sweats, Georgina O'Merkhin herself wouldn't turn a head," she said, referring to the current flavor-of-the-month holo sex-kitten star.

"We need to get one of them to want to come with us, not bore one to death. Go back to your room and put on a pair of your dance tights, at least. And put this on," she added, reaching to the floor and picking up one of her small tops that she had dropped there.

"Really?" Michi asked, dangling the top from one finger. "Don't you think it's a little small?"

"Of course it is, girl. You've got a little more to stuff inside than I do, but so what? You want him to be thinking about something else before you go all highlander samurai on his ass."

Michi laughed out loud at that. "Highlander samurai?"

"Yeah, I thought of it last night. Brills, right? You're First Family, and Clan. You've got them both by birth, and samurais are pretty kick-ass."

Tamara was excited, and her voice was a pitch higher than normal. The thought of going out and jumping a jack had hyped her up.

Michi went back into her room, slid off her sweats, then rooted around her dance kit for a pair of clean tights. All were dirty, so she took the pair with the least amount of smell and put them on. The top Tamara had given her was another story, though. It was tiny! She pulled it over her head and worked it down, trying to put everything in place. She took a quick look in the mirror and almost took it right back off. It didn't cover much of anything, and while not a prude, Michi was still Clan, and as such, she was not as open as her roommate. In the end, she just zipped up her cozy, hiding the mini-top from view.

"That's better," Tamara said as Michi came out. "Let's go get this done."

Michi was still hesitant about this "mission," as Tamara kept referring to it. Last time, she had been running on emotion and a mindless drive for vengeance. Now, she wasn't as driven. Killing the jack had extinguished part of the flame that burned within her. She had never envisioned actually killing a man, but now that it had happened, she was nervous as the two left the apartment and started downtown.

This was not a "kill" mission, however, as she had stressed to Tamara. In the first place, killing the jack before had been a fluke. Unless you used a weapon of some sort, killing with one blow almost never happened, despite what was shown in the flicks. It took endless pummelings to have the potential for death.

In the second place, Michi realized that she really didn't have the stomach for it. She hated the jacks and all they stood for, but killing someone took a person into another realm, one to which she really didn't want to travel. Michi still clung to her past self: the dancer, the treasured First Family girl, the student, the fiancé. She liked that life, and she was afraid of the violent undertow which threatened to sweep her into a darker, more sinister world.

Without Tamara, she probably would have never ventured out again like this, eventually going back to her family and apologizing. She knew they would embrace her return. Instead, she was following her half-crazy roomie out into the night to jump a jack. Maybe she was the half-crazy one for agreeing to it.

They made their way towards the Gut again. The lack of working surveillance vaulted it to the top of their preferred hunting grounds. The shrine Michi had used before was on the other side of the Slab, so this time, they stopped a few blocks short of the Gut, gave each other a kiss on the cheek as if parting (for the sake of any surveillance recordings), and then split up. Michi went into an industrial parts store where she changed cozies in the toilet before coming out and walking into the Gut itself.

There was an old statue of some ancient Scottish hero in the middle of the Gut, a testament to when this was a high-end neighborhood. The fine townhomes had fallen a long way into disrepair. Michi stopped at the foot of the statue and waited for Tamara.

"You want Light?" a furtive voice whispered to her.

Michi ignored the bundled person, unsure if the pusher was a man or woman, young or old. She kept glancing around, wondering how long she should wait. She felt far more vulnerable this time than before. She knew it was all in her mind, but that didn't make her feelings any less impactful.

Tamara finally sauntered up in a bright pink cozy with silver spangles. She stood out like a bird of paradise. The rentgirls and boys tended to the colorful, but Tamara put them all to shame.

"Not too conspicuous there, are you?" Michi asked as they met up.

"Don't you ever read the spy novels?" Tamara asked. "With all this glitter, who's gonna remember my face?"

"If we're planning this based on novels and flicks, then we're in trouble before we even begin," Michi grumbled without acknowledging that what Tamara had said made sense, garnered from a fictional spy story or not.

The two women started aimlessly walking, trying to look like they fit in. The Gut was not totally devoted to activities that pressed the boundaries of legality—or broke right through them, for that matter. The office buildings in the center of town rose to the west of the Gut, and some of the newly renovated condos so high in demand were just to the east, so the upscale workers simply walked through the Gut to and from their condos. It wouldn't be long before the real estate on which the Gut perched would be taken over for more condos, coffee shops, and hookah bars.

At this hour, most of the workers were already snug in their condos. There were some stragglers, however, mostly people who had stayed for dinner or to put in the late hours in their attempt to rise through the drek to the upper echelons of power. They walked with their heads down, ignoring the jetsam and flotsam that flowed throughout the Gut. Michi wondered if they were afraid that if they looked, they'd see a fellow worker indulging in what the Gut had to offer.

"Check this out," Tamara whispered before flouncing up to one head-down walker.

"Hey there, stud, you up for a drink?" she asked the man who merely put his head down further and sped up his pace.

"Told you this stuff works," she said to Michi as she came back, using one hand to sweep over her pink cozy. "I know that guy. He hit on me last year at one of our recertification courses."

Michi had to stifle a laugh. Tamara was one surprise after another. The girl had no filter.

They wandered about the Gut for over an hour, dismissing several prospects for various reasons ranging from one jack's wedding ring catching the light as he walked his rounds to another being joined by two more jacks just before the two hunters closed in.

Michi had felt uncomfortable when they first started walking. The Gut was not the kind of place she ever really thought she would be exploring. But as they hunted for a victim, she forgot about the seediness of the hunting grounds as her excitement started to take over. She had always been competitive, but this took it to a new level, one that quite frankly gave her a rush.

A few years ago, a cousin had come back on leave from where he served as a captain in the Marines. At a family gathering, he had started on his "sea stories," as he called them. He had been in the fighting during the Trinocular War, and to the rapt attention of the younger cousins, said that the thrill of combat was addictive, that nothing else matched up to it. At the time, Michi thought that was just bluster, but as she searched the warrens for her prey, she thought she just might understand what he'd been trying to say.

Michi had been reticent about Tamara's mission, but now that she was on the hunt, she was eager to get to it.

"Over there, at your eleven o'clock," she whispered to Tamara, when she finally spotted a likely target.

"Eleven freakin' what?"

Eleven o'clock. Like in the flicks. Twelve is right in front of us. Eleven is ahead and just to the left. Over there, across the street."

"Why didn't you just say that instead of going Hollywood on me," Tamara grumbled. Then, "Ah, I see what you mean. Mr. Jack seems interested in us."

"Mr. Jack" was a thirty-something, lower-level security specialist, based on the patch on his shoulder. He was a little old for his rank, and Michi saw something in his eyes as he took in the two women that made her positive he was the type to throw around what little authority he possessed.

Tamara immediately started crossing the street, and Michi had to hurry to catch up. The jack's eyes lit up as the two walked up to him.

"And what are you two ladies doing out and about this fine evening?" he asked them as Michi could feel his gaze peeling off their cozies as he openly looked them up and down.

"Nothing, sir," Tamara said. "Just out for some fun. Crunching actuarial numbers all day is *so* boring, and we need a little excitement."

With a number of insurance firms downtown, that little comment could throw suspicion in that direction, if it came to that. Michi had to give her roommate props. Michi hadn't even thought to come up with a backstory.

"Excitement? Plenty of places for that, ladies. The Gut, though, can be a little rough for office girls."

"Oh, me and Stacy like it rough," Tamara said with a throaty laugh. "Maybe you know someplace, though, where we can go to find something exciting?"

"Maybe I do and maybe I don't," he said with a laugh.

"Oh, you security guys are supposed to know all the naughty places, right? Where things happen? Maybe one where we could go but that's not, too, well, dangerous?"

The jack was eyeing both of them. Michi wondered if she should have unzipped her cozy a little, but doing that now would be too blatant. They had to tease this fish before setting the hook.

Michi was glad Tamara was the one doing the talking. This wasn't her style. Michi would rather have simply called out the man and gone at it. Finesse was not something she had in her bag of tricks.

"What about her?" the man asked Tamara, pointing at Michi.

"Oh, she's a quiet one, she is, out in public, but get her behind closed doors, she's a tiger," Tamara told him.

"Well, can you help us? Where should we go? But remember, we want it naughty, but not where we're going to get in any trouble. You know how the insurance companies are about moral standing."

The jack seemed to be considering it for a moment before making up his mind. He got on his radio and said, "Helmon, I'm taking my 30 now. You've got it."

He turned to Tamara and said, "Yeah, I know. I run this section," which Michi knew was a gross exaggeration, "so I know all the places. But two ladies like you can get into trouble getting there, so I'm going to escort you there and let them know you're under my protection, OK?"

Hook set.

"Oh, you'd do that?" Tamara asked excitedly. "Stacy, you hear that? I told you this would be sparking!

"Lead on my knight," she said, taking the jack by his arm. "I'm so excited."

"You excited too?" the jack asked Michi over his shoulder.

You don't know how much, she thought.

Michi didn't know what the jack had planned. It was doubtful that he would have actually led the two into danger, and 30 minutes wasn't much time for anything. He probably wanted to impress them with his importance and then set up something after he was off duty. It didn't matter. The guy was slimy, and Michi felt her endorphins kick in.

The jack led the two down Julian Street, which was far too open for Michi to strike. She wondered if she was going to have to fake the need to take a pee when the jack turned down a smaller alley.

"This is a shortcut, so don't be too scared," he said, full of self-importance. "I'm here with you, but don't try this way alone."

Michi decided she hated him. Not that hating him was necessary, but it added a certain spice to what was going to happen.

Halfway down the alley, Michi coughed twice. It was corny, but that was their signal.

"Oh, my shoe's coming undone," she said, stopping and bending at the waist as if to tie her shoe.

The jack stood over her, taking an unabashed look at her ass.

"Hey, jack," Michi said.

The jack looked up just as Michi's roundhouse kick caught him flush on the side of his face. The jack stumbled, but didn't go down.

"What . . .?" he started, coming back with his fist cocked to swing at her.

Michi leveled a front kick at his stomach, missing and hitting him on his chest harness, but knocking him back a full meter.

"You bitch!" he gasped out, looking at Michi with unveiled hate. He swayed as Michi just took in the sight, all hesitation about their mission now gone.

She should have attacked again and closed the deal instead of admiring her handiwork. He stepped back and reached for his Jamison, pulling it out. Michi tried to close the distance, hoping to connect before the woozy jack could pull the trigger. She was afraid she would be too late.

She just started to leap into a superman punch when the jack crumbled in a heap. Michi was so focused on him that she didn't realize what was going on. It took her a moment to take in Tamara, all 40 kg of her, standing above the jack with a truncheon in her hand. She had a huge smile on her face.

"That was fucking brills," she said, looking down in awe at the weighted leather club in her hand.

"Who's the samurai now, sister?" Michi asked, totally taken off guard.

Nowhere in their admittedly spotty plan had Tamara been involved in the fighting. She was supposed to set it up and Michi was supposed to close the deal. And where had that nasty truncheon come from?

"Where did you have that thing?" Michi asked.

"My bammers leave nothing to the imagination, but the cozy's pretty loose. And like I told you, no one gets past the glitter."

"I gotta give you cred," Michi told her. "I think you saved my ass."

"I think I did, too! You may be the Samurai Highlander, but I can sure be your robin,[8]" she said. "Every hero's gotta have her robin."

"OK, you've got the job." Michi said as she nudged the jack with her foot.

He was breathing smoothly, to Michi's relief.

Some freedom fighter I am, she thought. *Happy when a target lives.*

She bent over and took the Jamison out of its holster. She looked it over for a moment before sliding it inside her cozy.

"Uh, as my second robin duty, you do know that you can't fire that. It's keyed to that guy's bios."

"Yeah, I know that."

"And if you power it up, they can track it to you."

"What, you think I'm stupid?" Michi said as her heart fluttered.

Actually, she hadn't known either of those two pertinent facts. She had even thought about trying the first Jamison out after she had gotten it home. If what Tamara was saying was true, and Michi was sure it was, she would have had a platoon of jacks descending on her house, ready to take both her family and her into custody. First Family or not, murder was a capital offense.

"So why do you want it?" Tamara asked.

Michi knew she should have put it back, but she was not going to back down. It was the MacCailín stubborn streak.

"Just as a souvenir, nothing more."

"OK, it's your call," Tamara said.

---

[8] Robbin: a hero's sidekick

Michi instantly felt bad. "Her call" would bring the weapon into Tamara's condo.

"I've got a place I'll ditch it for safekeeping. But I want to send a message that this wasn't some random mugging. Shall we get out of here?"

"Yeah, that's probably a pretty good idea," Tamara said before walking over to look at the unconscious man.

Michi thought she might kick the man, but instead, she leaned over and kissed him right on the lips.

"It's only fair," Tamara said with a shrug before the two left the alley.

They made their way back to the statue before silently splitting up. Michi sat down on the statue's base, just a citizen taking in the sights. Tamara was supposed to leave first, but after surreptitiously ditching the pink cozy, Michi watched her approach two young salarymen. Within a minute, she had her arm hooked around one of them as they started off. She looked back at Michi and gave her a wink before getting into a deep conservation with her new companion.

Michi didn't know how far Tamara was going to take it. She did like her fun, and she had been pretty hyped after hitting the jack, Michi knew. She also realized that a man and a woman leaving the Gut together would be less conspicuous than two single women leaving. Was Tamara merely using the guy as camouflage, or was he going to be her release of pent-up energy?

Michi watched Tamara go into a bar with the man, waited another 15 minutes, then got up and slowly made her way out of the Gut. She was still pretty jazzed, and as she walked home, she was already planning her next strike.

Chapter 11

"Saint Chuck's ass," Tamara said as they watched the news feed. "Is that because of us?"

The feed showed riot-geared jacks rounding up people in the Gut. As indentureds didn't have the credits to play there, other than a few moonlighting on the service side of the equation, most of the people getting rounded up were free citizens.

"Do you know who I am?" screamed one florid-faced middle-aged man in the background behind the reporter. "I'll have your job," he said before being dragged off in zipties, anything else he had to say lost to the feed.

Their jumping of the jack the night before had gone unreported on any news feed, but this was a new development. Jacks tended to keep their hands off free citizens. They had full enforcement rights over anyone on the planet, theoretically even to the company execs, but this type of round-up just wasn't done.

"It has to be," Michi answered. "They're telling us, you and me, I guess, that they are going to play rough."

"I don't think people are going to stand for it. Don't they need probable cause to arrest people like that?"

"I think so. I'd have to take a look at the charter, though," Michi said. As a First Family, Michi had never much considered how the law was upheld on Kakurega.

"So maybe we need to lay low? No more missions for awhile?" Tamara asked.

"Lay low? How about lay off. We hit them, but I think we're done. Let's take this as a victory and leave it at that, OK?" Michi said as she watched the jacks haul off person after person.

"Quit? Completely? Some Highland Samurai you are?" Tamara grumbled, but without conviction.

Jumping a jack had seemed to be an adventure, a way to strike back. But they should have known the security forces wouldn't just meekly stand by while their own were targeted. One could have been a freak occurrence. Two, and two where Jamison's were taken, were a pattern, one that the jacks had to address. They had to know that they were arresting people who had nothing to do with the attack on the jack. Oh, maybe they thought they could get lucky and find the culprit during interrogation, but this was a message, pure and simple.

You don't mess with Propitious Interstellar's security forces.

Chapter 12

Michi's feet hurt as she made her way down Hallison Street. She had spent two hours at the studio, the first time she'd danced since Franz was killed, and her feet had paid the price for her absence. It was a good hurt, though, a familiar one. And familiarity was what she sought.

She'd had enough of hanging out at Tamara's condo and wanted to get a taste of her old life. She'd stopped by her family's house first, ostensibly to pick up some personal belongings, but in reality, it was just to see the place. Her parents weren't home, but as she sat in the kitchen munching on some of Talla's raspberry-mint tarts, the family maid let her know that her parents talked about her, and that they would welcome her back.

She was tempted to just stay until her parents came home. She wanted to turn back the clock, to go back three weeks when she had a fiancé, a life she loved, and no worries. But Franz was gone, and nothing was going to bring him back. She chatted with Talla, eating a few more tarts than she should have just to prolong the visit. Finally, though, she left and went to the studio.

A few of the others welcomed her back, and Melinda expressed her condolences on Franz' death, but most of the dancers there left her alone. Most probably just didn't know what to say, she knew, but still, Michi felt ignored. Michi lost herself in her positions, dancing until her feet cried for relief. She stopped and sat up against one of the mirrors, listening to the thuds and squeaks of the feet of the other dancers on the studio floor, smelling the familiar odor of human exertion. The smell, more than anything else, resonated with her, reminding her of the life she wanted back.

She tended to her feet, put her cozy over her dance clothes, and left the studio to make her way back to Tamara's. She wished she still had her Sullivan. A cold wind was picking up, and it would be a 45-minute walk on aching feet until she got there.

She tightened up the cozy hood around her face and neck, put her head down, and walked into the wind, lost in her thoughts. It would be so much easier to just go home and apologize. Unfortunately, she had a stubborn streak that wouldn't let her forgive and forget that easily. She had lost her love, and her family didn't seem to care.

With her hood up and her mind wandering, she didn't notice the growing crowd noise until she came around the corner and into Prosperity Square. Surprised, she stopped to see what was happening. There had been several protests about the wholesale arrests over the last few days, but this had a much more organized feel to it. There had to be 400 people in the square, all protesting Propitious Interstellar. Quite a few people had placards decrying security force heavy-handedness, and more than a few held aloft placards with Franz' photo on it and the date of his death.

That hit Michi hard. She felt his loss every day, but she had never come out in public forcing people to remember him. Yet here, at least 20 people were carrying his image, not letting the jacks forget what had happened.

"Excuse me," she said, approaching an elderly man who was carrying Franz' photo. "Where did you get that?"

"Up there," he responded pointing to the right of the crowd and down 8th Street, one of the streets that radiated out from the square. "It was a shame about the young man, so I chose this one."

Michi looked to where he was pointing, but she couldn't see anything. She thanked the man, and then walked in that direction, leaving the square itself before spotting a van, the back doors open. She shouldn't have been surprised, but it was Cheri at the van, handing out ready-made placards. Michi made her way through the crowd and approached Cheri.

"Can I have one of those?" she asked.

"Sure, which one?" Cheri asked before looking up and seeing who was asking. "Michi! It's good to see you again. How are you holding up?"

Michi neglected to mention that they hadn't seen each other at Cheri's request, not hers.

"I'm fine," she said instead. "I'm surprised to see this going on, and I'm even more surprised to see Franz' face being carried by so many people. You could have told me."

"Oh, Michi, dear. We didn't want to bother you. Franz' loss was shocking, and it hit so many of us. And now, with the jacks abrogating the charter and arresting people without probable cause, well, more and more people are getting involved. We need to show Propitious Interstellar that they can't run roughshod over us."

"No, it's OK. I just wish I'd known," Michi said. "Well, can I have one of those?"

"Oh, of course, dear. Let me get you one."

Cheri reached into the back of the van and brought one out, handing it to her. Michi stared at it for a moment before recognizing the photo. It was one she had taken herself at a picnic. Franz was smiling at her, looking younger than his years. Michi choked back any reaction as she took it, wondering where they had gotten the photo.

"Come on back when we break up, OK? We can catch up on things," Cheri said.

Michi took the sign and held it up, walking back to join the crowd. She edged into the back, only then noticing the line of jacks arrayed in front of them. This looked eerily like how they were positioned before Franz was killed, and she momentarily took a step back.

Hell! They don't scare me, she reminded herself. *I've taken a few of them down.*

She pushed back up, picking up the "No Jack Authority!" chant being voiced by the crowd.

There was no stage this time, no set speakers. But someone out of Michi's sight obviously had a bullhorn, and he was changing the chants every few minutes. Michi spent the next 30 minutes chanting herself hoarse, yelling with every fiber of her body. She shook Franz' picture as she chanted, using it as an exclamation mark. Despite the chill, her energy and the close proximity of the crowd kept her warm.

She knew that the jacks' crowd surveillance would have already identified her as a participant, and this was not what she should be doing if she wanted to go back home, but she didn't care.

When the blast exploded, she felt the rush of heat go over her head. It didn't register for a moment, but the screams that started up did. Ahead of her, a number of jacks were down hard while others struggled back to their feet. Within moments, some of them opened fire on the protesters. Michi saw a dozen or more protesters in the front ranks fall as they were hit.

People started to turn and run, a stampede to get away from the carnage. The human current took Michi with it. Not everyone ran, though. A figure in a ski mask and dressed in black stepped forward against the crowd, people parting alongside of him as he raised some sort of weapon and fired back in the direction of the jacks.

Michi was almost pushed into his line of fire, but she was able to squirm back and to his side. He pumped out three more shots, then pushed his way forward and out of sight.

Michi stumbled over a prone body. She bent down to help the man up and was almost knocked down herself. Another man stopped, and with both of them taking an arm, they picked the fallen man up and dragged him out of the way.

Shots continued to ring out, some close by, some from the jacks. Michi risked a glance back as she helped drag the man to one of the side streets. Twenty or thirty bodies littered the square, most looking like protesters. The man in black, the one who was firing, continued to advance, now that he was not blocked by the mass of people. He kept firing, but then he stumbled and went down.

Michi turned her attention to getting away and out of the line of fire. She lost sight of the square as she helped pull the man out and onto one of the side streets. People were rushing by when the man struggled to his feet, wheezing, but assuring them he was OK. The other man that was helping looked at Michi and snapped his head indicating that they should get out of there. Michi could hear the stomping of feet, feet moving in formation from the square. She looked at the man she'd helped.

"I'm fine, thanks to you. Get out of here," he told her.

Michi took the hint. She started sprinting, only then realizing she was still carrying Franz' picture. She knew she should drop it, but she couldn't. Holding it in her right hand, she took off, ignoring the pain that still radiated from her feet. Behind her, she could hear the firing die off while a voice coming out of a speaker in the sky ordered everyone to stop and lie on the ground.

Hell with that!

She quickly passed others who were also fleeing and didn't slow down until she reached Tamara's building. She ran up the stairwell instead of waiting for the elevator, and made it inside the condo.

It was then that the trembling started, and didn't stop until Tamara got home from work, unaware yet of what had just happened.

Chapter 13

With martial law declared, sporadic fighting broke out. "Fighting" might not be the best description of it. There was occasional sniping against company targets, and several mini-drone bombs were unleashed. Surprisingly, for a company as large and rich as Propitious Interstellar, they didn't have any defense for the mini-drones. The jacks had to resort to firing their Jamisons or the few energy weapons they possessed to knock the drones down. Even jamming the frequencies had little effect as whoever was flying them skipped frequencies all the way into the target.

The payloads on the 500 gram drones were not very powerful, so other than causing some minor damage, there was not much in the way of tangible effects. Psychologically, though, PI knew that the people, at least some of the people, had finally had enough to warrant action against the company.

The news feeds, which were all controlled by PI, were the only sources of information that were available on the holos, and they didn't show much. The key clip seemed to be one where an indentured maintenance worker at Plant 5 had been burnt by a mini-drone strike. The man was obviously in pain, and the holo camera lingered over him as he cried out in anguish while the reporter castigated the "terrorist" act that had caused the injuries.

The indentureds had been confined to their factories, and even the Class I employees were threatened with termination if they didn't show up for work. There was a curfew in effect from 8:00 PM until 6:00 AM for anyone not on company business. This was not just for PI employees; it pertained to everyone on the planet. Michi was out of the loop, but she knew the First Families would be up in arms. They treasured their independence, and their rights were specified in the charter—a charter that Propitious Interstellar seemed to be ignoring.

Company jacks held several raids. A news crew had been with them for one such raid on an indentured dormitory. All it showed was the jacks man-handling the Class 4s while turning up no weapons. The PR honchos must have stepped in after that as there was no more coverage of raids. However, Michi was able to watch several vids of additional raids by going through her proxy and accessing off-world sites. One of the most downloaded vids was one of a young boy, probably around 10 years old, sitting dazed in a dormitory ladderwell, his face bloody.

Without showing the vid, Propitious Interstellar denied that it was even taken on Kakurega, claiming it was a fake meant to discredit the company's security forces. Michi wouldn't put it past someone like Tamberlain, or even Hokkam, to put out some faked footage, but some of the other vids and holos showed jacks in the company uniforms meting out some severe treatment to unresisting people.

All of this galvanized the population. PI was making a big mistake, though, in Michi's opinion, that is, if they really believed their news releases. According to the company, the "unrest" was a result of off-world agitators rallying the indentureds using misinformation (not that they used the term "indentureds—with them, it was always "Class 4 employees"). Michi didn't think the company really thought it was off-worlders, but if they thought this was an indentured issue, Michi was sure they had misinterpreted the situation. From the zips[9] she was getting from friends, this "unrest" was far broader than that.

A low explosion sounded outside the window, and Michi got up off the couch where she had been watching holos and looked out. A plume of black smoke was rising up several blocks to the west. Tamara would be coming back home about now, and her route would be close to the smoke. Michi contemplated going out to see if she could find her roommate, but decided it was better to stay in the condo and let Tamara come to her.

Still, it was a tense 45 minutes as she waited, changing her mind back and forth on leaving, until Tamara came in the door in an agitated state.

---

[9] Zips: a social media transmission format where small messages, either written, spoken, or with video, can be easily and quickly sent to individuals or groups.

"Did they show any of it in the news feeds?" she asked breathlessly, looking over to where Michi had been watching them.

"Show what?"

"The fight! The jacks were pulling another raid on the indentureds, but they should have shown up with more. They were dragging three out of the dorm when at least 50 indentureds jumped them. I saw it all from the walkway," she said, referring to the elevated walkway on which employees who worked in Buildings Four, Five, and Six left the campus and which ran between some of the Class Four dormitories.

"They were beating the crap out of them. I captured some of it on my phone, but I could see the cavalry arriving, so I got the heck out of there. And then, right on the corner of Orville and Mendoza, the friggin' building blew up, the one with the noodle shop. I was only a block away!"

Michi took Tamara by the hand and sat her down on the couch.

"It blew up?"

"Yeah, kaboom! It's a fucking war out there, Michi. A war!"

Chapter 14

Two days later, two days in which clashes had become more frequent, and as Michi and Tamara were sipping tea on their small balcony during a lull in the fighting, several dark shapes flew overhead towards the company campus. Painted on the fuselage, Michi could clearly see the UFMC flash.

The Marines had landed.

Chapter 15

Michi and Tamara walked into a WRP office bustling with activity. The arrival of the Marines had thrown the planet into a tizzy, as could be expected. Not much of substance was being passed over the newsfeeds, only that the Marines were there to restore order and provide security for the "good citizens" of Kakurega. Estranged from her family, Michi did not have any other information sources available to her, so she and Tamara decided to see what the WRP knew about what was going on.

Michi hadn't even seen a Marine in person yet. There were too few of them around to make much of a physical impact, but the psychological impact was something entirely different. Michi could feel a sense of impending doom in the air, as if father was now home and ready to punish the offending children.

The fact that that Captain Ryck Lysander, the posterboy of the Marines, was one of the commanders of the battalion that landed only heightened the tension. The newsfeeds almost crowed about his presence, going into detail about his history and his "hero" status.

"Look, there's Cheri," Tamara pointed out. "Let's go see what she knows."

Cheri looked up from a conversation she was having with a young man as the two came up. "Tamara, Michi, how are you?" she asked, leaning forward to kiss each one on the cheek.

"We're holding out," Tamara said. "But we're pretty much in the dark. Anything you can tell us?"

"I, well, um . . . Danny, can you give me a moment here?" she asked the young man who nodded and walked off.

"I've been meaning to talk to you, Michi, but you know, with all of this, it's been a little hard."

"About what?"

"Ah . . . maybe here's not a good place, but I need to get this done. Can I come by tonight before curfew?"

"Uh, sure," Michi and Tamara said, almost in unison.

"OK, see you then," she said, looking around as if trying to see who might be watching. "Maybe you should go, and I've got a lot to do here before then. See you later."

She quickly walked off as the two women stared at each other. Michi started to ask what that was all about, but Tamara held up a hand, stopping her.

"Well, it's good to see everyone," Tamara said to Michi, but loud enough for anyone trying to overhear to do so. "But you promised me a bubble tea, so let's boogie."

She took Michi's arm in hers and turned around, heading for the door. They stopped only to greet two other people they knew and exchanged banal pleasantries, but within a minute, they were out the door and into the street.

"Bubble tea? You don't even like it," Michi said quietly as they walked.

"So sue me. It was all I could think of," Tamara whispered. "I should have said coffee, but we'd better stop for some tea."

"Don't you think all this cloak-and-dagger stuff is a little much?" Michi whispered back, wishing she had spoken aloud but spooked by Tamara's actions.

"If it's too much, no harm, no foul. As it is, better safe than sorry."

They made their way to the closest tea shop and sat outside in the spring sunshine, sipping their tea. Tamara didn't like bubble tea much, but Michi loved sucking up the little tapioca balls at the bottom of the cup. Twice, she tried to ask Tamara what was going on, but both times, her roommate changed the subject. Michi thought it was all too much, but she was willing to play along.

They left the tea shop to do some window shopping, ignoring the presence of large numbers of jacks. Along Manteo Drive, with all the high-end shops, the jacks didn't intrude, but even there, the two women felt eyes on them. Michi found it surprisingly awkward to try and act innocent, as if they were doing nothing.

Eventually, with Tamara controlling the pace, they made it back to the condo.

"So what's going on?" Michi demanded as soon as the front door closed.

"You didn't feel the vibe in there with Cheri?" Tamara asked.

"She was stressed, sure. But wouldn't you be? What with the Marines tipping the Federation's hand on where they stood?"

"I think it was more than that. Just call it a gut feeling. Anyway, she'll be here in an hour. Let's get ready to dial up a dinner. Maybe the *bœuf bourguignon*?" she asked, pulling out the keypad on the fabricator. "Why don't you get a bottle of shiraz and make up some sangria. Cheri is rather partial to that, you know."

Michi frowned. She had known Cheri for over a year and had dined with her, yet she didn't know Cheri drank sangria. She wondered just how close Cheri and Tamara really were.

The pitcher of sangria was already down two glasses when the door chimed. Tamara poured a fresh glass and went to let Cheri in.

"Oh, you know me, girl," Cheri said, gratefully taking the drink.

She took a swallow, gave a happy sigh, then sank down on the overstuffed chair next to the couch.

"So what couldn't you say at WRP?" Tamara bluntly asked without preamble.

"Getting right to it, huh? You always were direct," Cheri said.

She took another sip of her drink,and then turned to Michi.

"Michi dear, this is going to be hard, really hard. But I want you to think back to when Franz was killed. Tell me exactly what happened."

Michi stared at Cheri. Whatever she expected, this was not it. And she had been trying over the last month-and-a-half to move beyond that day, to move beyond the point when her life changed.

"I know this is hard. But please, tell me, what did you see?"

Michi tried to gather her thoughts. She took several deep breaths before starting.

"I was at the studio, practicing—"

"Skip ahead, dear, to when the trouble started."

"Huh? OK, well, the first two people spoke, and then it was Franz' turn. He said something funny, and the crowd laughed. You know, like he always does. Did," she corrected herself, a lump forming in her throat. "He said something about Henry Jugos coming, then started on about how PI needs their workers. You know, like you told me Hokkam wanted. Then the jacks started moving about, like they were nervous or something."

"And?" Cheri prompted her.

"Franz tried to calm down the jacks. He said we were doing nothing wrong. But it seemed like they might want to arrest him, so I started forward. I wanted to be there. Franz told everyone not to resist, and he even held out his hands like he wanted to be cuffed. Then one of the jacks fired, and Franz shouted out that he was surrendering."

"Did you actually see a jack firing?" Cheri asked.

"Well, no. But it had to be one of them, right?"

"OK, go on."

"Well, then, Franz was screaming at the jacks, and, uh . . ."

"What happened next," Cheri asked as both she and Tamara leaned in.

"You were there," Michi said angrily, pissed that she had to relive it. "His head exploded. They murdered him!"

Cherie leaned forward, taking Michi's hands in hers. "Michi, dear, think carefully. I know this is hard, but just how did he get hit?"

"They shot him in the forehead. I saw it. One moment he was shouting, the next his forehead was gone."

"And which way was he facing?"

"I told you. He was shouting at the jacks, and they shot him in the head."

Michi gulped in the air, trying not to break down. Cheri just looked at her in sympathy.

"You happy now?" Michi asked, pulling back from the woman.

"Michi, when a bullet hits, it makes a small entry wound. When it exits the body, it makes a huge, catastrophic wound, just like what happened to Franz."

Michi stared at Cheri, then simply asked "What?"

Tamara sucked in some air as she seemed to realize what Cheri was inferring.

"Michi, Franz was shot from behind the crowd. He was not shot by the jacks."

"Bullshit! I was there! I saw it."

"Michi, dear, most of the jacks were armed with their Jamisons, not projectile weapons. And none carried the caliber of weapon that probably took Franz' life. The PI report absolved the security forces, but we weren't sure."

"Of course those bastards would absolve the jacks."

"All of the security recordings are classified, and we have tried to hack them, but what you just said confirms what PI reported, and from what we are getting from our sources inside. Franz was not killed by the jacks."

"But . . . but maybe they sent one of them to the back of the crowd to kill him, to confuse people," Michi said, not willing to let go of her convictions.

She had killed a jack because of what happened to Franz. They *had* to be guilty.

"That could be. It might even be probable. But we don't know."

"Who else would want him dead? No, it was the jacks, and if not them personally, it was Propitious Interstellar."

"I agree with Michi," Tamara offered. "Who else had the motive?"

Cheri looked at the other two for a moment and seemed to come to a decision. "We don't know. It probably is the company, but it also seems we have a traitor in WRP."

The two roommates looked at Cheri in stunned silence.

"That's why I wanted to come here and not talk at the office. There have been too many coincidences, starting with that rally. We changed the position of the stage from what we had been permitted due to the planting of the spring flowers. We never submitted that change."

"Yet someone knew where to get into position to shoot down Franz," Tamara said as understanding dawned on her.

"Exactly! And there have been other things as well—too many to be purely bad luck."

"Who is it," Michi asked in a steely voice, her thoughts drifting back towards vengeance again.

"We don't know. I don't know. I am getting paranoid, suspecting everyone," Cheri admitted.

"Someone inside the WRP had Franz murdered?" Michi asked, her voice rising, bordering on hysteria.

"I'm not saying that. I still think it was the company, or even the Federation itself. It's just that they had help from inside," Cheri said.

"If it goes as high as the Federation, that explains the Marines," Tamara noted. "They needed an excuse to send in their enforcers, and by us acting out, we handed it to them. This could be another Ellison or Fu Sing."

"What? Ellison and Fu Sing?" Michi asked in a confused voice.

"Geez, Michi. Don't you follow anything? Both planets had worker protests put down, and it was the Marines who did it. On Fu Sing, the Navy even bombarded the refugee camps. Maybe 50,000 were killed," Tamara said.

"I think I remember that one, but wasn't that a revolt? Didn't the Navy and the Marines have to rescue the people there?"

Tamara snorted as Cheri said, "Really, Michi, dear, do you even have to ask that? You've seen the newsfeeds here. Is that what's really happening, or is that what the Federation propagandists want you to believe. Do you think it was any different for those two planets?"

Michiko sat for a moment, digesting what she had just been told.

"So, killing Franz was just a set-up, to create a situation where the Marines could be called in?" she asked.

"We think so. I think so, at least," Cheri said.

"And I gave them that excuse," Michi said, more to herself than to the other two.

"*You* gave them? What do you mean?" Cheri asked.

"Michiko!" Tamara warned.

Michi held up a hand, palm outwards, stopping her roommate. "No, she needs to know."

"Know what?" Cheri asked, obviously confused.

"You know those two jacks? The one that got killed? Gerile Fountainhead? And there was another that got mugged, his

Jamison stolen. We did that, Tamara and me. Or we did the second jack. I killed the first one."

Cheri slid back into her chair, looking at Michi in stunned silence.

Michi looked down at her hands, examining the fingernails as she waited for some sort of reaction.

"You what?"

"I killed the first guy. Broke his neck. I don't think I planned that, but maybe I did. We, Tamara and me, we jumped a second jack, right before they declared martial law. We did that. We gave them the excuse to come here with the Marines."

"Why? I mean, I know why, but we figured that that Fountainhead lad wasn't just some drug deal gone bad, but we thought it must have been the NIP[10] who did it, deny it all they wanted. But you? You're a—"

"I'm a First Family, from both sides, Clan and *Kaitakusya*, I know. But they took my Franz, and that's all that mattered. I might as well have given the Marines an engraved invitation," she said bitterly.

Cheri edged forward, putting a hand on Michi's knee. "It was coming anyway, dear. You may have sped the process up, but you didn't cause it. If Franz was killed by them, and I completely believe that to be so, this was a long time planning. If it wasn't you, it would be something else. Now, we just have to think of what to do with it."

"It should be obvious," Tamara, said. "We have to nip this in the bud. No freakin' Marines are going to be allowed to run over us. We've got our Highlander Samurai here, our Jeanne d'Arc. She's a marketing miracle, so use her. Let's push them back off Kakurega."

Cheri listened to Tamara's rant and seemed to consider it. Michi could almost see Cheri's thoughts war against each other across her face.

"Actually, that falls in line with what some of the WRP think, and certainly the NIP agrees with that. We've been discussing it, to be honest. The trick is to make it uncomfortable enough for them to

---

[10] NIP: National Independence Party, an armed organization dedicated to independence for the planet.

leave, but not go over the line and invoke a severe retaliation," Cheri said. "Michi, I want you to tell me exactly what you did, every step along the way. Don't leave anything out." She looked at her watch. "And it looks like you've got a guest tonight. I won't make curfew."

For the next three hours, with Cheri being surprisingly thorough in her questioning, Michi and Tamara related everything they could remember. Michi knew that Cheri was high up in the WRP, but she'd always been sort of a slightly eccentric aunt to her. Only now, could Michi see the organized, driven leader Cheri really was.

"OK, I know that was tiring," Cheri said as she had finally wrung all she could from the two roommates. "The question is, what do we do next?"

"It's obvious what we do next. We jump a Marine," Tamara declared. "We don't kill him, but we let them know that we aren't going to meekly stand by and let the company throw the charter out the window."

"You know, I think you're right, and that surprises me. I do think we need to make a statement," Cheri said. "Do you think you can do it?"

"No problem," Michi said, determination in her voice.

"A couple of things different, though. No more cozies for camouflage. I'm going to send someone over, someone I trust. He'll have something a little better for you. And I want backup. No two lone rangers out there. Let me work some things out, and do not, I repeat do not, attempt anything until I get back to you. Agreed?"

"You can count on the Highlander Samurai and the Tattooed Avenger," Tamara said in an excited voice.

"This isn't fun and games, Tammy," Cheri said. "This is serious shit, so no grandstanding. Am I clear?"

"Yeah, yeah, I know."

Cheri turned to Michi and asked in the same serious tone, "Am I clear, Michiko MacCailín, blood of the First Families."

Cheri, not being First Family herself, didn't have the power to invoke a First Family honor-binding, but Michi didn't care. She didn't need to be honor-bound to tell the truth.

"If you will give me the means to get revenge, then I am your woman. I will do as you say."

Chapter 16

"Oh, that's pure dead belter,"[11] Michiko said as she stared in the mirror, looking at the stranger's face staring back at her.

The "stranger" had red hair and a pale, round face sprinkled with freckles across the nose. Her body was essentially Michi's, but the face was that of a 15th Century Scottish lass, not the darker First Family countenance that Michi had grown used to over her 19 years. She reached up with a hand and touched the round, pug nose she saw, but felt her own smaller, familiar nose.

"OK, OK, I mean, this can't be penetrated by anything in the electromagnetic spectrum, I promise you that," Doug Taggart said excitedly. "It can be jammed, of course, but that would take a directed beam transmitter, not the surveillance equipment we have here on Kakurega."

"My turn, Michi. I want to see who I'm going to be," Tamara said.

Tamara pushed Michi away from the mirror, took a breath, then turned on the facial recognition spoofer attached to her collar. Michi thought it was freaky to see Tamara's short brown locks and round face immediately switch to an exotic, dark-skinned stranger with close-cropped corn-rowed hair. Both girls had put on T's for the test, and the top of Tamara's jungle-scene tattoo disappeared, slightly coming back as her skin color faded lower into her chest. From under her bikini panties, her normal tattooed palette ran down her legs to her pale ankles and feet.

Michi stepped to stand beside her, both taking in the sight of two strangers looking back at them.

"Dougie, my boy, you done good," Tamara said, awestruck for once.

"This is a pretty new development," Doug started. "It was started as an application for psychoanalysis, of all things, but

[11] Pure dead belter: something that is exceptionally brilliant or amazing.

progression with TET-cells made miniaturization and more refined refractory lanes—"

Tamara cut him off. "Slow down there, boy. I don't really care how it works, just that it does," she said, before turning to the redhead Michi. "Think of it, Michi, we can set our look in the recipe, then just turn it on in the morning. No make-up, just instant glamorous me."

"Well, I guess that would be possible," Doug started. "Let's see, if we . . ."

Michi looked at her black roommate in the mirror, and both of them broke out laughing as Doug went on. They had met Doug only two hours before. If Hollywood had cast a resident geek, this is who they would have come up with. Doug was earnest, gangly, and overwhelmingly devoted to technology. He was like a puppy, eager to please. He had almost started stammering when the two roommates had stripped to T's and panties, but once he had attached the small spoofing units, he had forgotten the fact that the girls were only half-dressed as he became engrossed in his toys.

Doug worked for the company, probably as they were the only ones on Kakurega with a big enough lab to interest him. Somehow, though, Cheri had recruited him. Michi wished she knew how Cheri had done that. Doug didn't seem like the political sort. But he had come through. If the face-spoofers, for lack of a better term, could spoof the surveillance cams as well as they fooled the eyes, then no more pulled up cozies. This was brills.

They had met at a local shawarma stand, and before anything was said, Doug had handed Tamara an envelope. There was no subterfuge, no attempt at a covert hand-off. He just said hi and passed the envelope.

The handwritten note told the two roommates that no one else at WRP knew about "anything," and that Doug's presence was also a secret, known only to Cheri. Once they had finished reading, Doug opened his mouth to speak when Tamara hushed him. Evidently, Doug was not a fan of spy flicks. Neither woman was anything close to a real spy, but both knew you just didn't openly discuss potential illegal actions at a café table on a public street.

They finished their shawarmas, then walked back to their condo, Tamara's arm in Doug's as if he were her boyfriend with Michi trailing behind. Even in a make-believe world, Michi was a third wheel, she thought to herself ruefully.

Once back in the condo, Michi found herself liking the eccentric young man. Actually, he was some seven years older than her, but something about him spoke little brother, rather than big.

Eccentric geek or not, his little toys, which he had modified to be portable and with a two-hour battery life, were invaluable. They would make it that much easier for Michi to strike back at the Marines, and through them, the Federation.

Chapter 17

It was an unseasonably warm evening, and Michi and Tamara strolled through some of the small cafes around the Riverwalk. They had contemplated going back to the Gut, but with their face-spoofers, they decided they didn't need to search the Gut's warrens for a victim.

Michi kept glancing at Tamara, trying to get used to her roommate's appearance. The face-spoofer only changed the area around the head (although Doug kept insisting he would get that range extended), so Tamara could not show as much skin as she might have wanted, but in her zebra-striped unitard, she combined the exotic look of old Africa with the lithe body of a sprite or elf. Tamara had insisted that Michi was quite a looker as well, but perhaps conditioned by her time in the dance studio, she felt big and ungainly alongside her smaller friend.

She consciously worked to sway her hips as they walked, trying to give the picture of two young girls out for some fun. So far, the two had received a few interested glances, but from locals. No Marines were out and about, despite Cheri telling them that this was one area where a few Marines had been spotted while off-duty.

The day before, Michi had seen her first Marines. Four of them had marched down Harrison in their combat suits, two-and-a-half meter tall monstrosities that moved with surprising grace. That sobered Michi; there was no way she could do anything to one of them. She just hoped the information she had been given was accurate. She could deal with a Marine who had snuck out for a drink or two. From what she had heard, it wasn't as if the Marines in the city were restricted from the stadium where they had set up a base camp. The newsfeeds had shown them playing with the kids at the company-run orphanage and playing basketball against the Lipper University team. Generally, though, the Marines seemed to stick to the stadium when not on duty.

Michi wiggled her shoulders, trying to loosen up. She had to be ready when the opportunity presented itself. She had to remember that they were the enemy.

"You look like you're pissed off," Tamara whispered to her. "Smile, at least. Act like you're having fun."

Michi tried to take off her war face and smile. She probably had been scowling.

"Not much better, there. Now it looks like you've got constipation."

Michi broke out into a laugh. Tamara had her way about her.

"Ah, there you go. Now keep it up if we're going to catch us a Marine."

Two middle-aged men walked up to them, and Tamara flirted with them for a few minutes before promising to meet up with them later at the Belly Up, a well known music venue.

"Done wasting time?" Michi grumbled.

"If we're supposed to look like we are out on the town, we can't very well ignore everyone, right? 'Sides, the Belly Up? Knossis is playing there tonight, and they suck. You wouldn't catch me dead listening to that crap."

They slowly wandered through the small streets and alleys, stopping for coffee or tea. They needed to keep alert, so no alcohol. The coffee was getting to Michi, though, and she had to pee when she spotted a man sitting alone at an outside table, a burger and a stein of beer in front of him. Something about him was different, and he just didn't fit in. It might have been the clothes: they were decidedly out-of-date, and even if Michi was not a fashion zombie, she knew you didn't wear socks and sandals with champs. It might have been the close-cropped hair. More than those, though, Michi thought it was the air about him. He was only eating and drinking a beer, but he had a look of utmost confidence.

After a few minor clashes when they first arrived, ones in which no Marines were reportedly hurt, things had been fairly quiet. Curfew had even been extended to 10:00 PM. But still, this was "enemy territory" to the Marines, and Michi would have imagined that anyone sneaking off for a beer would be more obviously alert.

Seeing this man, though, changed Michi's opinion. He just seemed too confident, as if no one could offer him a credible threat.

Michi was convinced he was a Marine, and his arrogant attitude angered her. She felt her fight come on. The Marine looked tough, true, but Michi was confident of her abilities. With the element of surprise, she didn't think anyone, no matter how strong, could stand up to her roundhouse.

"Over there, sitting at the third table, I think that's our man," she whispered to Tamara.

Tamara didn't stare, but let her gaze cross over him. "Could be, I guess. What say we grab a table and see."

They wandered over, and took a seat. "Order me an ale," she told Tamara. "I've got to pee."

Tamara looked surprised, but the man still had half of his burger left, and if he was a Marine and their target for the night, Michi didn't want to fight with a full bladder.

There was a drink waiting for her when she got back. She brought it to her mouth and acted like she was taking a sip. They were sitting two tables from the man, but he was more interested in his meal than in them. He was dipping his fries in what looked to be mayo, then putting each one into his mouth, sucking off the mayo, then popping the fry into his mouth as well.

"That's pretty disgusting," Tamara whispered as she lifted her own glass.

Unless she was dumping some on the ground, it looked like she had taken a few swallows of her beer. Well, it wasn't as if she was going to be doing any fighting, so maybe it was OK.

Michi picked up her PA and dialed Doug. Doug was their "back-up," as Cheri had made them promise to have. Michi wasn't sure how much good having Doug around was, but with Cheri's fear that there was a spy in the WRP, neither Michi nor Tamara wanted to bring anyone else in on their plan.

"Hey, Danielle. We're at Yancy's Café, over on Calamus Two," she told Doug over the PA.

"I'm on Calamus Four, so let me move over. Do you have someone?" Doug asked.

"Maybe, but don't you worry. We'll let you know if we leave here," Michi said before cutting the connection.

"Duty done," she whispered to Tamara, bringing up the glass to cover her mouth.

"Ah, yes, Danielle is such a sweetie," Tamara said with a laugh.

The laugh sounded a little forced, so Michi knew Tamara was getting amped. The girl had a mean streak in her, and Michi was glad they were friends. She didn't think Tamara would make a good enemy.

As the man finished his burger, he asked for a check, his off-world accent clearly reaching them.

"Bingo!" Tamara said.

Whether he heard her or not, he looked up, catching her eye. Tamara smiled and lifted her glass up in a toast. The man nodded and lifted his up in return before breaking the contact.

"I already paid," Tamara told her. When he leaves, let's follow him. If he starts to head towards the stadium, then he's our man."

The man sat at the table for another 20 minutes, seemingly happy to just relax while Michi got more and more tense. She was ready, and she wanted to get at it. When the man finally got up, Tamara had to put out a restraining arm to keep Michi from immediately jumping up to follow.

The man started to walk deeper down Calamus Two, which was a good sign. The stadium was only five hundred meters or so through the winding small roads that made up this restaurant district. At the point where the river bent around, there was a footbridge, and over that was the more open plaza where the stadium, museum, and opera house stood. If they were going to jump him, it had to be before he got to the bridge.

The two roommates trailed the man, and when he stopped to ask directions on how to get out of the district, that cemented it. This was their target. They were getting close to the outer river walk and the bridge, so they had to move.

They picked up their pace. They were still 10 meters in back of the man as he came within sight of the river walk.

"Hey!" Tamara called out.

The man, *the Marine*, turned around. "I was wondering when you two were going to say something," he said in his off-world accent.

"What do you mean?" Tamara asked, using the time to close the distance.

"Well, you've been following me since the café."

"Well, did you have to make it that difficult for a girl, then?" she asked, reaching out to take one of his hands in hers.

"Difficult is all relative, don't you think? Anyway, I'm afraid that as much as I find the both of you fine specimens of Kauregan womanhood, whatever you had planned won't come to fruition."

"Specimens?" Michi thought as she maneuvered in back of the man, just off his right shoulder. *I'll show him "specimens."*

The man gently disengaged his hand from Tamara's as she started to protest. He cut her off. "Look, I'm trying to be polite, but whether you're looking for some fun or you've got some scam going, it isn't happening tonight. So why don't you two—"

Whatever he was going to say was lost as Michi's roundhouse kick connected solidly on the side of his head. Michi could feel the force jolt up her leg, and she reveled in the power of it.

Only, the Marine didn't go down. He staggered a step into Tamara, then spun around.

This time, Michi was not going to be caught just looking. She was surprised he was not down yet, but she launched into a back kick. The Marine whipped up his arm and deflected it, knocking Michi off balance.

"So that's your game, girlies. Not a smart move. I don't have many credits on me, so even if you could get them, I don't think it would be worth the effort, so what say you two just turn around and find someone else to rob."

The way he just stood there, not even protecting himself, infuriated Michi, and she suddenly spun into a spinning back fist, anxious to smash his smug face. Only his face wasn't there as she came around. His right fist was, however, swinging into a short uppercut to Michi's chin, stunning her. She went to one knee, fighting to get back up.

The Marine wasn't following through. He stood there, looking down at her with a look of, could it be pity?

"No one pities me!" she screamed as she struggled to her feet.

The Marine suddenly sprouted an extra pair of arms, it seemed to Michi's still-fuzzy mind. It took her a moment to realize that Tamara had launched herself into the fray, and just as quickly, the Marine had thrown her off to crumble into a heap against the wall of the building beside them.

"Have you had enough?" the Marine asked her.

With a wordless shout, Michi rushed the man, wanting to tear him apart. Forget about Cheri telling them that this was to be a simple mugging—she was going to kill him.

His resigned look and the big fist coming at her face were the last things Michi remembered.

Chapter 18

Michi rang the buzzer, and a few moments later, the door opened. She climbed the steps to the third floor and opened the door to Apartment G. A small counter blocked her way, a 30-something man leaning over it, looking at her expectantly.

"You Seth MacPruitt?" she asked.

"Yeah, and who might you be, angry young woman?" he answered.

He was observant, at least. Michi was angry. More than that, she was humiliated. It had been a day since they had tried to jump the Marine, and the bruise on her face still showed. She hadn't gone to a doctor, so she had to rely on NovaSkin, which was great for small cuts, but didn't work as well with subcutaneous bleeding.

The bruised face meant nothing, though. It was her pride that had been damaged. She had been so sure of herself, and even with complete surprise, she had gotten her ass whipped. Worse than that, she was still free.

Oh, she was glad she hadn't woken up in jail. But the fact that the Marine hadn't even considered them enough of a threat to call the jacks was the utmost degree of disrespect. No, not disrespect. That, at least, required that the Marine thought something of them. He just didn't care. They were nothing.

"My name really isn't important right now. I hear you still do MMA training."

"Which would explain the mats and punchin' bags behind me," he said.

Seth MacPruitt was First Family, even if the MacPruitts were considered somewhat on the low end of the Clan totem pole. But as a young man Seth had managed to win not one, but two Kakurega MMA championships and had even taken runner up at the sectional tournament. The fact that he had then joined the Marines had given Michi pause, but the rumor was that he left the Marines on less-than-favorable terms.

"Well, given the fadin' bruise on your face, I'd be sayin' you're here to get some revenge on a beatin'. The thing is, I don' take on no wannabes."

"I can fight," she protested.

"Not well enough, evidently."

"Look, I can't pay you much," Michi started.

"You're Clan, cousin, I can smell it on you. And you can't pay much?"

MacPruitt and Michi were not related, as far as she knew, but some Clan liked to call each other cousin as a sort of endearment. MacPruitt, though, used it sarcastically, as if to emphasize their different positions in life.

"Uh, well, I'm sort of on my own now," Michi admitted.

"Ah, you pissed off your family? Interestin'. Maybe you've got some balls, girl. Tell you what. Hop around the counter, and let's roll around on the mat. Let me see what you've got."

Michi walked around the counter and started to step onto the mat when Seth stopped her. "Take off those Clodders. I don't need you tearing up my mat. There's a locker room in the back. Get dressed, then we'll see."

As Michi crossed the worn mat, she saw various photos on the wall, some of Seth in action, several at the awards ceremony, and one of him teaching what had to be Marines. There was even his discharge certificate framed and on the wall. Was she coming to the enemy for help?

She was changed and back in a few moments, standing in front of the relaxed Seth. She came to the balls of her feet, ready for whatever he might have for her.

"Well, don't waste my time, girl, show me you're worth it."

Michi immediately launched into a superman punch, knee up to change to a kick if the opportunity presented itself. She was taller than Seth, and the superman punch was a good way to close the distance.

In an instant, she brought her fist down towards his nose, and an instant later, she was on the mat, her right arm being extended and cranked back.

"Tap, tap!" she shouted, using her left hand to tap Seth's back.

He let her up while she tried to shake out the strain on her arm. "You done?" he asked her.

In response, she flicked out with a front kick, which barely touched his chest. She hopped up to come down with an axe kick, which he easily batted away before dropping down and punching her between the legs. The punch hit her squarely in the crotch, and pain flooded her senses. With a shout, she dove at him, grabbing him and driving him back, striving to mount him so she could get to the ground and pound. She felt a momentary thrill as she felt him go down, but somehow, he ended up on top, and within moments, she was in a crucifix, pinned.

He didn't pummel at her, as she expected, but he thrust his pelvis into her face once before letting her go and looking at her expectantly.

She felt the *radge* start to rise, but she fought it down. She knew his little balls-in-the-face was an attempt to get her to lose it. It would take more than that to get to her, she promised herself.

She stood back up, brought her fists up, and started circling, leaving anger and emotion to focus on technique. She thought she saw Seth slightly nod as he closed in. They sparred for another 20 minutes, giving and taking, although Michi was taking much more. She managed to reverse Seth once, and she caught him with an elbow, but that was about it. If he'd wanted to, he could have destroyed her, she realized.

He called a halt, walked over to an old, beat-up fridge, and pulled out two waters, throwing her one. She gratefully took it, trying to drink between heavy breaths.

"Well, you ain't very good, are you?" he asked.

She started to protest, but he held up a hand and continued, "But you're ungodly strong, and you're aggressive. You've got some potential. I can't believe I'm saying this, but come around at 3:00 tomorrow, and we'll see what we can do. Pay me what you can, and if it ain't enough, you can clean up the place after, give it a good scrubbin'. Deal?"

Michi wasn't a maid, and cleaning wasn't her thing. And she owed him for the crotch shot, which still hurt. But she needed to get better, and this was her best shot.

"Deal," she said as she shook his hand.

Chapter 19

"You've got to be kidding me," Michi said as she looked in the mirror. She had on her own face, but she was very unsure of the outfit Tamara and Cheri had come up with.

"Look, this top is about five sizes too small," she told them, trying to stretch it out to give it more coverage.

"We went over this, Michi, dear," Cheri said. "The Federation government and military are the last bastions of misogyny. Women need to be protected, so they say, and that keeps us from all the opportunities offered men. If you, as a woman, take down one of theirs, that should shame them."

"I get all of that, and I agreed to this mission, but why do I have to look like an exotic dancer? I'm not comfortable with that at all."

"Suck it up, big girl. 'Sides, we need there to be no doubt in anyone's mind that it's a sister doing the deed, and your twins there are going to take care of that," Tamara said.

"Easy for you to say. You're not going," Michi grumbled.

"First, I don't have the assets you do, and second, I've got to be at work. Someone's got to pay the bills around here."

"I . . . but what about the boots? And the gloves? How can I fight in these things?" she asked, pointing at the thigh-high faux-leather boots Cheri had brought.

"I told you, this time, you won't be fighting. I've got the three guys to meet you there, and they'll do the restraining. You've just got to look fierce and deliver the message," Cheri started.

"But—"

"If you feel uncomfortable in them, we'll fix them after. But we've got to strike now before one of them gets tired of the other."

"Them" was Marine Lance Corporal Thane Regent and Kelli Mae Osterson, a local girl hired as a food service contractor to help feed the Marines. The two had managed to hook up, and they were meeting every Monday and Wednesday afternoon at her apartment for a discreet liaison; only it was not so discreet that Cheri and the WRP had not found out.

The decision had been made to break into their little tryst, capture the Marine, and record a message for distribution. The decision had also been made that the person doing the recording was to be female, and Cheri had volunteered Michi without revealing her identity.

Cheri had come over to the condo the evening before to set it up, telling them that this was a better plan than trying to jump a Marine somewhere. Michi and Tamara hadn't batted an eye at that. None of the three involved had told Cheri about their disaster the week before.

Tamara mentioned the need for a "look," and with Cheri quickly on board, the two of them concocted this warped fantasy outfit.

Michi took a deep knee bend. The boots restricted her flexibility."

"Uh, that might be a little revealing, I guess," Tamara said, pointing to Michi's ass as she squatted.

Michi jumped up, pulling up on the back of the low-riding pants.

"Don't worry, we'll fix that, too. For a first try, though, you look pretty bitching, if I say so myself."

"Michi, we've got to go. Just follow the plan. I've got the overalls over there on the table. Be sure not to take them off until you are in the building, and don't put them back on until you are on the roof. Doug is sure he can control any overhead surveillance and inside the building, but not all the security cams in the area."

Both Tamara and Cheri kissed her on the cheek.

"Kick some ass," Tamara said as the two left for their jobs.

Michi sat down, feeling alone. She turned on the holo and tried to watch a show on how T-cells were replicated to fight the constantly evolving virus threats, but she couldn't focus. She got up and practiced some of her kicks with the boots on. Her favorite roundhouse was doable, but some of the others would be difficult and less than effective.

At 10:00, she fixed some soup, but she could only finish half of it. She threw the rest out, then called Seth to tell him she was not feeling well and would miss that afternoon's session.

She regretted that. In only a week, she felt that she had really progressed. She was earning the increased skill, though. Seth was not holding back, and each lesson was a journey into pain.

The day crept on, but finally, it was time. She slid on the blue company overalls worn by utility teams. PI Services was not part of the company proper, but rather a purportedly independent spin-off that managed the water, sewage, and power for the planet. The overalls looked like the real deal. The boots sticking out from the bottom of her cuffs were not, though. She flipped on the face-spoofer, and her redhead alter ego appeared. She put on the uniform cap and pulled it down low over her eyes.

No one seemed to notice anything as she walked outside and over to the tram line. No one seemed to notice as she sat on the tram, going to the other side of town. No one seemed to notice when she got out and made the ten-minute walk to Kelli Mae's apartment building.

As she walked up, three men in the same blue overalls stepped out from the side alley. One threw her a tool kit, which she caught and slung over her shoulder. One of the men swiped an access card, and the apartment door opened. Talking about the latest V-Game, they entered the building and went up three flights of stairs, ignoring the elevator.

"OK, you ready?" the first man asked her.

Michi didn't know any of the men, and she hoped they didn't know her. She nodded, though, and slid off her overalls and stuffed them in her tool kit. She thought she caught the briefest flicker of prurient interest from at least two of them as they slid out of their overalls, revealing black military-looking uniforms, but no one said a word. Each of the men had a wicked looking handgun strapped to his thigh, and the shortest of the three handed Michi one in a belted holster. She started to put it on backwards, and without a word, the short guy helped her get it attached. Michi looked down at it. She didn't have a clue how to fire it if it came to that, but it did feel reassuring as it hung on her hip. No one was supposed to get hurt, but they had come prepared.

They silently climbed up two more flights, then slipped into a utility closet. Standing there, half-naked, at least in her mind, in close proximity to three men, Michi wondered how she got to this position. Just two months ago, her main concerns were ballet and planning a wedding. Now she was hiding in a closet, waiting to attack a Federation Marine.

One of the men, the swarthy-looking guy, Michi thought, had horrible breath. Michi thought she was going to gag as it filled the closet. Then, to make things worse, the short guy, the one who had handed her the handgun, let out a quiet fart. That broke the tension. No one laughed out loud, but there was a sense of normalcy about it. Suddenly, Michi felt OK.

It was only five or so more minutes before they heard movement outside. There was a quiet knock, then a whispered greeting. The four of them waited another five minutes before creeping out and moving to Kelli Mae's door.

The tallest of the three put his ear to the door and listened: no high-tech gear, just an ear to the door. He nodded and motioned to the stairwell, and the bad-breath guy left and disappeared down it. He was their security.

The three left got into position. Michi knew what she was supposed to do, but it would have been nice to rehearse it at least once. She nervously waited behind the two men as the tall guy took out a small rectangular box that he held up to the lock. Red lights blinked for a few seconds before turning green.

For a moment, Michi wondered what his name was. It seemed impersonal to refer to him only as "the tall guy." Then there was no time to wonder. He pushed open the door and the three of them barged in.

The Marine was at full throttle, pounding away at Kelli Mae, whose feet were up in the air straddling her thrusting paramour. He had time to glance behind him and start to dive off of her before both of Michi's companions were on him, dragging the young man to the floor. Michi could see they needed no help, so she jumped on the bed, straddling the sweaty girl and placing a hand over her mouth.

"Shh," she said, holding a finger over her mouth. "Stay quiet, and no one is going to get hurt.

The Marine was struggling, and he managed to get up to a sitting position. Michi contemplated joining the fight when the tall guy managed to ziptie the Marine's hands in back of him and slap a pressure gag on his mouth. They hauled him up, avoiding his kicks. The shorter guy stepped in back of the Marine, put him in a choke hold, and began to apply pressure before easing off. The Marine got the message and stopped struggling.

He was glaring bloody murder, though, and Michi had no question on what he would do to them if he could. He stood there, stark naked, being held, yet he was not cowed. He was no longer rampant, and his dick still had Kelli Mae on it, but he stood as if he had on full battle gear.

Kelli Mae, on the other hand, squirmed under Michi, not to escape, but to pull up a sheet to try to cover herself. She didn't speak, but terror showed in her eyes. Michi felt a moment of compassion for her, but they had a job to do, and she was going to get it done.

"Over here, with the bed in the background," she said. The shorter man nodded and brought the Marine over to the foot of the bed.

The other man reached in his tool kit and pulled out a small, high-def holocam. He stood in front of Michi, ready to go.

"Look, lance corporal, you are going to be let free if you cooperate," Michi said. "I want you to stand beside me while we record something. That's it. Then you and your girlfriend will be free to go. If you make a move, if you try anything, not only will you fail, but Kelli Mae will pay the price. Do you understand, and do you agree?"

Michi would not hurt the girl no matter what happened, but the Marine didn't need to know that.

"Nod your head if you agree."

"Thane!" Kelli Mae pleaded.

"Shut up!" Michi ordered, not turning around to look at the girl.

The Marine looked beyond Michi at Kelli, and Michi could see the capitulation. He nodded.

"Good. Stand here," she said, pulling him over as her short companion stepped just out of cam range, but close enough to move in if need be. He pulled out his handgun and kept it loosely aimed at the bed.

Michi looked back at Kelli Mae, who had managed to cover herself. Michi knelt on the bed, then turned the girl slightly to the side, pulling back the sheet to reveal a long expanse of her side and legs. She let the girl keep the sheet over her front, but Michi wanted there to be no question as to what had been happening.

"You can put your head down so no one can see your face," she whispered to the girl before getting off the bed to stand next to the Marine.

She nodded at the tall guy, and when the record light came on, she started.

"I am a member of the Free Kakurega Militia. We have been formed to protect our rights under our Federation Charter, rights that have been abrogated by Propitious Interstellar Fabrication, Inc. Not only have they broken the charter, but they have brought in Federation Marines to crush our legal right to protest.

"Today, we have stopped one of their Marines, Lance Corporal Thane Regent, from abusing a free citizen of Kakurega."

At Michi's use of "abusing," The Marine stirred, but Michi's short companion raised his weapon and pointed it at Kelli Mae, who thankfully didn't see it as her face was still buried. The Marine saw it though, and he got the message and stood still.

"The Federation Marines have the power here. They killed three of our citizens when they arrived. They are enforcing martial law. And now they take our citizens for their own perverted pleasure.

"It is up to you, people of Kakurega. Will you stand for this? From First Families and all Free Citizens, from employees and indentureds, this is our home, and Propitious Interstellar cannot break the charter as they deem fit.

"If you agree, on this Saturday, at 9:00 AM in the city, we urge all of you to take to the streets. We are not advocating violence. We leave that to the Marines and Propitious Interstellar security forces. But let your voices be heard. Let the Federation know we will not stand for this."

With that, she swept one hand back to indicate Kelli Mae. This was adlibbed, but the tall guy took the hint and zoomed in. Kelli Mae's sobs shook her body, and Michi knew this was good footage. She made the cut motion, and the tall guy cut out.

"It's OK, Kelli Mae. It's over. You did fine," she said, reaching over to put her hand on the girl's shoulder.

The girl flinched, and looked up. "It's not fine, you bitch. We love each other. It's not like you said," she spewed with anger.

The Marine, hands still bound behind him, climbed into bed and leaned up against his lover, who put her hands protectively around him.

Suddenly, Michi felt dirty. Very dirty.

She wanted to say something about the greater good, but their security came running into the apartment.

"Trouble! We've got jacks swarming."

Michi's heart fell. How had they found out so quickly?

The tall guy pointed up, and all four of them sprinted out the door, leaving the two lovers, and over to the stairwell. Taking the stairs three steps at a time, they climbed to the tenth floor and out onto the roof. Michi automatically looked up, hoping that Doug had been able to gain control of any overhead surveillance in the area.

Each of the four had his or her own escape route, but both Michi and the tall guy had the same initial first step. The tall guy stopped to wordlessly shake Michi's hand before he took off. Michi followed and was on his tail as they jumped the alley to the roof of the next building. Michi barely made it, falling down and rolling on the other roof, cursing her ungainly boots. The tall guy turned to the right and was gone while Michi scrambled up to keep going straight to the next building over.

Below her and back at Kelli Mae's building, she heard shouting and sirens. She didn't have much time. She wondered if she had twisted an ankle, so despite the urgency, she approached the edge of the building cautiously. The next building was a story shorter than this one, and she had to make sure of where she landed.

The helmeted jack who appeared in front of her, climbing the fire escape, took her by surprise. Instinctively, she flowed into her favorite roundhouse kick. The jack saw it coming and tried to duck, but hanging on the fire escape limited him, and she caught him up high, knocking him off the ladder.

Michi rushed forward and looked down. Four or five meters below her, another jack was clinging with one hand to the ladder, the other holding the dangling jack Michi had just kicked. The one still on the ladder looked up, hate in his eyes. Michi knew he would shoot her if he could, but he needed both hands to hang on and keep his friend from plummeting to his death. Michi briefly considered dropping something on them, but that would be a wasted gesture, and one that would cost her time.

She took a few steps back and launched herself over the alley. Her ankle cried out, but she pushed beyond the pain and landed cleanly on the other side. Maybe getting beat up by Seth was doing her some good.

She took a right and ran down the length of the building, dodging air conditioning units and running around a rooftop garden, then stepping up to the next building. Somebody had already placed a rough steel grate between the two, so it was an easy transition.

These apartment buildings were part of Propitious Interstellar's second expansion, constructed when they needed rooms for their workers. The buildings were generally cheap and close together with fire codes only loosely followed. Some buildings were connected to each other, others had ten foot alleys between them. By jumping, Michi was able to quickly move five buildings over. She risked a glance behind her. If two jacks had been climbing, others would be, too, and face-spoofer or not, Doug could not hide her from direct human vision. Just as she reached her stairway down, she saw the first jack making it to the top of Kelli Mae's building. He was a good 70 meters away, but Michi was clearly visible if he turned around.

Praying that the door was open, she yanked herself off-balance and almost fell inside just as the jack started to turn. She didn't know if he saw her. She was supposed to stay as her redhead alter-ego, but the two kids and at least one jack had seen her bright red hair, so she turned her face-spoofer off and pulled out her overalls, struggling to get them over her stupid costume. The boots almost got her killed. She considered leaving them there, but walking around barefoot while in overalls would draw attention, and despite them being sprayed with a derma-barrier, she wasn't confident that a forensic lab could not find some of her DNA if she left it to be found.

Calm down, calm down. You're just a worker going about her business, she kept telling herself.

She casually made her way down the stairs, too scared to use the elevator despite being several buildings away. She nodded to an old lady at the building's front door, holding it open for her. Then she was out in the sunshine. There were sirens, and overhead, a chopper came screaming up. Michi resisted the urge to watch it and instead kept walking, trying not to look suspicious. People had come out of the buildings to warily watch the commotion. They had to be curious, but this was still a martial law situation, and no one wanted to be caught in any crossfire that might erupt.

Michi didn't start to relax until she was on the tram heading home. She hoped her three unnamed companions had made it out safely. It had been close, but she thought they had gotten out in time.

That left the question as to how the jacks had responded so quickly. They could have been spotted inside the building, she acknowledged, but Doug had been confident on blocking off anything inside. And if he hadn't that was still a very quick reaction.

No, there was only one logical explanation. Cheri had been right in her suspicions. There was a traitor within the WRP.

Chapter 20

Michi and Tamara sat on the couch, focused on Michi's manifesto. The signal wavered once or twice as the broadcast company tried to regain control over the feed, but whoever was hacking it was able to keep the clip running.

Michi knew it was her on the holo, but with the different face and voice, it was easy to feel it was someone else, a stranger. That somehow enabled her to really look at it, to analyze it.

The obvious, in-your-face aspect was that Tamara and Cheri had been right. She, the redhead Michi, looked great. Michi didn't know if holo had been brushed up or not, but the outfit, the face Doug had given her, even her earnest but intense voice created an image of a strong, capable woman, with the emphasis on *woman*. When she had put on the top, in particular, she thought it too small, but on the holo, it emphasized her curves and femininity. Michi rarely felt feminine anymore after she outgrew her dance partners, and she liked the feeling.

As the holo came on, Tamara had exclaimed, "Balls, girl, you look pure dead hot," and for once, Michi accepted that.

The boots, the ones she hated, worked well, too. They took away from the camouflage bammers that clung to her legs and ass and gave her a more military air. With the handgun hanging from her waist, she looked decidedly warrior-like. She decided she liked the look, even if she was going to have to work on the boots' utility.

The Marine standing beside her looked deflated. The small flinch he'd made when Michi had said "abusing" had been edited out. It was hard to look tough when naked, and with his head hanging down, he simply looked defeated.

Then there was Kelli Mae. Michi knew that her family had been contacted and informed that it would be *best* for everyone if she did not volunteer that it was her in the holo. Sitting on the bed in back of Michi, head down, she was the perfect picture of an abused woman. The sobs that wracked her body showed up perfectly on the holo, and even knowing the truth, Michi felt a twinge of pity for the poor, abused girl.

Of course, the abuse was at the hands of Michi and her three companions. Kelli Mae had done nothing wrong other than fall in love, and what she had gone through was at the hands of Cheri and Michi. Michi did feel guilty about that, but it was for the greater good, right?"

"Stars above, we've got to watch that again," Tamara said as the holo faded it. She hit the playback, and the two roommates re-watched it, pausing it a couple of times to point out details.

"Powerful stuff, that," Tamara said, serious for once. "I think it's a glove to the face of the Federation. I just hope it rallies, the people for Saturday."

"Do you think it will?" Michi asked.

"Well, it will sure rally the male population and more than a few of the female, girl," she said, the irreverent Tamara back as she punched Michi in the arm. "They may not understand the cause, but they'll follow you, looking like that."

They watched the replay several times, and when they switched back to the live feed, a response was already being aired. The company, of course, decried the act of "terrorism." A Marine spokesman issued a statement asserting that the so-called abuse was a case of consenting adults, and a chagrined-looking Thane Regent was trotted out where he insisted that he had been with his girlfriend.

When a reporter asked for the name of the girlfriend, the spokesman stepped back in and said for privacy reasons, they could not reveal that. Michi had half-expected the Marines to release Kelli Mae's name, but the organization's arcane sense of honor evidently got in the way of that. And by not releasing her name, it made their statement seem like a cover-up. They were telling the truth, Michi knew, but they certainly seemed guilty.

Despite an almost disastrous conclusion, the mission looked to be a success. The real test was on Saturday, though. Would the people rally to the cause? Without massive public support, anything they did was just pissing in the wind.

Chapter 21

"Feelin' better?" Seth asked as Michi came through the door.

"Oh, yeah, much better," she said, for a moment forgetting that she had called in sick the day before.

She was glad to get back. With two more days before the planned rally, she had pent up nervous energy, and a session with Seth seemed like the perfect antidote.

She stripped to her unitard, left her Clodders and outerwear on the counter, and got on the mat where without warming up, Seth was on her. Fifteen sweaty minutes later, Seth released his kimura lock and slid away to sit while Michi caught her breath.

"You seem fine, considerin' your health."

"Oh, like I said, I'm better, and it really wasn't much."

"Good to know. Your health is number one, am I right?"

"Yeah, right," Michi said, wondering at the direction Seth was taking. He never seemed too concerned about her health before.

"What did you think about that holo yesterday, the one where that Marine was called out for abusing that poor lass?" he said, switching topics.

"Uh, it was disgusting," she said, the response she had decided upon in case anyone asked her.

"Yeah, Marines are always chasin' pussy, you know. Gets them in more trouble. But that woman in the holo, she was something else, am I right?"

"I . . . I guess so," she got out.

"A redhead, too. Not many around here, and I always was partial to redheads. And she was a big girl. I like that. Nice big tits."

Despite herself, Michi started to color. "I wouldn't know about that."

"Oh, of course not. Excuse me if I was a little crude there. Just statin' facts," Seth went on. "'Sides, there are lots of big, strong women around. Like you, for example.

"You know, I had a visit from the jacks about two months ago. Remember the jack who got himself kilt in that drug deal?"

"I think so," Michi said, trying not to let her rising apprehension show.

"Well, first, they wanted to know where I was when he got zeroed. Seems, that as a discharged Marine and someone who knows his way in a fight, they thought I might be a suspect. Luckily, I had an alibi, so then they asked me for my opinion. I looked at the holos, and I told them it had to be a big, strong man who zeroed the guy. His neck was broken, and from one hit. No other damage."

"Yeah, a strong guy, that makes sense."

"But I been thinkin', why only a guy? A big strong girl could do it, too, like that girl on the holo, 'specially one who knew some fightin' means, and 'specially if she was wearin' heavy boots. I don't think she could do it with a punch, but maybe a kick, like the roundhouse you like to throw. A good kick, with boots, iffen she got lucky, that could do it."

Seth broke his gaze on her to stare at Michi's clods where she had left them on the counter.

"You got sometin' to tell me?" he asked.

Michi wanted to leave, but she tried to sound casual as she replied, "No. You might be right, but I wouldn't know."

"Do you think I'm a huddy, girl? 'Cause I'm a MacPruitt and not one of you high-side Clan families? I may not be as good-speakin' as you, I may not be as educated, but I can see what's in front of my own eyes."

Michi said nothing, staring down at her hands.

"I did some research. Your fiancé was that indentured who was killed. As they say, in the cop holos, you've got the motive. You wear those Clodders, and I'm thinking that with your roundhouse and your strength, iffen you caught some jack unawares, you could possibly break his neck. But most of all, I've been all over you on this mat. I've had my hands on you. I know your body. I know that little dark spot on your hip. When they changed your face in editin', they forgot one thing. That, good cousin, was you on the holo. Deny it if you can."

Michi wanted to deny it. She wanted to jump up and run out.

Instead, she meekly asked, “What are you going to do?”

“Me? What are *you* goin’ to do is the real question. Are you here to get some revenge? If you are, you’re wasting your time.”

For a moment, Michi had hoped she could enlist Seth as an ally. But he was rejecting her.

“I’m sorry, I thought I could . . . I just don’t know.”

“Look, girl, I knew that was you on the holo, but I was guessing about the jack. You got lucky, damn lucky with that. You try that amateur shit with the Marines here, you’re going to get crushed.”

Michi shuddered, thinking of the ass-whipping she and Tamara had received.

“You are too, too First Family, all right and proper, all by the rules. You don’t have the killer instinct.”

“I do so,” she protested.

“No, you don’t. What did I do when we first fought here?”

“You know what you did,” she bristled. “You hit me, well, down there.”

“Damn, you can’t even say it, can you? I hit your freakin’ fud, girl. Smack in your pussy. And what did you do about it? Nothin’. Then in the crucifix, what’d I do?”

Michi thought back, then remembered his driving his crotch in her face before letting her up.

“You pushed your . . . your . . . *balls* in my face,” she almost shouted.

“And what did you do about it?”

“Nothing! What could I do about it? You had me in a crucifix!”

“Bullshit! You can always do something. You could have bitten me, taken a chunk out of my knob!” he said, his voicing rising in emphasis.

“You . . . you wanted me to bite your dick?”

“No, I wanted you to try. I wanted to see where your spirit was. You weren’t gonna succeed, but I wanted to see you resort to what you could. But no, that would get you disqualified from an MMA match? And you’d never do that, am I right? Let me tell you, girl, that won’t cut it in a fight with a Marine. He’ll do everythin’ he can to win, and there are no rules. Even Saint Lysander, he's resorted to some underhanded shit despite what the Marine propaganda machine would lead you to believe."

"You mean that commander they talk about on the newsfeeds?"

"Yeah, that commander. Captain Ryck Lysander, hero of the Corps."

"You know him?" she asked.

"Unfortunately, yes. We went to boot together, and served in the fleet. I even broke his arm once. He's an arrogant bastard, I can tell you."

"You broke his arm? Why?" she asked curiosity overtaking her anxiety for a moment.

"Call it payback. But forget him. Any Marine's gonna fight dirty if that's what it takes. You can't play by no fuckin' rules if you want to survive. And you, cousin dear, don't have it in you.

"Look, I love MMA. It pulled me up and gave me my shot at a better life. It got me into the Marines, before I screwed that. It pays my bills now. But it's a freakin' sport, not battle. And until you get that there are no rules in a fight, you are gonna get crushed."

"What about you?" Michi asked excitedly. "Why don't you join us?"

"Join you? Fat fuckin' chance of that!" he said with a snort.

"Why not? You don't like the Marines, I can tell. You can't support the company. Who do you support?"

"I support me. I always have. I'm Clan, but not Clan. None of us MacPruitts matter squat to the rest of you. I joined the Marines, but I never fit in. The company doesn't want much to do with me, neither. I'll just make my own way like I always do."

"But this is your chance to hit back. What about that commander? Get back at him. Get back at the Marines, at least," she continued.

Seth leaned forward and grabbed her wrist, bending her arm back.

"The Marine Corps and me may have not parted on the best of terms, but that was my fault. The day I pinned on my sergeant's chevrons was the second best day of my life. I just couldn't play by the rules until it was too late. And Captain Lysander? He's an arrogant asshole, but he's a good Marine, and I respect him. I don't like him, but I would follow him into combat. No matter what, no matter what silly-arse games you play with the company, be sure of one thing—I will never lift my hand against another Marine."

He let go of her arm, and she brought it back to her lap, rubbing it to restore the circulation he'd cut off.

"What about me? What are you going to do?"

"I ain't gonna do nothing. I don't care what you do, and I won't stop you from getting yourself zeroed, 'cause that's exactly what's gonna happen iffen you try and play by the rules against the Marines."

She sat there, looking at Seth. She didn't understand him, but she could sense his conviction.

"Can I at least keep coming to your dojo?" she quietly asked.

"I don't think so, Michiko. You need to forget about MMA as a sport."

"But you can help me with that."

"Yeah, I could. But I won't. I won't stand in your way, but I ain't gonna help you, neither. And when you fail, I don't want them to trace you back to me. I don't got no dog in this fight.

"I think it's time for you to leave."

Michi sighed, then slowly stood up. She picked up her outer clothes on the counter, and with one look back at Seth sitting on the mat, she turned and opened the door.

"Go with God, cousin," she heard him say without his usual sarcasm as the door closed behind her.

Chapter 22

Seth had been right about one thing, Michi conceded. Neither she nor anyone else was going to force the issue by getting into fistfights. This was not a refereed fight in a ring going three five-minute rounds. This was real life, and if Michi wanted to get the Marines off Kakurega, she had to use more than a roundhouse kick.

As she came home from Seth's dojo, his words echoed in her mind. Maybe she was biting off more than she could chew, but she had never actually analyzed that. She had just acted willy-nilly on her emotions.

Despite the apparent success of their little mission to Kelli Mae's home, Michi realized that they were amateurs, and that almost got the four of them arrested—or worse. If she was going to continue opposing the company and the Federation occupation, that had to be addressed. She decided to take the bull by the horns and called Doug, asking him to stop by on his way to work in the morning.

Tamara was still asleep when Doug showed up, eager to see what Michi wanted. Michi took Doug to the kitchen table, poured him a cup of coffee, and sat him down.

"What's up," he asked.

"Did you tell anyone you were coming?"

"No, I did as you asked. What's with all the secrecy?" he asked, a puzzled look on his face.

"You know that our little mission the other day almost ended up as a disaster, right?"

"Yeah, I was monitoring it. Close call, huh?"

"Did you wonder why, how the jacks knew to come?"

"I guess someone spotted you on the way in?" he offered.

"No one spotted us. The jacks were tipped off by someone in the WRP. And you are going to help me flush him or her out."

"I, uh, what? What am I going to do?"

"I figured it out last night. There's a traitor in the organization, and we're going to find out who it is. That's why no one else can get wind of it. Look, who's the leader of the NIP?" she asked.

"The National Independence Party? No one knows. It's a secret. That's how they keep going," he said.

"Exactly, but with the big rally tomorrow, don't you think they might want to have a hand in it? And wouldn't they maybe reach out to the WRP?"

"Yes, but so what? How does that help you find this traitor you think is there?"

"I don't think. I know!" she said with conviction. "Look, this is what I want you to do. Can you send out, say, eight different messages, all saying that the leader of the NIP wants to meet, but he wants to meet only one person in absolute secrecy?"

"Sure, that's easy. But what will that get you?"

"I want each meeting place in a different spot, somewhere where we can monitor and see if the jacks show up," she said.

"Ah, kilo-brills! I get it. So if there really is a traitor, and if the jacks show up, that's our man. Or woman, I mean."

"So, can you set that up? I was thinking if we stagger the supposed meetings and put them close together, like at Morning Star, we could keep an eye on all of them," Michi offered.

"Morning Star is compact, so if you wanted to physically stake out a place, sure, that apartment complex would work. But get with the times, Michiko! We don't need to be there at all. Tennyson I and II are easy hacks, and we can sit right here and watch each meeting spot. There's no way we can miss them," Doug said with just a hint of condescension in his voice.

Michi let it slide. This was Doug's arena, and she let him take charge. He muttered to himself for the next twenty minutes before asking Michi how many meeting sites she wanted.

"I'm not sure. We need enough to cover anyone who might have the information that the company wants, but they would have to be high enough for the NIP leader to want to meet."

"Well, I can think of a few. Rosario, for sure. He's in charge of security, and he would have the easiest time. I never did like him, anyway. Gabriella, Su, and Rangle. They're all on the board, but Su hasn't been active lately."

"No, keep Su on the list," Michi told him.

"I guess you want Hokkam, too?"

"Yep. He's in position."

"OK, that would be five so far," Doug said.

"And Cheri," Michi said with conviction.

"You think Cheri could be a traitor?" Doug asked surprised. "She hooked the three of us up."

"No, I don't think she is, but we need to be sure," Michi said, ashamed for even doubting her.

But Seth said you had to be ruthless to succeed, and she'd be damned if the person who either ordered or allowed Franz to be killed got away with it.

"OK, that's six. Any more?"

"Maybe Sven Tyler. He seems to be in everyone's hair. Can you handle seven?"

"No problem. I could handle more than that," he said confidently.

"No, if we don't get a bite on this attempt, we might go down the list and try again. Let's work on the wording of the message itself."

They went back and forth on that for a good half an hour, trying to make it compelling, but not going overboard. They stressed that the meeting had to be extremely confidential, that the "leader" only wanted to meet one person. Michi didn't want anyone to start comparing notes about the liaison. Finally, between the two of them, they had something they thought would work. Michi thought someone might suspect a trap, but Doug pointed out that a real traitor would have communications with the company, and he or she would know it wasn't some company trick. If any of the others suspected something, then it wouldn't matter anyway.

"OK, send it out," she told him.

It only took a few minutes before he broke out into a broad smile and said, "Done and done!"

"Done and done what?" Tamara said, coming out of her bedroom and rubbing her eyes. "What are you doing here so early, Dougie?"

"Ah, we've been—"

"We've been working on some new ideas for the face-spoofer, you know, so it can change more of the body, too," Michi said, stepping firmly on Doug's foot under the table.

"And this had to be done now?" she asked as she reached over for Doug's coffee, took a sip, and made a face.

"You need to freshen that up," she said, tossing the cold coffee in the sink and getting a refill from the brewmaster. She took a sip. "There, that's better," she said before giving the cup back to him.

"OK, you two have fun. I need a shower," she said with a yawn as she went to the bathroom.

"You think Tamara could be the traitor?" Doug asked incredulously.

"No, I don't," she said, even if she felt a touch of guilt because no, at the moment, she didn't trust anyone 100%. If she hadn't needed him, she would have done this without Doug, too. "But what she doesn't know, she can't be implicated in it."

"I guess so, but it seems weird. We're like the Three Musketeers, aren't we?"

He seemed so earnest that she had to assure him that yes, they were a team. All three of them.

"OK, while she's in the shower, give me a rundown on how to monitor these things," she told him.

"No reason, to. I'll be doing it, so there'll be no screw-up," he told her.

"We set this up for this afternoon. Don't you have work?"

"Oh ye of little faith, my queen. As I sit here, I am at work. Little packets of information are going out: key strokes, messages, some unauthorized surfing. If anyone checks, I am at my desk right now."

"Really? Well what happens if someone tries to find you to talk?"

"Like in person? For real? No one does that, and if they did and saw me missing from my cubbyhole, they'd think I was in the lab or in the field. I do this all the time, and no one has ever caught on."

"You do? What do you do when you're playing hooky?"

"Oh, you know. All sorts of things. Sleeping in. Seeing a flick. Going to a game."

"A game? What sports do you watch?" she said with a disbelieving laugh.

"Oh, I get it Miss MMA superfighter. Just because I like tech means I can't like sports, right? For your information, I'm a Gryphons fan, always have been. I've had season tickets since I was 18," he told her, a hint of anger in his voice.

Michi felt bad about that. There had been no reason for her attitude.

"Sorry," she said, trying to fix things. "Of course you like sports. It's just you never talk about them, and most guys, you can't shut them up about this team or that."

"Umpf. Maybe," he said, only slightly mollified.

"The Gryphons suck, by the way," she added. "You need to root for a real team, like the Desecrators!"

"Desecrators? Oh, let me tell you about the Desecrators . . ."

That started at least 20 minutes of smack talk. Tamara came out, listened for a moment, then shook her head and left for work without a word. They ended up agreeing to disagree, as most sports arguments ended, and turned on the holo. They settled on watching an old Frank Garrison comedy, one both had seen before but still got them laughing. Frank G was so stupid that he shouldn't be funny to anyone with an IQ over 60, but still, they both enjoyed the flick.

When it was over, Michi looked at Tamara's cuckoo clock. The analog hands showed it was only 9:20. Michi groaned. They had almost five hours to go.

Time crawled while every possible thing that could go wrong was brought up and discussed. Maybe two of their targets started talking. Maybe they weren't even checking their messages. Three of them worked for the company, and if they did access their private zips, they might not be able to get away. Michi and Doug realized that they should have made the meeting for the evening, instead.

Their brainstorming revealed one possible hole in their plan, though. If the jacks did react, and then when there was no NIB leader there, they would certainly contact their spy. They decided to block all messages to the traitor, then they ginned up a "success" message that Doug would send if the jacks did react. That should calm the traitor and keep him or her from bolting.

They made noodles for lunch, but after one bite, Michi couldn't eat any more. She was too wound up. Finally, 2:30, the time of the first meeting was approaching. Doug put his PA on an easel and turned on the seven surveillance cams into which he'd hacked. Each one had the name of the target person to whom that apartment number had been given. There was some movement, and Michi jumped from where she was standing looking over Doug's shoulder.

It was a woman with a small child on her arm. She made her way to the door, swiped it, then went inside. If the jacks broke into her apartment, she would be terrified.

"Just whose apartments did you pick?" she asked.

"Don't know. I never looked at the occupant lists. I just wanted apartments where I had good coverage."

She was the one who was supposed to be hardened by necessity, but she worried about a woman and child while it was Doug who focused on the mission. She shook her head and went back to watching the monitors.

Nothing was happening, and Michi thought that their traitor either wasn't one of the seven or hadn't taken the bait. She was about to give up when three of the feeds flickered.

"We've got something here," Doug said, checking a fast scrolling file that appeared at the corner of his PA screen. "Someone else is onboard. This is building 2002."

"Do they know you're there, too?" she asked him.

"No reason they would. I'm passive here."

They waited anxiously for several minutes, then just at the edge of cam range on one of the feeds, several sets of military-like boots could be seen. Slowly, the riot-equipped jacks edged along the wall until they flanked the target door. Another man in a StarEx uniform came up to the door, just a deliveryman making his rounds. He even had a package under his arm. He tried the bell first, and when there was no answer, knocked.

He finally stepped back and shook his head. One of the jacks leaned forward, holding a master lock to the door. The lock light flashed green, and the jacks rushed in.

Doug needlessly pointed at the name at the top of the feed. Michi had been well aware of who was the traitor.

"Send the success message, then block anything else except from me. I've got a few people I need to contact about this. Good job, Doug, we won this fight."

The only thing was that it didn't feel like a win.

Chapter 23

Michi tried to calm her expression. She was just there for a visit before the big rally, right? She gave herself a body shake, then opened the door to the WRP office spaces.

It was almost 6:00 PM, and those who had been at work all day were straggling in. There was an air of building excitement. WRP's official mission statement was to monitor the treatment of workers, particularly Class 3s and 4s, but over the last year, rallies had become a big part of what they did, and the members hoped that tomorrow's rally would be their biggest yet. It was reasonable that Michi, even if she was not officially a member of the organization, would stop by and see how things were going.

"Michiko, it's good to see you," Gabriella said, looking up. She came around some desks and gave Michi a kiss on the cheek.

Gabriella was the chapter quartermaster, in charge of accounting. That also placed her on the board. Michi hugged her back, returned the kiss, and tried to show nothing on her face as she slipped a small, printed note into Gabriella's side pocket.

"Just coming by to say hi and see how things are going for tomorrow," she said.

"You can imagine," Gabriella told her. "Things are rather hectic. Let's catch up after this is over, OK?"

Michi had to hold back a smile. Yes, they would be meeting sooner than perhaps Gabriella expected.

Michi made the rounds, stopping to chat with people she knew. There were many people she didn't recognize. Evidently, the Federation's latest actions had inspired a good number of people to join the cause.

As expected, Su was not there, but she exchanged pleasantries with both Rangle and Rosario, slipping each one his own note. Neither noticed her doing it, which had been a concern. She didn't want any discussion in public.

She tracked down Sven in the computer room. Passing his note was easy. His nose was so buried in some messages that Michi didn't think anything would register with him.

Michi didn't want to seem too purposeful, so it was ten or fifteen minutes before she stuck her head in Hokkam's office. As expected, Cheri was also there along with two people Michi didn't recognize.

"Michiko," Hokkam said, rising to greet her. "How are you?"

He was wearing his usual Dashi one-piece, with its sealed pockets. Michi, expecting that, had his slip in her hand, and she passed it directly to his as he reached out to pull her in for a kiss. He didn't bat an eye as she turned around and gave Cheri a hug, slipping the last piece of paper into her back pocket.

"Good to see you, dear," Cheri said.

"Greg, K'to, this is Michiko MacCailín, a friend of the chapter. Michiko, Greg and K'to are from Earth Headquarters."

Greg had started to greet Michi, but his face took a downturn as Hokkam told Michi who he was.

"Oh, don't worry Greg. Michiko can be trusted. She was Franz Galipili's fiancé," Hokkam told him.

"Oh, sorry for your loss. He was a valued member of the WRP family," Greg said.

Michi thanked him and made nice for a minute before Hokkam said, "Michiko, it's nice to see you again, but we've got quite a bit to do before tomorrow. Will you be coming?"

"Yes, I wouldn't miss it. I'm sorry for disturbing you, and I'll let you get back to work."

She left Hokkam's office, greeted a few more people, and left the outer office. In the hallway outside, she started trembling and leaned back against the wall, taking some deep breaths. That had been more difficult than she had expected. Slipping the notes and leaving traces of her DNA had been the easiest part. It was just being in there, knowing what she knew, and acting like a good and loyal friend that had taxed her emotions.

Ever-conscious of surveillance, Michi centered herself and walked out of the building. Down the street was an upscale café owned by a cousin—an actual blood relative, not the casual use of the term. She walked in, chatted with Bridgette, and had a cup of Lastermay tea. Bridgette would have been well aware that Michi was not living at home—family matters were hard to keep private, and gossip was traded like gold amongst the First Families—but Bridgette never let on as they talked. First Families like their profit even more than gossip, and even a simple cup of tea added to the day's take.

Michi hung out, listening to what gossip Bridgette was dishing out—and getting interested despite herself—before finally making her goodbyes at about 7:15. She stepped out into the dusk and made her way towards the Gut, stopping several blocks short. Checking for any obvious surveillance cams, she flicked on her face-spoofer.

When she had asked Doug if there was another face she could use, he had eagerly shown her over a dozen he'd already prepared. She selected one with Indian features. Without a mirror, she hoped that was what she looked like.

Then she took a can of a derma-barrier and started to spray her hands and face. Derma-barriers were used by medical personnel to keep them from contracting their patients' diseases, but as a side-effect, they kept skin flakes and other bodily detritus from littering the area. Hair could still fall, and that could be tested for DNA, but the spray lessened the amount of Michi that could be found by a forensic team. And if they did find anything, well, that is why she had gone to the office earlier and hugged everyone. Finally, she took out a new silk scarf and wrapped it around her head. If a hair would betray her and fall, it would have to work to make it to the ground. Finally, she took a disposable rain poncho out of her pocket and put it on.

With a new face and as safe as she could make herself, she continued on into the Gut and to the statue. Three jacks walked by on patrol, but they didn't give her a second glance. She felt a stirring of pride knowing that is was because of her actions that the jacks weren't allowed to walk alone anymore. Doug had assured her that the spot in back of the statue was clear of surveillance, so she switched off the face-spoofer and was Michi again. Then she waited. And waited. She kept looking at her watch. Curfew was approaching, and she wondered if the notes had been a good idea.

Her first inclination had been to send a regular message to everyone, but despite Doug's assurances that they could not be traced, she figured if he could trace something like that, so could someone else. So she switched to printed notes.

If no one found the notes, though then it had been a waste of time.

"Michiko, I assume this is as important as you indicated," a voice said from in back of her. "And all this cloak and dagger was really necessary?"

Michi spun around to see Hokkam standing in back of her. At least he'd read the note. She looked around, but no one was with him.

"Yes, it is very important, and I couldn't say it at the office. I've got something vital to tell you, and after that, it's up to you on what you want to do."

Hokkam gave her a condescending look and asked, "So what's so important? Curfew's in 25 minutes, and we've got a big day tomorrow."

Michi looked around as if to check for eavesdroppers. "Not here. Come," she said, taking his arm and leading him to the small alley where the trash bins for Franny's were lined up.

"Michiko, just tell me. If you really know something important, then I can take care of whatever it is," he protested as he resisted her pull. "Stop pulling me. I'm not taking another step until you tell me what it is!"

Michi spun him around, shoving him between two of the trash bins. She jumped forward, putting her forearm under his throat, cutting off any potential cry for help.

"Cheri told me she thought there was a traitor in the chapter, and she was right," she hissed as Hokkam's eyes grew large with the onset of panic. "But you knew that," she said as she pulled Tamara's 10cm chef's knife from her belly pocket and thrust it into Hokkam's belly.

He let out an "oof" sound that escaped past Michi's arm, and he tried to struggle. He was not a small man, but he couldn't move his killer.

"I should have known it was you. I saw you edging away from the rest back on the day Franz was murdered, but before any shots were fired. You knew what was coming, didn't you? Because it was you who set it up."

Hokkam tried to shake his head, probably to deny it. But he couldn't deny that it was to his supposed meeting place that the jacks had shown up that afternoon.

Michi rammed the knife in deeper, then twisted it and started slowly pulling it across and down Hokkam's belly, only stopping when the knife hung up on his belt.

A sudden smell of blood, shit, and piss assaulted her nose. This is what death smelled like up close and personal. She stared into Hokkam's eyes as they faded and went dull.

She wanted to feel something as she looked into his dead face. She wanted triumph, revenge, anger: anything. Instead, she felt nothing. She stepped back and let the body slide to the ground.

Working quickly, she bent over and started sawing through his neck. No one was going to get him into regen, she vowed. It was much more difficult to separate his head, though, using a kitchen knife than she had expected. It took partly cutting, partly sawing, and partly brute strength to yank the head free.

She had to work quickly. She was basically out of sight from the road, but anyone—from the bar staff to a jack patrol—could happen by.

She looked down at her gore covered legs. Hokkam had had a lot of blood in him. She quickly stripped off the rain poncho and dropped it to the ground. Then off came her slacks. She had liberally applied the derma-barrier to her legs earlier, and it seemed to have worked in keeping the gore in the slacks and not sticking to her skin. She pulled down the legs of the minishorts she had on underneath the slacks.

Her shoes, though! She hadn't thought that through. They were covered. Michi bent down, grabbed the slacks, and using the cleaner area around the butt, used them to clean off as much of Hokkam from her shoes as she could. It wasn't a great job, but it would have to do.

As she stood up, another problem made itself known. Even in the darkness, a bloody footprint could be seen.

Reaching into her belly pocket, she took out the glass bottle that Doug had given her before she left. Very carefully, she poured it on the pile with her slacks and poncho. A vile-smelling smoke arose from the pile as the molecular-debonder reacted to break down the clothing. She had to add a few drops here and there to keep the reaction going. But within a minute, all that was left of the pile were some component chemicals. A good forensic investigator could determine what had been broken down, but identifying DNA should be impossible.

After considering her shoes, she poured a few drops of the remaining reagent on the footprint she had left, then carefully stepped on the sizzling ground. She hoped there wasn't enough of it to eat all the way through the shoes and into her feet, but she really didn't want to leave recognizable footprints.

To her relief, her feet weren't eaten away.

Michi coughed as the fumes from the destruction of her clothes ate at the back of her throat. She had to get out of there. Without a look back at the decapitated Hokkam, she pulled down at the hem of her shorts once more, turned off her face-spoofer, and walked down the alley and out into the street by the statue.

Two men with bottles of beer in their hands spotted her, and one shouted "Hey, where're you headed?" then "Don't be like that," as she ignored them and walked on. Neither followed her, though.

It took almost 35 minutes on the convoluted route she took to get back to the condo, which was well past curfew, but no one stopped her. Tamara wasn't in. She'd had a date, and Michi guessed it had gone well based on the short "I won't be making it back" message on the house PA that was cut off with a laugh.

Michi took the knife from her belly pocket. This was a high-end knife with a serial number. She couldn't leave it at the scene. She shouldn't even have used it, but this was a thrown-together plan, and she had run out of time. The knife went into the dishwasher, and she started the clean cycle.

Then it was her turn. She put some lilac bath salts in the tub and filled it, stripping out of her clothes and slipping in. She let the salts soothe her, body and mind. As the water began to cool, she got out and emptied the tub. She took her shorts, shirt, underwear, and shoes and placed them in the tub, then poured the remainder of Doug's solution over them. Doug had assured her the reagent would not harm the tub's surface, and with the toilet exhaust fan on, most of the fumes went up and out of the bathroom.

Not quite everything was eaten away, however. Michi turned on the showerhead and thoroughly rinsed the tiny scraps left before picking them up and putting them in a trash bag.

She was done.

It was still early, but she went to her small bedroom and got into bed, pulling the sheet up to her chin. She lay there, wide awake for almost 20 minutes before she started to cry. Within moments, she was sobbing, and it was another five minutes before she stopped.

She wasn't crying over Hokkam. Hokkam meant nothing to her—and that was why she was crying. The first jack had been an accident. Michi had attacked him with violent intentions, but she hadn't planned to kill him. The thought really hadn't crossed her mind.

But Hokkam was different. She knew him, she planned out his death, and she had killed him in cold blood while watching his life fade as she stared into his eyes. A normal person would feel something after taking a life in such an intimate manner. It could be sorrow or regret. It could be exultation or thrill. It could be anger or bitterness. But it should be something.

Michi felt nothing.

Michiko MacCailín had been a love-struck teenager, a ballet dancer, a First Family girl with whatever future she wanted. That Michi would have been horror-struck at the idea of taking any life, much less a human life.

That Michi was gone, though, probably forever. And the new Michi cried when she realized that. She wanted the old Michi back, and she was sure she despised the new person she had become.

Chapter 24

Michi waited at Bridgette's restaurant in a corner table, out of the way of the rest of the patrons, an untouched Danish in front of her. She wondered if the rest of her notes had been read. The rally was scheduled to start in an hour, and all the WRP staff would be there, but she hoped that she had convinced them to see her first. If not, she would contact the council members after, but if Hokkam had any planned role in the rally, then Cheri and the rest should know that he would be a no-show.

At 8:35, just when she had about given up hope, Cheri, Rangle, Sven, and Gabriella came in together. Gabriella spotted Michi first, and all four came over and sat down beside her.

"You wrote that this was vital," Rangle said, sounding as if he was being put upon. "We're a mite busy today."

"What is it, dear?" Cheri asked. "Why didn't you just tell us yesterday instead of all the mystery? We compared notes, and you gave us all the same thing. Rosario said he had more important things to do this morning, we couldn't contact Su, and Hokkam's probably already at the rally."

"No, he isn't," Michi calmly told the three board members. "And he won't be coming. I wanted to let you know before the rally started that you needed to elect a new chairman."

"Why, has Hokkam resigned?" Gabriella asked. "He never told me he was considering anything like that."

Cheri stared into Michi's eyes for a moment. She saw something in the young woman that spoke more than mere words could. "It was necessary?" she asked.

Michi nodded.

"What was necessary? What are you talking about?" Gabriella asked, her irritation beginning to show.

"Rangle, you are the acting chairman for this. If need be, you will talk. You wrote the talking points for Hokkam, so you are the most familiar with them," Cheri said, taking charge.

"But what about Hokkam? Can somebody please tell me what is going on?" Gabriella persisted.

"There's no time for that now, Gabby. Hokkam's gone, and we'll leave it at that. And no, you cannot call him. We've got a rally going on, and I suggest we get there.

"Gabby, get a hold of Su. Tell her to get to the office for an emergency meeting at 6:00."

She held up a hand when Gabriella started to protest. "Not now, Gabby. Let's get to the square. Michi, are you coming with us?"

"What the hell's going on?" Rangle muttered as they left, but he followed Cheri's commands.

The five made their way to the square, but even from two blocks away, people filled the street, making progress almost impossible.

"We cut that too close," Cheri said, awe in her voice evidence that the numbers of people who showed up was a surprise to her. "Rangle, try and worm your way up. Tamberlane and Fort will already be there."

"Fort" was Fortitude Fein-Simak, their rally master. He was part stage director, part cheerleader, and he was nominally in charge of the rally. However, this was not just a WRP event. Other organizations had been approached, and several had already sent reps to the WRP office to help plan, and more than a few had probably just shown up to take part.

A person holding a placard turned back, and Michi saw the image printed on it. It was her, in her red-headed glory, looking particularly fierce. The words "Red Athena" were printed under her photograph.

"That's pretty impressive. Tamberlane's doing?" Michi asked Cheri.

"No, ours says 'The People's Valkyrie,'" Cheri told her. "And the photo is a little different. That means your performance must have caught on. That's reassuring."

The three women worked their way forward, keeping close to the buildings lining the street. Up ahead, they could hear chanting, but it wasn't until they managed to worm their way into the square itself that Michi could make out what the chant was.

"Red Athena! Red Athena!" the crowd yelled out.

"Looks like Fort went with the other name," Cheri said matter-of-factly. "His call, and whatever catches on. The 'Valkyrie' was my idea, though. Oh, well."

Michi felt uncomfortable seeing so many placards with her photo on it. The overtly sexual flair to the WRP version bothered her. At least it was that of her redhead alter-ego, and that put some psychological distance to it. She was glad when the chant shifted to "Worker Justice Now!"

Crowd chanting was a science. Fort might be leading the chants, but he had a team scattered around the rally, taking measurements of the volume and intensity of the crowd. All of that was fed to an AI that calculated when to change chants and when to try new ones. It might seem like mob rule, but it was a carefully choreographed and continually changing ballet.

At 8:15, Fort stopped the chanting, and through his bullhorn, told everyone that it was time for the Propitious Interstellar anthem. The crowd booed him unmercifully, but as the recorded music played, most of the people joined in, singing as far out of key as possible and changing more than a few of the words.

After the anthem, Rangle took the bullhorn and welcomed the crowd in the name of the WRP. He stressed that this was to be a peaceful rally, to which some people booed. He spoke for a few minutes, seemingly as ease. Michi wasn't sure she could have pulled off speaking in front of so many people with so little advanced warning.

He turned the bullhorn over to representatives from some of the other organizations that had gone public in opposition to martial law and the presence of the Marines. Michi listened to them with only half an ear. She jumped up on a fire hydrant and looked at the line of jacks blocking B Street. Unlike at the rally in which Franz had been killed, this time they were backed up by about 30 Marines in their armored combat suits, "PICS," they called them. The stood motionless behind the jacks, looking impressive, Michi had to admit. Michi wondered what options they had if it came to an open confrontation with them.

A camcording of Henry Jugos, the same human rights champion whose arrival had been announced back when Franz had spoken, was replayed for the crowd. In it he urged them not to back down and to demand their charter be honored. When martial law had been declared, the PI lawyers argued that this allowed them to nullify Jugos' visa, and so it was back to court.

Scotty MacScotty, an irreverent comedian whose real name was a loosely-held secret, was next, and he had the crowd roaring as he skewered the company. Michi normally thought he was funny, if a little crude for her taste, but this time, she let the humor pass her by. She was watching the jacks and the Marines for any sign of action.

"There's trouble in Dundee," Cheri relayed to them in a whisper, one hand over the ear into which her PA bud was inserted. "The crowd tried to take over the company office, and the Marines pushed them back. There are some dead, but I don't know who or how many there are yet."

Dundee was Kakurega's second largest city, the planetary capital, and the site of PI's Plant 4, where large items were fabricated. There was a higher percentage of indentureds and fewer PI management at that factory than at perhaps any other company facility.

"We knew that was a possibility when we set this up," Gabriella said quietly as she took a glance to see if anyone was listening in. "Hokkam said that we might need a spark to get the fire going."

"Hokkam is out of the equation now," Cheri answered. "So it doesn't matter what he said. We might have that fire, but will it engulf us all?"

Behind the Marines, Michi saw movement. It was one of the T2000 forklifts, the big ones used to move vats of base materials. It stopped in back of the Marines, and someone climbed onto the forks. The operator raised them, lifting the passenger above the Marines and jacks and in view of the crowd.

It was Dr. Keller, the deputy mayor. The fact that a public official was sitting on a yellow forklift with "Propitious Interstellar" was a telling connection that did not slip past Michi.

"People of Tay Station, this gathering is illegal and you are ordered to withdraw. Despite no permits being issued, we have used patience as a show of good will. That good will has been exhausted, so as law abiding citizens, you must go home.

"If you have reasonable grievances, you may come down to the city offices during normal working hours and file them.

"As a member of the city council, I am issuing the order to cease and desist as per City Proclamation 19.815.3062, the previously declared imposition of martial law. Failure to do so can result in arrest and imprisonment for a period of no more than ten years."

As if in a Hollywood flick, a round, red object sailed from the crowd and arched over to strike the mayor on his thigh. The tomato had been ripe enough to splatter, covering him in juice and seeds.

The crowd roared with laughter and the deputy mayor hurriedly motioned for the operator to lower him. The laughter broke off and faded to nothing as the jacks, who had been lining B Street, split in the middle of the line and marched smartly to each side of the street, leaving the center open. A few people moved forward as if to enter the opening the jacks had made.

"Get out of here," Michi said to Cheri and Gabriella, pushing them back.

They didn't argue, probably thinking of what had just transpired in Dundee. A few other people started to edge back as well, but the bulk of the crowd just stared to see what would unfold.

Michi was not surprised when the Marines started moving in their huge combat suits. For something so big and unwieldy-looking, each Marine smoothly stepped forward, each rank in unison as they passed the jacks, then spread out, shoulder to shoulder, completely blocking B Street and extending along the entire west side of the square.

A voice came out of some unseen speaker, "This is your last warning. Leave the square now and return to your homes or you will be forcibly evicted."

A number of people turned to push their way out, but the sheer number in the square made that difficult. A person holding one of the rally signs tried to push past Michi, dropping the placard. Michi saw her own face as the sign fell, hitting her in the head before it fell between the people onto the ground. Michi might have thought the irony of getting hit with her own photo was funny hadn't the Marines then started a slow march forward.

Screams erupted from the crowd as people tried to get out of the way. The Marines did not fire any weapons, but merely walked forward in lockstep, using their combat suits as bulldozers. A few young bloods tried to hit the Marines with rally signs, and one young man jumped up on top of a Marine only to be casually plucked off as if he was an errant kitten and tossed aside.

Behind the Marines, the jacks had formed back up. Several of them pounced on the young man who'd just been tossed. A few people lost their footing. Michi became incensed when the Marines kept marching, stepping on those on the ground. An older lady fell, and a Marine stepped squarely on her. The woman went still.

"They're not resisting!" she shouted, her voice lost in the bedlam.

She wanted to strike out at the Marines, and she had to fight the impulse to wade into them. Her blood boiled, but the rational part of her mind argued that she couldn't do any good in jail. She wavered for a few moments as the Marine line moved inexorably forward, the eager jacks rushing to arrest anyone who was left as the Marines stomped over them. Finally, the rational Michi gained control, and she turned to flee.

She would leave the square to the Marines and bring the fight to them another day and on her terms, not theirs.

Chapter 25

The three friends jumped at the chime.

"Check it, please, Doug," Michi said, trying to sound calm.

They were in an apartment into which Doug had gotten access. It was furnished, if somewhat tacky, and from hints Doug had made, it was used as a secret getaway for higher ups in the company technical division when they wanted discreet liaisons. Doug guaranteed there was no surveillance leading to or inside the getaway. Michi thought it ironic that they were using what PI management had set up for secrecy, be it for an amorous reason, to possibly plot against the company.

"It's them," Doug said, checking the wall screen. "At least it's Ms. Balilies and two men."

"Am I OK?" Michi asked Tamara after switching on her face-spoofer. When Tamara said yes, Michi nodded at her, and Tamara opened the door.

Michi had been standing regally in the front hallway, her back highlighted by the afternoon sun. The effect, which the three of them had worked out, was spoiled by Rosario pushing her aside and quickly checking the apartment. Cheri and their guest came in, but Rosario held up his hand to keep them from talking while he took a portable scanner out of his pocket and checked for whatever he suspected.

"OK, it looks clear," he finally said with a scowl on his face.

Isn't he ever happy? Michi wondered before turning to greet her guest.

The man standing in front of her looked to be in his mid-thirties, stood about 2 meters, and was a trim 85 kg. He was supposedly an accountant for Jericho Trading, responsible for accounts payable to Propitious Interstellar. Jericho Trading was a Brotherhood company, just one of the many, many companies who bought PI goods and kept an office in the city. In reality, "Mr. Samuels" was a bishop in the Brotherhood military, if their information was right, and he wanted to meet the "Red Athena."

The fact that he was in the military but undercover made Tamara declare that he was a bonafide spy. Michi had to agree, but Tamara seemed too excited over the fact. She had been in the condo when Doug had suggested the location for the meeting, and she was adamant that she was coming, too.

Michi was in full costume for the meeting, which had taken over a day to set up. The location proved problematic, what with Mr. Samuels being unable to visit the WRP offices and Michi not willing to go out in public in persona. It was Doug who came to the rescue with his division's little sex hide-away.

Mr. Samuels had extremely white teeth, Michi noted as he held out a hand.

"Thank you for meeting with me," he said, smile dazzling. "Should I call you Athena?" he asked with just the right degree of lightheartedness.

"Valkyrie was better," Cheri muttered.

Cheri was now the chairman of the WRP. She had been the unanimous choice, and Tamberlane, who had always been in on most chapter decisions anyway, and been elevated to full board status.

"Sure," Michi said. "And should I just call you 'Bishop?'"

"Touché, young lady, touché. But I think Mr. Samuels will be fine," he said with a chuckle.

"Ms. Baliles has been kind enough to show me some of your recent recordings. I have to say you cut an impressive figure."

Michi wondered if that had been a double entendre, but she simply asked, "So I can assume your interest in us means your, uh, *company*, might be willing to render assistance?"

"While my company appreciates your situation, and while we philosophically stand for human rights and freedom of speech and actions, sometimes our support is more of a moral type rather than the material."

"So you mean you will root for us, but in secret so as to not upset the Federation."

"M—uh, Athena, it's not that easy," Cheri snapped, eyes blazing.

Michi didn't care. Cheri was her friend, but this pompous ass came to ogle her in her costume, see the "Red Athena," and maybe ask for a photo with her, and he offers nothing?

"No, Ms. Baliles, she's only saying what is evident," he said to Cheri before turning back to Michi. "No, we are not ready to offer overt aid. However, we can offer some information when it is feasible, and we will be monitoring the situation. If it escalates to a certain point," he held up a hand as Michi was about to interrupt, "and what that point is, I frankly don't know. But if it reaches there, we would be forced, on humanitarian grounds, to assist. Exactly how or in what form? I don't know. My job now is to gather information so that we are able to react quickly if and when necessary."

Michi started to protest again, but as she thought about it, what the bishop said made sense. She could not expect the Brotherhood to risk war over worker conditions on a Federation planet. They fact that they were even monitoring it was gratifying.

"And why did you want to meet me? I'm not a decision maker," she asked, slightly mollified.

"Because I wanted to see the face of the worker movement. I wanted to get a feel for you. And something tells me that you are not the mere figurehead you let yourself on to be. There is more fire in you than that," he said.

He's a smooth talker, Michi admitted, feeling herself calm down.

She had been frustrated over the last week. She was the one who had eliminated the traitor, but she had no say now in what was happening. The WRP was moving slowly while Michi knew in her heart that they had to push while the momentum was still there and before it dissipated. There had been impromptu protests, but with 23 killed in Dundee and two in Tay Station, and with over 40 in varying degrees of regen, the protests had a tentative feel, and the numbers were not overly impressive.

All she had done in the meantime was record four short camcordings, all done to a script that was handed to her. She had felt awkward and not vested in what was being said. To have the bishop tell her she was more than that was a needed boost to her ego.

They spoke for only a few more minutes, the bishop asking, Michi responding. She didn't totally understand the point of each of his questions, but she tried to answer in all candor.

"Well, Ms. Athena, I want to thank you for meeting with me, but I've got to get back," he said, shaking her hand. He didn't let it go, but stared at her face for a few moments before saying, "Not a bad job on your disguise. I can barely tell where it leaves off and where you begin. I can't quite see what method you are using, but if you want a slight bit of advice, though, you might want to up your frequency. Certain surveillance devices available to any military might be able to mesh with your transmitter and essential see what is underneath. A shifting frequency might even be safer."

Michi heard an intake of breath from Doug. She almost had to smile. Doug had been so proud of his spoofer, but evidently it was not quite as unique as he had thought.

"Thank you," Cheri whispered as she turned to leave, probably relieved that the meeting had not gone too poorly.

Rosario hung back, and as the two stepped out the door, he grabbed Michi by the arm and pulled her in close to quietly snarl, "I know who you are now, and I know what you did to Hokkam. Remember one thing. I am in charge of security, and your amateur actions could have blown up in our faces, still might, and that puts all of us in danger. If you find out anything else that affects us, you come to me and let me handle it. Understood?"

Michi glared back and ripped her arm out of his grasp. "Have a good day," she said forcibly.

He looked at her for another moment before Cheri's voice came in from the hall, "You coming?"

"Remember what I said," he whispered as he turned and left.

Michi took a deep breath as the door closed and turned around to face her two friends. Doug was staring at her, either upset about the comment about his spoofer or because he heard part of what Rosario had said. Tamara, on the other hand, had a goofy smile on her face.

"Did you see him?" she asked. "That's enough to make a girl weak at the knees."

"What?" Michi asked, taken by surprise by the direction of her roommate's comment.

"Oh, come on, Michi. A handsome hunk like that? Did you see his teeth? And a spy? Didn't he make you," she paused to dramatically put her hands over Doug's ears, "make you just the teensiest bit wet?"

Doug winced and recoiled from what he'd heard, while Michi protested, "What? No!"

"Oh, come on. Have you gone all dried up and dusty inside?"

That innocent comment hit Michi hard. She had felt dark and "dusty" inside, not in a sexual way, but in her heart. Tamara was talking about sex, but it went much deeper than that to Michi. She feared she was losing her humanity.

"You're losing it, girlfriend, and you need to get it back. You need to get laid and soon. Tell you what, I'll step back and leave Mr. Spy to you."

"No! I mean, I'm not interested!"

"OK, then anyone. Hey Dougie, you got anyone for the ice princess here? Someone who can give her a good fucking?" she asked, using her arm and fist to pump back and forth.

"Tamara! Stop it!" Michi shouted. "I'm serious!"

"OK, sorry. I was just joking," Tamara said, sounding miffed.

"You can be a real bitch," Doug said quietly to her.

"What a bunch of limpies," Tamara said in response, but more to herself than to anyone else.

Michi needed to move on, to get the subject off of her. The bishop had said there was more to her, and Michi grasped at that like a life ring in a storm.

"Both of you, get serious and come sit down. Doug, how long do we have this place?"

"Uh, I don't know. At least until evening, maybe longer."

"OK, Tamara, put on some coffee, and let's get to work. We've got some planning to do."

Chapter 26

"What do you mean you can't get their schedules? I thought you could hack into anything?" Michi asked in exasperation.

"I told you, I can get anywhere into the company or the government here because when we put in the security, I managed to insert a back door. I've got the key, and I can get in anytime I want. But you're talking about the military. They've got Gen 10 security, and there's no way I can break in."

"Just hack it," Tamara said.

"You're not getting me. I couldn't hack PI without the back door. As far as military? There's just no way!"

two hours later . . .

"So that won't work either," Michi said with disappointment as she read the web article. "The PICS are shielded against some pretty powerful energy weapons, so a simple electric current, no matter how powerful, won't knock one out."

"I thought it might work, but I guess that would be too easy," Doug said with a sigh. "Well, back to the drawing board."

another hour . . .

"Yech! The coffee's cold! Tamara, how about contributing and brewing up a fresh pot!" Mich said.

Two more . . .

"I already took care of that. As far as anyone knows, you live in apartment 307 in Building 1002, Franklin Manor," Doug said.

"And that will fly?"

"It should. You've been burning power, watching the holo, going online. I even had you download your speech about the Marine and his girlfriend."

"Was that smart? I mean, downloading it was illegal. What if they come to check on me?" Michi asked.

"Sister, *everyone* downloaded that." Tamara said.

"Tamara's right. Almost everyone undoubtedly did. There are probably programs out there to see who didn't. Anyone too clean raises red flags," Doug agreed. "You even filed a report on noisy neighbors."

"So as far as anyone knows, I don't stay at Tamara's? And when did you do all of that?"

"When I first met you two. It just seemed like appropriate precautions."

Tamara gave him a hug and kissed his forehead. "Oh, you care, Dougie!"

Doug shrugged off her arms and muttered, "Just being safe is all."

But his face was turning red.

2:30 AM

"Well, theoretically, that might work. My mind's a bit fuzzy now, but let me go over the calculations," Doug said as Tamara snored beside him.

"Even if it might work, the question is where?" Michi asked.

"That might take some more digging. But let's look at the numbers first. No use getting excited about it. Look at how much time we wasted on the electrical shock idea."

5:09 AM

"Well?" Michi asked, waiting once again to hear why this one wouldn't work, either.

"I . . . I think we have a plan!" Doug said.

Chapter 27

"Can you get it?" Michi asked while Doug grunted a few steps into the tunnel.

"It's a lot harder than it looks!" he complained.

They had to cut open the lock, or their whole plan had to be scrapped. The lock was to an old access tunnel to the power station, and that was their way out of the park.

Ledges Park was just to the east of the city along the River Tay. Eons ago, there had been a waterfall at the park, but over the years, the river had eaten its way through, leaving a canyon and some rapids as it made its way to the lower plains. The first Scottish settlers had selected the location for Tay Station because of the rapids. They provided the power they needed to build and run their city. After Propitious Interstellar arrived and built more modern, efficient, and reliable power plants, the old hydro-electric plant was shut down, and the canyon became a public park. The old access tunnels, though, still existed, and they offered another way out of the park to those who knew the tunnels.

"Here, let me try," Michi said, pushing past Doug and taking the bolt-cutters.

She got the jaws around a link in the chain, and with a shout, put all her strength in back of it. It didn't look like it would be enough, but then, with a snap, the chain parted.

Doug rolled his eyes but said nothing.

"Let's get back so you can do your thing," Michi hastened to say.

Doug was not an "Ugh, me man, you woman"-type, but still, having Michi open what he couldn't had to sting at least a little.

They strolled arm in arm back to the running path, two lovers out enjoying the sunny day. The park was not in much use during the week, and with martial law, even the evening joggers were few and far between, but on the weekends, it would be packed with people.

They saw two Marines in their combat suits on patrol. Michi laughed as if Doug had said something funny, then wanted to kick herself for looking too fake. But the Marines continued on their way. The best Doug had been able to find out was that there were four Marines in the park during the day, then eight at night.

Michi spread out a blanket on the grass where a finger of the cliff jutted out closer to the river. From rock face to the river was less than ten meters, and that included the running trail. Michi and Doug took off their shirts and lay back on the blanket. On her bikini strap, Michi retained her spoofer, set on another of Doug's faces for her, this one with close to her real skin color. Doug had Tamara's spoofer, this one set for a face not too different from his own.

"Wow, boy, you need to get out in the sun more," she whispered to Doug, taking in his pale skin.

"Yeah, yeah, I know. You can dispense with the ghost jokes now."

Michi wanted to get going, but if there were eyes on them, they had to act natural. She lay in the sun, feeling the warmth seep into her. It felt good, and it forced her to relax. Without meaning to, she fell asleep.

"Hey, I need to go take a pee," Doug said, waking her up with a start. She sat up and yawned.

"Take your pack and use the cream," she said as planned.

Michi didn't know what cream she would have meant, but on the off-chance that they were being overheard, they had wanted a reason for him to take his pack.

"Don't nag," he said as he shouldered his backpack.

As he disappeared behind her, she adjusted her bikini top and looked out over the river. She wondered if there was anyone out there observing them, and if so, were they watching Doug or her? It seemed as if her contribution to the cause always had her half-naked, and that ate at her. She was more than a dress-up doll. It had been Tamara's idea for the sun-bathing; but then again, Tamara's mind was always in the gutter.

Two Marines came down the running trail. She couldn't see them through their combat suits' visors, but she nodded at them as they passed only a couple of meters from her. She could actually feel the ground shake as they walked by.

It seemed to be forever, but finally, Doug reappeared. He nodded to Michi as he sat down. Now, they waited.

With two Marines just having passed, they knew it might be awhile. The Marines didn't seem to have a schedule, but still, it could take 30 minutes or more for the other team or the same team to come by again. After 20 minutes, Doug put his arm around Michi's shoulders and nuzzled her ear.

"Damn, Doug! You need to learn how to do that better," she said quietly while lifting her chin and smiling. She turned, stood up, and reached down to take him by his hand, guiding him up.

She felt totally weird trying to act like a woman in lust when she felt nothing. If they were under observation, she hoped it looked natural.

The two of them walked slowly back alongside the cliff finger to the denser foliage at the base of the farther-back cliff face, the same brush that hid the entrance to the access tunnel. She put her arms around Doug's neck, then pulled him down to the ground.

Immediately the two parted and went to their bellies. Doug reached out and parted the brush slightly so they could see out. One moment, they were lovers ready for passion; the next they were soldiers in the ambush.

Michi reached into Doug's pack. It had carried the explosives, but it also carried her costume. Off came the bikini top and on came the Red Athena's top. She peeled off her loose pants to reveal the camouflaged bammers she'd had on underneath. Then came the boots and the pistol belt. Finally, she pulled out the handgun and the rifle, and with three practiced pulls, snapped it to its full length. The last two were risky. These were the weapons with which she had been making her recordings, but by telling Cheri that she was going to work on more recordings, she had been allowed to keep them for the day. If they had been stopped for any reason and the weapons had been found in Doug's pack, there would have been no reasonable explanation.

All of this had been done lying in the dirt beside Doug. He ignored her gymnastics and watched the running path.

"Here they come," he whispered, excitement in his voice.

Two Marines were striding down the path, each stride seemingly gobbling up meters. They looked powerful, and Michi had sudden misgivings. What if things went wrong?

But it was too late. As they strode into the kill zone, Doug pulled on the wire.

And nothing happened.

He pulled again, and the wire came to him easily. There was no explosion.

"What the fuck?" he asked as the Marines passed on.

"You've got to check what happened," Michi told him. "I can't go out like this. Go to the picnic basket and act like you are getting something for us to drink, then take another pee. And here," she said, rubbing some dirt on his body. "We've been rolling around back here, remember?"

Doug made his way out of the brush, stretched, and with a satisfied insolence, strolled back to the blanket and their food basket. If Michi didn't know better, she would have sworn the guy just got laid. Who would've known he could act so well?

He picked up the blanket and two bottles of beer. The blanket was a good touch. It would have been reasonable to have taken it with them in the first place. Then he wandered off to the bushes at the side of the cliff and disappeared. A minute or two later, he came out zipping up his fly. He sauntered over to Michi and got on his hands and knees to crawl in with her.

"The wire came undone. I fastened it tighter this time," he told her.

Doug had made the explosives with some common ingredients. Sensors shouldn't pick up anything unless they were looking specifically for that combination. But any commercial fuze would be picked up by the Marine's combat suits, so Doug had rigged up a simple mechanical fuze. With one good tug, a spring-loaded hammer would fall, striking a small percussion cap and igniting the explosives.

"Let's hope it works this time," she said as they settled in to wait.

They lay in silence, watching for movement. Finally, two Marines, either the same ones or two others, made their appearance. Doug got ready.

"No, stop!" Michi hissed as the Marines approached the picnic basket and discarded shirts they had left as markers.

Two joggers were coming the other way, and they would be in the kill zone as well. They had to wait again.

Just as the Marines passed the kill zone, one of them glanced to where Doug and Michi were hiding. It was a quick look, but Michi knew then that their ruse had been necessary. The Marine had been hoping to catch a glimpse of some action.

"Did you see that?" Doug asked.

"Sure did. He must think you're some sort of stud. What's it been? Forty-five minutes now?"

"Yeah, that's me. Stud," he said sarcastically. "And now we wait yet again."

They were running out of time. They weren't sure what time the other Marines would arrive, but they didn't want to deal with them. Four was too many as it was.

The two Marines had only been gone less than ten minutes when two more appeared. That meant the other two were still close, and that increased the risk.

"Well?" Doug asked.

Michi ached to strike, but was the increased risk worth it? She went back and forth in her mind.

"Now or never, Michi."

She made up her mind. "Do it!"

Doug pulled back on the wire, and the entire cliff face on the point seemed to erupt. Rocks and clouds of dust plummeted to the ground, hiding the two Marines from view. Doug and Michi burst from the brush and rushed forward, Michi with her rifle at the ready, not that it would do any good against a combat-armored Marine.

As the dust started to clear, they looked frantically for any sign of the Marines. Doug pulled out a sensor and swept the area.

"I've got one. He's under there," he said, pointing at a pile of rubble. "He's alive."

"Can he get out?" Michi asked.

"Well, we'll find out, won't we, if he can," Doug said logically.

Michi spotted a shape as the dust settled. Her heart lurched, but the shape was still.

"Over there," she shouted, sprinting to the edge of the river where a Marine was lying face up.

He wasn't moving. As Michi got closer, she could see that the lower half of his combat suit was crushed. The Marine was dead.

How can he be dead when the one under all the rubble is still alive? she wondered.

"Quick, over there, from his head," she told Doug. "I want them to be able to see him."

As Doug scrambled over the rocks that littered the river bank, Michi put her foot on the Marine's head, then moved to beside the Marine, then finally decided on a foot on the chest.

"How do I look?" she asked Doug as he raised his recorder.

"Uh, your face!"

"No, this is what I want," she said, not turning on the spoofer.

"You sure?"

"Yes!" she almost screamed. "Hurry up! We don't have much time!"

The red light came on, and Michi calmed herself. She turned to stare into the camera with her best warrior look.

"My name is Michiko MacCailín. Some of you know me as The Red Athena. I was born and raised here on Kakurega, and this is my home, a home under siege. Propitious Interstellar has not only broken the charter, but they have murdered our citizens, not the least being my fiancé, Franz Galipoli. When we resisted, they called in the Federation to rescue them with the Marines. Make no doubt about it, we have been invaded, and we must fight back. The Marines are not invincible, as you can see. We can win. All sons and daughters of Kakurega, rise up and throw the invaders off our home!"

"Michi, we need to go," Doug said, pulling down the recorder.

There was a strange sound coming from the direction in which the other two Marines had marched. It sounded like a cross between a cargo truck and a plane.

Doug was already scrambling up the bank. Michi gave him a hand up, and both sprinted to brush that hid the access door. They were still 10 or 15 meters away when two shapes burst past the cliff point and into the rubble field.

"Go!" Doug shouted, pushing Michi forward into the bushes. Michi saw the cliff face and thought they had made it when the bushes disintegrated and chips started flying from the rock face. Several chips hit her as she fell more than dove into the entrance and scrambled on her hands and knees to the gate. Her ears were ringing as she reached up to push the gate open.

She took a moment to look back for Doug when he plowed into her, knocking both of them past the gate and onto the dank floor.

Michi lay there, trying to catch her breath when Doug picked her up, shouting "Go, go!" They stumbled forward, the only light coming from the entrance in back of them.

When the light behind them went dark, Michi thought they had gone far enough, but Doug pushed her down to the rock floor. A moment later, all hell broke out over them. A dip in the floor protected them, but chips of rock fell on top of them as rounds impacted, and then Michi felt the tingle of a side lobe of some sort of energy weapon.

"Keep low, but crawl," Doug told her.

Both of them, Michi in the lead and Doug literally on her butt, managed to scoot farther down the passage. When Michi felt the opening to the left, she knew they had reached their route out. She pulled Doug in, and they both sat up, gasping for air.

"Why did you use your real face for the recording?" Doug asked in the darkness as a few rounds zipped past the opening and farther down the first tunnel. "They're going to know who you are as soon as we broadcast it."

"Have you ever heard the word *arinomamade*?" she asked him as her heart started to slow down its frantic beating.

"No. Is that Japanese?"

"Yeah. My grandmother used to say it. It means the way something is, or maybe 'it is what it is.' It's kinda hard to put exactly in Standard. But it fits why I did that."

Some stone chips knocked free by the Marines firing managed to ricochet into their side tunnel, and both friends scooted in another three meters.

"It is what it is?" Doug prompted.

"Yeah. I am not the Red Athena. I'm me, a First Family citizen of Kakurega. I'm me, Michiko MacCailín, whose fiancé was murdered by the company. I'm me, a girl who won't stand for that anymore. That's who I am, and I'm not going to hide behind a disguise. If people are going to listen to me, they deserve it to be me, not some comic book construct. *Arinomamade!*"

"I guess I understand, but your life just got levels more difficult. I hope you realize that. Think about it, OK? I don't have to release this if you change your mind," he said, patting his recorder where he'd hooked it to his belt.

"I won't. I didn't quite say what I had planned out there, but what I said was me, too. I want you to run with it."

"Your call, Michi. I'll ask you again before I do, though."

The firing down the entry tunnel stopped. The Marines must have given up, Michi figured..

"Good thing those guys are too big to get in here," Doug said as what had happened sunk in.

"That saved us," Michi said before another thought struck her. "But the specs said they can molt out of them. What if they come in after us on foot?"

"Shit. I didn't think of that. Let's get moving."

He pulled a flashlight out of his pocket, and the two of them started off at a slow jog down the tunnel. It would take awhile for the Marines to access the plans, as Doug had erased all copies on Kakurega. They would have Federation copies, but it would take them some time to realize that. Within 20 minutes, the two would be at their exit and changing into the clothes they had left there earlier.

Michiko had kept her promise. She had taken it to the Marines on her own terms and won!

Chapter 28

How about Hanggaju Gozen?" Doug said, looking up from his PA. "That's in keeping with Tamara's Highlander Samurai theme. It says here she was an *onna bugeisha*, or female warrior. Oh, not wait, she was captured and forced to marry the shogun. We don't want you and the CEO hooking up."

The three were sitting in the condo, watching the net as Michi's camcording was the subject of most social media. The company blocked all official access, but the under-net could not be blocked without shutting down the entire planet, something the company could not do and maintain production. They'd issued one statement, that there had been a "manufactured" camcording released, but that it was all CGI.

On GC109, a popular forum, one poster had written that given the latest recording, the name 'The Red Athena" was somewhat inaccurate. That was probably a little too far for even the normally light-handed moderators of the forum, but the three had read it before it was deleted and were lazily discussing a public name for Michi.

"I still think the Highlander Samurai is brills," Tamara said, refusing to give up.

"Some people are calling you, the Kakurega Jeanne d'Arc, you know," Doug went on.

"I saw that," Michi said, "and my ancestors are probably rolling over in their graves. A French heroine? If anyone, it should at least be a good Celtic girl, like Boudica."

"Not everyone has your vaunted Scottish ancestry, and no one knows about her. I wouldn't have, if you hadn't pointed her out on the history holo," Tamara said.

"Here's another: Tomoe Gozen. Seems she was a vaunted warrior and cut off the head of some enemy general," Doug started.

Michi almost flinched at the "cutting off the head," part. Both Doug and Tamara knew that she had killed Hokkam, but the security report never mentioned her beheading him, and she had kept that to herself.

"She's been popular over the ages in anime, so some people should know her. Oh, wait, she was this other guy's concubine. What is it with these Japanese fighters? Maybe those Celtic goddesses we found would be better," Doug went on.

"I already told you I've already decided. I made myself pretty clear. I'm Michiko MacCailín. I don't need a Celtic goddess or Japanese samurai to give me credibility."

"Oh, you're no fun," Tamara said sourly. "If you're going by your real name, how can I be 'The Tattooed Avenger?'"

She got off the couch and stomped off to the bathroom.

"Do you think she likes that guy?" Doug asked.

"What guy?"

"You know, the Brotherhood spy," Doug said.

"Him? Tamara 'likes' almost everyone, and she has a pretty active appetite. You know that. Would she play hide-in-the-cupboard with him? I don't know. Probably, if the opportunity presented itself," Michi responded. "Why?"

"Just wondering."

"Is the boyfriend getting jealous?" Michi asked with a laugh.

With Doug constantly coming over, they had decided a little over a week ago that Doug and Tamara should become a "thing." They ate lunches together at work and came home together when their schedules coincided. And Doug slept over more often than he went home. He slept on the couch, and inside the condo, it was the same as always, but they hoped to anyone on the outside that it would seem the two had a real relationship.

"No!" Doug protested. "I, well, I just want to make sure everything looks right. That's all."

His vehement denial gave Michi pause. Did Doug really like her?

That line of thought disappeared as an undernet feed chimed on both of their PAs. A vid of Marines moving through some buildings could be seen, and a voice said that there had been violence again in Dundee. The vid was choppy and unsteady, but it zoomed in past the Marines to what were unmistakably bodies. The voice reported that over 100 were killed as they assaulted a Marine unit.

"What's up?" Tamara said as she came out of the bathroom.

"People are fighting the Marines," Doug said soberly. "I guess they listened."

Michi stared at the dead bodies. She knew, she hoped, it would come to this. But seeing the bodies, well, that brought it into focus. Those people were alive this morning, kissing lovers and playing with children. Now, because of Michi, they were dead.

The price of war hit Michi hard.

Chapter 29

"OK, we're running late. Stand up and take off your shirt," Doug said as he and Tamara came in the door.

"What?" she asked, standing up, but not taking off her T.

"Come on, girl. Your shirt, take it off," Tamara said, reaching over to help.

Michi didn't resist, but she didn't help much either as the shorter Tamara struggled to get the T over her head.

"Bra, too, girl. Come on, off!" Tamara said impatiently.

Michi glanced at Doug. Despite him now living on the couch, she had not paraded naked in the condo. She had changed from the bikini to her Red Athena shirt in the park, but that had been a quick switch while Doug watched the kill zone. Now, Doug was standing there, watching and waiting. With a sigh, she shrugged and touched the two release buds, and her bra cups fell to the ground.

Doug handed Tamara what looked to be a large roll of gauze, like medics and nurses used.

"Hands up," she told Michi.

Michi felt exposed like that, and she wished she knew what the two had prepared for her. She knew she needed a disguise, but what that had to do with her standing exposed like that was beyond her.

Tamara put the leading edge of the gauze against Michi's side. "Doug, help me. Hold this here."

Michi stared over Doug's bent head as he reached forward, pressing the leading edge against her. Tamara started walking in back of Michi, unrolling the gauze. She came to the front again, pulling the gauze tight against Michi's breasts. Then it became clear. They were binding her! OK, that made some sense.

It took a few minutes, but finally Tamara stepped back and looked at Michi's chest. "What do you think?" she asked Doug.

"She's still not petite, but I think it's enough," Doug said.

Michi, hands still up, looked down. Her chest was not small, but her breasts had been flattened pretty well. She lowered her arms and then swung them around to see if the gauze would stay in place.

"That feel OK?" Tamara asked.

"Uh, yeah. Weird, but OK."

"Let me have the pad," Tamara told Doug, who handed over what looked like a warped pillow. "I don't know. The duct tape?"

"Yeah, I think the gauze might shift," Doug said as they stared at her as if she was a mannequin.

"This might hurt a little when it comes off," Tamara told her as she and Doug put the pad around her belly and over her hips and duct taped it into place.

It was tight, and it restricted Michi's breathing just a bit, but it wasn't too bad.

"Drop the shorts," Tamara told her, but with the duct tape around her belly, Michi couldn't bend over that well, and her shorts hung up on her knees.

Tamara had to reach over and knock them down so Michi could step out. Doug and Tamara then proceeded to tape pads to her thighs and butt, leaving bulges where previously there had been none. When they were finished, they both stepped back to check their work.

"I don't know, it might be enough. Let's get her dressed," Tamara said.

"Hey, 'her' is right here in front of you," Michi grumbled, but without conviction.

Wrapped up, Michi couldn't dress herself, so both of her roommates had to pull on the pants and shirt being careful to leave all the pads in place. She sat down as Doug pulled a pair of Giraffes out of a bag.

Oh great, with me all bundled up, they want me to wear 12 cm platforms? She thought.

But when Doug slid on the shoes, she was surprised that her feet went in farther than she expected. She stood up, and she felt like she was standing on the floor itself, not on the elevated soles.

"Hollowed out," Doug said with a smile. "Makes you look shorter than you really are to any surveillance."

"Is all of this really necessary?" Michi asked. "Isn't this overkill? You've got me a new face, after all."

"I told you this would change your life. They've got recordings of you, and your body, your posture, your gait, everything will have been entered into the system. All the surveillance cameras will have been programmed to alert on anyone who fits those parameters. So it's not just the face. We have to change everything."

He took the shoes back off, put something inside each one, then put them back on her.

"OK, walk," he told her.

"Ow!" she exclaimed as something dug into her feet. "What did you put in there?"

"Just an insert to make your gait different."

"You mean that really works?" Michi asked.

"Yeah, why?"

Doug never knew about the two attacks on jacks, and Michi and Tamara had decided to keep that secret.

"I don't know. I guess I thought that was only in the spy flicks," she said instead as Tamara silently mouthed "I told you" behind Doug's head.

"OK, I think we're ready. Go take a look in the mirror," Doug told her.

Michi walked into Tamara's room and to the big, full-length mirror there. In front of her was a slightly dumpy-looking girl, not really fat, but not slim either. She turned on the new spoofer face, and the dumpy-looking girl turned into a dumpy-looking middle-aged woman. The face was not too terribly different from hers, but it had lost the slightly Asian-cast her real face had.

"Yes, you're beautiful. But we've got to get going," Tamara said, leaning against the doorframe. "The NIP won't wait."

"You still think this is a good idea?" Michi asked her.

"No, I'm not sure. But risk and rewards, like Doug said. We've got to make a move sometime, and now, you're hot," Tamara responded.

"But you don't have to go. Why risk it?"

"I couldn't get to your little ambush, so it's my turn. 'Sides, if this is a trap, then they'll get my identity out of you."

"I wouldn't talk," Michi said.

"Everyone talks. Don't let the flicks fool you," Tamara said.

"You two done? We've got to get moving," Doug said, poking his head in the bedroom.

Michi and Tamara hugged, then Michi left the room and made her way to the street. The other two would be following in a few minutes. She slowly walked to the rendezvous point, just a woman on an afternoon stroll. She would have felt better meeting at night, but the curfew made that impossible.

She stopped for a doughnut, and there, sipping some coffee, was an old lady wearing a green neck scarf. Michi tried not to stare at her contact. She nibbled at her doughnut, but when the old woman got up, Michi was only half-finished. She slammed the rest down, and after a minute, left the shop.

The old lady was about 30 meters down the sidewalk and Michi slowly followed, looking in store windows, trying to seem inconspicuous. The woman turned the corner, and when Michi reached it, she saw the woman stepping into an apartment building. Michi hurried forward and stepped in as well. The woman was gone, the access door closed.

Michi didn't have a code, nor did she know an apartment number to ring to get buzzed up. She tentatively reached out and pushed the door, and to her relief, it opened. She stepped inside, and the old woman was waiting for an elevator. Michi joined her, and they rode to the 32nd floor. The woman got out without saying a word, and Michi, not knowing what else to do, followed her. Halfway down the hall, a door opened and an arm reached out to pull Michi in. Her heart pounded as a hooded man stood there. He quickly ran a portable scanner over her and must have been satisfied because he motioned for Michi to enter the apartment.

"Michi, dear. So glad to see you," Cheri said, giving Michi a kiss on each cheek.

This was the first time they had seen each other in person since the broadcast. Michi had made a recording, giving a full report, and that had been given to the chapter chairman, but they hadn't had time to discuss things in more detail.

"I'm not sure if you've heard anything yet, but your parents have been arrested, and your home's been razed," she told Michi, her voice not quite indicating sympathy.

Michi thought it might have been somewhat of an "I told you so," statement that Cheri should not have been kept out of the loop.

Michi was shocked at the revelation, though. Her parents? Her home? She knew coming out would have ramifications, but she didn't know her family would be affected like that. What was the probable cause? They were First Family, and the company could not run roughshod over any of them, at least according to the charter. But then again, the company had shown before that it was willing to break the charter to suit its needs.

She had been essentially disowned by her family, but still, blood ran thick. Their arrest was just one more thing on the list for which Michi planned on getting revenge.

"Michi, let me introduce you to Mike."

Just "Mike?" No last name? Michi wondered.

"Mike is an officer in the NIP, and he wanted to meet you."

"Shouldn't we wait for the other two?" Michi asked, speaking of Tamara and Doug.

"They won't be coming," Mike said. "They've been taken somewhere else." He held up a hand as Michi started to protest. "They will not be harmed. We just wanted to meet you privately, and when you insisted on your friends coming too, this was just easier."

Michi didn't like that. The other two were part of her conditions, and if this was the NIP, that didn't bode well for potential cooperation.

That was the crux, though. Were Mike and his unnamed companion really NIP? Each of the old board members knew that Michi had used the NIP as bait to identify the traitor, and Hokkam had brought the company in on the supposed meeting, too, so it was not any secret. They could have turned around and used the exact same tactic to capture Michi. But Cheri had insisted this was the real deal, so Michi had agreed.

"Can we see the real you?" Mike asked, pointing to Michi's face.

Michi had forgotten her spoofer. With a flip of the switch, she was back to being Michiko.

"That's better. Ms. Baliles here has already explained your disguise generator. It's an interesting application, perhaps a little dated, but that might have been to your advantage given surveillance technology," Mike went on.

Michi bristled at that. "Dated?" *Who was he to criticize?* The NIP had been organized almost 20 years before, and what had they accomplished during that time? Nothing!

"Ms. MacCailín, what now?" he asked.

What now? What now what? she wondered, confused by the question.

"I'm not sure what you mean."

"You've killed a Federation Marine and essentially called out the planet to go to war. So what are you going to do now?"

"Uh, well, I haven't discussed that with Cheri and the board yet, so I don't know of any concrete plans."

"But you are not actually a member of the Workers' Rights Party, if I understand correctly. So why are you waiting for them?" he asked.

"No. I mean yes. I am not a member. But we've been working together," Michi said.

"Have you thought about coming to us? We are the more, shall we say, active group in opposition to the company and Federation. We're not in it only for company employees—we are fighting for everyone on the planet, even including the First Families like your father and mother who are now in company holding cells."

"And why do you want me?" she asked him.

"To be blunt, because you've managed to incite a spark in the people, something we haven't been able to do. We've got weapons. We've got trained fighters. We've got plans upon plans. But we've not been able to draw the masses to the cause. We think you can."

Michi sat staring at him before looking to the other man. "And does your quiet friend think that, too?"

The two men looked at each other, and with a shrug, the second man reached up and pulled on his chin. A sheet of bioflesh lifted off, revealing the familiar face of the Right Reverend Duncan, the spiritual leader of The Kirk and the same man who had sat in her living room to grill her those months back.

"Yes, lass, I do," he said.

Michi stared at the man in shock. The NIP had a reputation of being obsessed crazies running around in the forest while playing militia. How could the Right Reverend be involved?

"You've probably got many questions, and if you want, you and I can sit and talk, but the question now is if you want to help."

"But you're the—"

"I'm this year's Right Reverend, aye. But righteousness is righteousness, and the Kirk has always protected the oppressed."

"But with guns?" she asked, still surprised.

"The sword of the Lord is wielded by mortal man, lass," he said gently.

She looked from the Right Reverend to Mike to Cheri.

"What do you think?" she asked Cheri.

"I wouldn't have agreed to the meeting if I were against it. Maybe, if the time is right, you can do more good with the NIP."

"And is the time right, Mike?" she asked.

"Well, to be honest, we had planned on something later, but that was before you took it upon yourself to take out a Marine and issue a call to arms. We have to be flexible if we are going to persevere, and you sort of kicked it all off. We want to take advantage of that," he said, all traces of self-importance gone from his voice.

Michi stood for a moment. The thought of striking back, really striking back, excited her. This was a moment where she could seize the momentum, seize the opportunity.

"And you are ready to strike?" she asked.

"Within a week, maybe two at the longest, yes," Mike told her.

"I'm in, but under some conditions."

"And what conditions," Mike asked, his voice suddenly wary.

"First, I am not a figurehead. When it comes to a fight, I will be at the forefront."

"And second?"

"Second, I am not some comic book figure. The costume goes. No more bare midriff, no low cut bammers. Whatever uniform you have, that's what I'll wear."

She saw the Right Reverend smile at that. No matter his willingness to fight, it seemed as if the First Family inherent cultural conservatism still held sway with him.

"Anything else?" Mike asked.

"Yes. When we win, I want my parent's house to be rebuilt. That's all."

Mike held out his hand, which Michi took. "Done and done," he said, his face breaking out into a smile.

Michi was elated. She was going to war!

Chapter 30

"We can fire 15 of these 25mm shells per minute, and they pack a pretty good punch," the man said with evident pride in his voice.

Michi tried to look attentive as she listened to the man extol the virtues of their three Donaldson field guns, small mobile artillery that could be employed by a two man team. The NIP had three of them, and these were the heaviest guns in their inventory. Or was it those rockets she'd seen only 20 minutes before?

Michi was having a hard time keeping everything straight. She pulled down her fatigue blouse where it kept riding up under her pistol belt and over her butt. The uniform was better than her super-hero costume, but despite her words, she was sure it had been tailored taking her figure into consideration. There were other women in the NIP army, and their fatigues were the same shapeless ones given to the men. Michi's, however, gathered at the waist and had slightly tapered legs. The difference was not so great, though, that Michi felt she had to protest. She was pragmatic enough to realize that even if she insisted she was not a figurehead, still, as one of the leaders of the small army, appearances mattered.

Most of her first four days with the NIP army had been spent bending the flesh and getting her bearings on the underground complex that served as the NIP headquarters and training area. It was located in an abandoned salt mine, and coupled with the best shielding they could buy, had been enough so far to keep the company, and now the Marines, off of them.

Michi would not turn 20 years old for another two weeks, but they had given her a general's star to wear on her collar. She wasn't in command but had been given the title of Assault Leader. Michi got the feeling that the position had been created just to appease her demand to be in on any coming action.

Michi thanked the ordinance technical two[12] and tried to cubbyhole his position in the army. *A "two" was the same as a*

---

[12] Ordinance technical two: NIP enlisted military ranks do not follow Marine, Legion, or militia ranks. They are based more on

sergeant, right? All of the unique structures to the 2,000 man force were confusing her, but she had to just smile and radiate an aura of confidence.

At least the rank-and-file seemed to embrace her. Even men and women in their 60's and 70's seemed to truly like her and expressed their willingness to follow her. The fact that she had killed a Marine, and that is how the soldiers considered it, gave her immediate credibility and warrior status.

The leadership, on the other hand, seemed to merely tolerate her presence. They were slightly condescending as if they found it amusing that the little girl wanted to play with the grown-ups.

Her "assistant" was Colonel Perseverance Hannrahan, but Michi had come to the conclusion that he was more of a baby-sitter than assistant. When she asked about the coming battle, he told her not to worry, he was on top of it, and he would tell her when things firmed up. Michi got the feeling that even if she were nominally in command of the assault, it would be Hannrahan giving the commands.

That pissed off Michi at first. But she had to admit that she knew next to nothing about military tactics, so it was probably better that the colonel issue orders. But Michi would observe and learn. The next time, Michi would be better prepared to command in her own right.

"You're supposed to go give a pep talk to the cooks," the colonel told her, "but I've just been told that Jessep wants to see you. Let's head on back, OK?"

He phrased that as a suggestion, but Michi knew she really didn't have much say in the matter. Jessep was General Jessep Alvarez, the man in charge of the army and one of the highest-ranking members within the NIP.

At first, Michi had been surprised at the way people were addressed, usually by their first names. She had envisioned people marching about, shouting "Yes, sir!" and "No, sir!" Instead, despite the rank insignia, things were rather casual. Michi didn't know if that disappointed or enthused her just yet.

---

navy ranks, with the type of job first, then a one, two, or three to indicate seniority

Michi had to stop several times on the way to the conference room as people came up to welcome her or congratulate her on the attack on the Marines. An older lady pulled Michi's hand to her forehead, where she held it as she recited what sounded like a prayer in a language Michi didn't recognize. When she was finished, she lowered Michi's hand to kiss it before letting her go, a beatific smile on her face. Michi knew the woman meant well, but that creeped her out. Why would a woman, obviously in her 70's or more, seem to almost worship a mere 19-year-old girl? Michi tried not to let her unease show and instead reached out to hug the woman.

As with any group, crowd dynamics were such that when anything big was up, there was an undercurrent of intensity that could be sensed. It could have been something as simple as the army leadership suddenly heading for the command center, or it could be some deep tribal perception that couldn't be explained. Whatever the reason, people started gathering close to the command center entrance. The number of people surprised Michi. She had been told that NIP had 2,000 soldiers, and they had been stepping up training since the Marines had landed. Michi didn't know if that meant actual combat soldiers or if that number included support personnel, leadership, or other members scattered across the planet.

As far as she knew, except for some of the leaders, and now Michi, most of the people who lived in the complex were indentureds who had run away. The free citizens came and went as they pleased. Michi had even recognized a few First Family members there, including one of her cousins. Michi thought that the constant comings and goings would be a security risk, but Hannrahan had laughed when she brought that up saying they "had that covered."

Several of the other leaders were already in the conference room, eating doughnuts and sipping coffee, when Michi and Hannrahan came in. Jessep saw her and smiled, motioning her to come.

"Michiko! I trust Perseverance has been getting you acclimated?" he asked, then going on before Michi could respond.

"Before we begin, I thought you might want to see this," he said, holding out his PA.

It was a reward notice with a copy of her university id holo. The Federation was offering a 300,000 credit reward for any information leading to her capture.

"300,000? For 'sedition?'" she asked, strangely disappointed.

She had known this was coming, but given the fact that she and Doug had taken out a Marine, she had expected something bigger, maybe even the max reward ever offered on Kakurega—a cool million. Although 300, 000 was not chump change, still, other rewards often exceeded that.

"Yes, I thought you would find that funny."

"But why sedition?" she asked, confused.

"Because officially, the dead Marine never happened. Remember, they said the recording was fake. So they gave you a high-enough reward to interest the bounty hunters, but not enough to give credence that some uni girl managed to take out a Federation Marine."

"But it's not fake, and they know that," Michi protested.

"They know that, and we know that, but they don't want the public to know that. And if a reporter had some balls, he or she would have tramped out to the Ledges and looked for the evidence like we did," Jessep told her.

"You went out there?" Michi asked, surprised.

"Of course we did, Michiko. Due diligence. We had to make sure before we approached you. And now, almost everyone is here, so why don't you take your seat."

Michi went to her seat and sat down. It was near the head of the table, but not at it. Hannrahan sat immediately behind her and up against the wall. Michi looked around at the other leaders of the NIP, nodding at both Mike and the Right Reverend. She had met some of the others, but really was not yet on chatting terms with any of them.

Jessep called the meeting to order, then jumped right into the reason he had called them together. "Friends, the time has come for us to finally level the first strike against those who oppress us. We have planned, trained, and given our all for the last 20 years, and other than a few small actions, some small acts of sabotage, we have merely been a gadfly to the company. That changes tomorrow.

"At 8:15 AM, we will launch a military attack on the Marines. Our target? None other than their hero, Captain Lysander, the scourge who attacked legal protestors on Soreau, the same Marine who tried to enforce illegal tariffs on Greater France, the same one who perpetuated the aggression on the trinoculars."

A holo of the captain appeared in the center of the table. He was standing in Prosperity Square, scowling at something out of holo range.

It was only a holo, and Michi had never met the man, but despite Seth's half-defense of him, Michi felt the bile rise in her throat. She would love to be part of the attack to take the man down.

"Captain Lysander's company is located at the old refining complex, as many of you know. He has 180 Marines with him, but we've got over 2,000 righteous soldiers who are anxious to defend our home.

"I'm going to turn this over to Dwantifor now for some of the details. Get comfortable, because you know how he is once he gets started," he said, just injecting the right amount of humor to break the tension, Michi thought.

The group chuckled, and then Jessep went on, "You can put away your PAs. We are now officially in lock-down. No one leaves and no communications. Dwantifor, you've got it."

There was a buzzing as the operations chief walked to the front.

"Pay attention," Hannrahan whispered, leaning in to her shoulder. "Not all of it will make sense to you, but pick up what you can. We're going to have a lot to go over tonight."

Michi nodded, too excited to speak. She watched the holo base, waiting for the holo itself to appear and eager to see what she would be doing. At last, no more little ticky-tack efforts. This was the real thing, and she was going to be part of it!

Chapter 31

Charlie Company, First Battalion, 11th Marines, commanded by Captain Ryck Lysander, was based at the old refinery where the first settlers cracked organics from oil and natural gas. It was located downstream from the city at a bow in the River Tay, where pollutants would have less of an impact, but close enough for easy logistics. With the arrival of Propitious Interstellar and their more advanced power generation emplaced, the old refinery grounds turned into an algae farm. The company's patented Blue-99 was their top organic base, used in everything from food products to plastics to cosmetics to liquid fuel for aircraft.

The Marine company's location was probably more due to protecting the algae farm than anything else, but it also provided a good base of operations for actions in the southern part of the city. Michi hadn't realized it when she and Doug had taken out the Marine, but the Ledges was in the company's "AO," or area of operations, as she learned it was termed.

With the river on three sides, that left only the eastern approach accessible over land. This was a concern, but both Generals Kyne Fuller and Loski Sonutta-Lyon, who had served with various mercenary companies in the past, seemed to think that with their huge advantage in manpower, and with the plan they had devised, the NIP could simply overwhelm the relatively small force inside the refinery.

The large force that would assault the entrance over the land, which Michi was nominally leading, was not the real breaching force, however. The assault force would initiate an attack to pin down the Marines, and then the real breaching force would emerge from the River Tay itself to hit the Marines from the rear. With that confusion, Michi's assault force could charge the refinery and roll right in.

The river commando force was their surprise element, and Michi though the plan was brilliant. No one would expect an underwater assault from a free-flowing river. But what the Marines didn't know was that the NIP had a number of commercial divers within its ranks, and with the heavy deep-sea suits they had been able to acquire and the firm bottom at the river's bow, even non-divers could simply walk across the river. The commando force would enter the river at a small lagoon that was out of sight to anyone at the refinery and would already be on its way, trudging the 500 meters to reach the first set of algae tubes at the leading edge of the river bank.

Michi looked around at those of her force who were in sight. They had stopped in the trees stopped well short of the broad expanse leading up to the refinery's front gate. Two Marines in combat suits were manning it, according to the reports coming in. Inside, there were probably 120-130 more Marines. The night patrols had already returned and were probably sacked out, and the day patrols had left. They would be non-factors in the coming assault. The NIP outnumbered the Marines fifteen-to-one, and from what she had been told, an attacking force only needed a five-to-one advantage to succeed.

"You ready for this?" Hannrahan asked her.

"I was born for this," Michi replied.

"Just remember, don't go charging off. We are here to attract their attention and fix the Marines in place so our commandos can breach the defenses. Only then, will we actually go into the attack ourselves."

"I understood that the last fifty times you told me" Michi muttered under her breath.

She glanced at her watch. They had fewer than five minutes to go. Her warrior spirit was clamoring for attention, and it was about time to let her out. She realized that she was still somewhat of a figurehead, but if she was getting into the fight, she could accept that.

She checked her rifle. It had still been packed when she got it, and she had felt like she was opening a Christmas present as she ripped away the plastic storage wrap. It was beautiful, a two kilojoule Leung Min pulse rifle. It didn't have as much range as that of most of her soldier's weapons, but it was simple to use, and within 15 meters, it was deadly. Aiming was not vital—a simple point-and-shoot was all she would need to shut down any Marine in her path. She had one extra powerpack, so she was good for about 100 shots, but the fight should be over before she could exhaust the rifle's charges.

Hannrahan was absorbed with his watch. He held up his other hand, then still looking at his watch, brought the free hand down in a chopping motion.

"OK, tell the arty to open up," he told her.

She flipped on her throat mic, cleared her throat, and gave the command that committed the people of Kakurega to war. "Donaldson team, commence fire."

Behind her, the three Donaldsons opened up, the outgoing rounds a sharp report. They were only 1,000 meters back, so within seconds, there were explosions to Michi's front as the rounds hit the refinery. The war was on!

She counted five outgoing volleys, and before Hannrahan could tell her, she shouted into her mic, "Assault force! Up and at 'em."

Michi had gone over in her mind what she might say when the time came, but in the end, decided that she didn't want anything too flowery, just a simple command.

She jumped up, pulling down on the bottom of her body armor, getting the collar off of the base of her throat. It was uncomfortable, didn't fit right, and restricted her breathing, but the command staff had insisted on it. Every piece of body armor they possessed had been passed out, with all of the first wave of the assault force getting it along with some of the second wave.

Hannrahan was speaking into his throat mic as he moved just to her front. Anger flared in Michi as she realized that he was controlling at least part of the assault. This was her command, not his! She pushed her anger down for the moment—she would confront him on that after the refinery was taken.

There was an explosion just off to Michi's left. Michi felt the shock wave, but didn't see anything through the trees. She was momentarily startled, but then pushed forward. Of course, the Marines wouldn't just let them waltz in. They were professionals, after all. But if the Marines were firing at them, then her assault force was doing its job by fixing the Marines in place. Within moments, the river commando breaching force would be hitting them through the algae farm.

Coming out of the trees, still some 300 meters from the front gate, the first rank ran up the slight bank of the roadbed for Highway 2. This was the major highway that ran along the river to the south to Gaberson and points beyond. Four lanes wide with a grassy median, it could be a kill zone if they let it. That wasn't going to happen. They wouldn't cross it in force until the Marines were focused on the breaching force. But to give that force a chance, the assault force had to act the part, and that was going to result in casualties.

The open area from the T-intersection to the refinery's gates was almost 400 meters wide and 300 meters long, with the river on the south side and trees on the north. The refinery sat like an ancient fort on the west side of the open area.

As Michi crested the roadbed and sprinted across the highway, she only had a glimpse of the front gates before all hell broke loose. Several explosions sounded just in front of her with plumes of smoke and dirt erupting into the air. The sound of gnats zinged past her ear, and she saw one of her men stumble and fall.

"Now!" Hannrahan yelled from a few meters off her side.

"Fall back!" she screamed, turning and running back to the far side of the highway and diving for the ground where the roadbed offered her slightly less than two meters of protection from direct fire.

She got up on an elbow and looked up and down the edge of the road. She had gone over the road with about 400 soldiers, and it looked like most of them had made it back. A body hurtled down the depression fifteen meters away from her, the soldier's neck half-torn open, blood spurting wildly several times before tapering off.

Michi stared at him. She knew some people would be killed, but seeing a man who had followed her into battle, trusting her to lead him to victory, die right before her eyes brought the seriousness home to her. This was not a lark. This was life and death.

"Send up a count," she heard someone call out.

"I'd hoped we could have gotten farther," Hannrahan said beside her.

"*Arinomamade," she* said quietly, looking up and down her line.

"What?" he started, but Michi waved him off, and he continued, "But I think this still might do the trick."

"Are they going to mortar us?" Michi asked.

"We'll find out pretty quickly, won't we?" Hannrahan said, sounding dismissive of her question.

One of the assumptions of the assault was that the Marines' ROE would not let them damage Highway 2. The company needed it to reach the cities and facilities to the south. Her first rank relied on that fact. The hope was that as the Marines knew they were there, and as they had acted like a disjointed force without the courage and fortitude to continue, the Marines would organize some sort of counter-attack. If that happened, the rest of the 1,100 assault force would pour from the forest into the attack. If the timing was right, the breaching force would be hitting the Marines from the rear at the same time. The Marines would be caught in a pincher and be destroyed.

Michi looked back to where the bulk of her force was hidden. Direct fire rounds were flying over their heads, the occasional clods of dirt and grass raining down on them. But something was missing, and it took Michi a moment to figure out what it was.

"Where's our arty?" she asked Hannrahan.

"Good question," he said, and without even pretending to go through her, he got on his throat mic.

The throat mics replied primarily on subvocalizations, so Michi couldn't hear more than a murmur, but from lip-reading, she could see him trying to raise the gun teams. He gave up and looked to Michi, shaking his head.

"Damn pieces of shit probably broke down," he said. "I told Jessep to get the KU-300's from Gentry.[13] But he wanted to save a few credits, and look now. Well, it is what it is, and we may not have any supporting arms."

---

[13] Gentry: A Congress of Free Worlds planet known for inexpensive but utterly reliable military and construction gear.

"Do we need them?" Michi asked.

She swore Hannrahan was about to roll his eyes, but he answered, "No, we don't *need* them. But casualties will be higher without them.

The head count came back to Michi then. Only 348 men and women had made it back to the depression that protected them now. Michi gulped. That mean 59 people had not made it. They were just over the lip of the road bed, wounded or dead.

A sudden thought hit her. "Will they be shooting our wounded? They're still firing!"

"Wouldn't put it past the bastards," Hannrahan conceded.

"Well, shouldn't we do something?" she asked with concern.

"Do what? Get more people hit? That's a kill zone there, just like we knew it would be. Let our river team get in before we sacrifice anyone else."

Michi looked at her watch, then asked, "But shouldn't they already be assaulting?"

Hannrahan looked at his. "Yeah, they should. But walking on a river bottom can be tricky. You can't see anything, so it'd be easy to get turned around," he said.

He put his hand to his throat mic, though, and contacted someone. Michi wasn't even upset anymore about him bypassing her. She just wanted answers.

"Uh, we've got some garbled messages from the breaching team. Command is trying to find out what's going on, and they'll get back to us in a moment."

"But they should have gotten in at least to the algae farm, right? The Marines won't attack in there."

"No plan lasts beyond the first shot in a battle. We have to be ready to improvise, and I'm guessing we'll be pulling back about now," he said.

"Pull back? But what about the Marines?" she protested.

"The fucking Marines are why we might have to pull back. If the breaching team failed, we can't conduct a frontal attack."

"Don't give me can't, colonel!" Michi screamed at him. "We've got almost 2,000 soldiers who came here to win, not to slink away with their tails between their legs! And if you don't have the balls to take the Marines on, I sure do!"

She stood up, ignoring the round impacting on the edge of the roadbed and showering the two of them with dirt.

On the far south side of her line, firing broke out. She slowly turned to look and saw a dozen or so combat-suited Marines emerge from the river, firing their weapons at her soldiers. She could see some of her men and women firing back, but only those at the very end of the line could fire without fear of hitting the others.

"Well, *colonel*, do you have any balls?" she asked before turning and starting to run down the line towards the fight.

"Follow me!" she screamed, her anger mounting. She would crush the Marines, then focus on the refinery.

Alongside her, soldiers were jumping up and running, a mass of unstoppable humanity. More of her men and women started pouring out of the forest to join them. There had to be 600 or more of them rushing down the 40 meter wide open area between the road and the edge of the forest.

Something hit her in the arm, knocking the rifle out of her hand and almost spinning her around, but she regained her feet and continued to run. Soldiers were falling around her, but she led the charge. They *would* close with and destroy the enemy. It was their destiny!

Suddenly, Michi was lifted into the air, heat and sound enveloping her. The sky, her soldiers, and the road rotated several times in her vision before the ground filled it one last time as she slammed down, and all went dark.

Chapter 32

A burst of pain forced its way into Michi's consciousness, pulling her from the depths to which she had descended. She struggled to make sense of her world, and another blow almost knocked her back into nothingness.

"Hey, the bitch's back with us," a voice registered.

Michi opened her eyes. A jack had her by the collar having pulled her to a sitting position. His arm was cocked back to hit her across the face again. She knew she wasn't dead. She hurt too much for that. The smell of blood, sweat, and shit was too strong for that. Michi might be in hell, but she wasn't dead.

"She doesn't look so tough now, does she?" another jack said as he came up to stare at her.

Michi focused on the second jack's bulging belly, which pulled open his shirt, leaving gaps between the buttons. She realized the guy's clothing didn't matter, but she needed an anchor on which to focus in an attempt to gather her thoughts.

"What . . . what happened?" she managed to get out.

"Ha! What happened? Derrick, she wants to know what happened!" the first jack said, the one who had slapped her face.

The second one stepped forward, and with a gloating smile creasing his face, said, "Well, Miss Red Athena, what happen was that you tugged on superman's cape and got your asses handed to you. The current count is that over 1,300 of you fucking rebels were killed, another 600 captured.

"What, you thought you might actually win?" he asked as he saw her jerk at the news. "You never had no chance. We had loyal people who infiltrated your vaunted NIP. We knew everything you were going to do. We wanted you to attack, in fact, once we had the Marines here. That way we could get you out in the open and stomp on you like cockroaches. Hell, with all those who got zeroed, you're lucky to even be alive."

"Oh, I don't know about that," the first jack said with an evil laugh. "About being lucky and all. Now that she's awake, she's got some 'splaining to do, and I don't think that's going to be pleasant, no I don't. She'll wish she had bought it with the rest before Fordyce and his team are done with her."

"I think you're right, there, Gunter, my man. I think you're right. I'll go tell Fordyce she's ready for him."

"Hey, ask him if we can watch!" the first jack asked his retreating friend.

He shifted his grip to Michi's hair and pulled her head up until she was only centimeters from his face.

He looked deeply into her eyes for a moment before saying, "You fucked up, girl, and now you're going to pay the price."

He let go, and her head thudded back onto whatever she was lying on. Sharp lances of pain radiated throughout her body as her head bounced.

She almost cried out, but she knew that was nothing. Whatever awaited her would be much, much worse.

Chapter 33

Michi was trying not to cry. Was he telling the truth? Did 1,300 soldiers really die? All of this had been her idea, all because the company murdered Franz. But her anger had cost 1,300 more people, people who had loved ones, people who had their own lives.

When the man who had to be Fordyce finally came in the little cell in which she was held, she merely looked up at him in resignation. Whatever his plans, she probably deserved them.

"Ah, you are awake, Miss MacCailín. Good. You and I are going to have a good time, together," he said, actually rubbing his hands together in anticipation. "I have some things to ask you, and you are going to give me the answers. I won't lie to you, though. Whether you tell me easily or hard, it won't make much difference to you because," he leaned forward to whisper into her ear, "I just enjoy it too fucking much."

The two previous jacks had evidently received permission to watch as they followed Fordyce in as did one other man. The one called Derrick had the decency to look nervous and uncomfortable, but the other three looked at her with unbridled eagerness.

Michi was lying on a metal table. Her right arm, the one that had been hit during the assault, was cuffed to one of the table supports. She didn't struggle as the four men surrounded her.

"Chen, you and you," he said, pointing at the other jack, Gunter, "take off her clothes."

Both men jumped forward, hands quickly stripping her down. With her arm attached to the table leg, they jerked on her shirt a few times, eliciting a gasp from her as they jarred her injured arm, before grabbing a knife and cutting the shirt off.

She had expected something along these lines, and she tried to ignore the growing feeling of vulnerability as the men gawked at her body. She tried to send her mind elsewhere. That worked in books and flicks, but it wasn't doing too much for her. She was very much rooted in a small cell, naked on a cold metal table.

"OK, my dear. My first question is where is the man you call Jessep? He wasn't captured, nor was he among the bodies. The many, many bodies, I might add. So where might he have gone?"

Michi couldn't tell them even if she wanted to. She didn't know. She suspected that Fordyce knew that she didn't know, too. But he smiled, took a short, wicked looking knife, and put the tip a centimeter from her left eye. Lowering it to her cheek, he lightly traced a line down her face and neck, over her clavicle, across her breast, and down her belly. He lingered with the knife tip alongside her inner thigh, and despite her resolve, Michi flinched. He almost chuckled, and then started the knife moving again. It went down her thigh. Michi couldn't tell if he was actually cutting her or not, but when he passed her knee, the pressure eased.

Michi let out a breath she hadn't realized she was holding. She started to relax her muscles, which she had involuntarily tensed, when fire sunk into her calf as Fordyce plunged the small knife up to its hilt. She let out a screech of pain.

"Oops! Sorry about that," he said with a laugh, a laugh echoed by at least two of the others. "It must have slipped.

"So, where were we?" he asked, pulling the knife out of her leg.

He moved in front of Michi and slowly licked her blood off the blade. If he was trying to unsettle her, it was working.

"Oh, I think I was asking you about Jessep. But we can come back to that. I see you have beautiful hands, and I want to play before we get to work."

Michi raised her head as he pulled out a pair of pliers from the bag the fourth man, Chen, held out for him. They were simple, ordinary household pliers. Michi had used similar ones a thousand times, never thinking about how evil they could be.

"What say you, right or left?" he made a show of asking the other three. "What, left you say? I am at your command."

Michi started breathing hard as Fordyce grabbed her free hand and held it up, admiring it as if it was a piece of art. Michi twisted and brought her arm forward, breaking free of his grasp. She punched out, but Fordyce ducked back out of the way.

"A fighter! All the better. Fighters last longer. You two, grab her arm and hold it down," he said.

Gunter and Chen stepped up to grab her arm. Michi struggled, and she managed to land a punch to Chen's nose, starting a flow of blood. Within seconds, however, they had her arm pinned to the table. Chen licked at the blood on his face, then with a smile, pushed his face onto her left breast, wiping some of his blood off.

"Ah, yes, now we have the hand trapped like a dove. And look, no ring on the finger. Wasn't she supposed to be married? What was his name? Franz Galipili? Did that man leave her at the altar?" he asked in mockery.

"Fuck you, you bastard," Michi blurted out, knowing she was playing into his hands.

"That's some mouth you have there, young lady. I was going to offer you to Chen here as a wife since you seem to be missing a man, but I don't know if he's going to want you now."

"Oh, I ken teach her manners, never you fear," said the man holding her arm down. He leaned forward and licked her face, from chin to eyebrow.

Michi tried to headbutt him, but he was too quick, and he jumped back out of the way.

"Temper, temper, Miss MacCailín. That will get you in trouble sometime," Fordyce said.

His play-acting was infuriating Michi, and she wanted to lash out. Then, somehow, the absurdity of that hit her. She'd been shot. Her calf was on fire after being stabbed. She was naked, and two men were holding her down while a third was threatening her hand, and she was worried about the personality game her torturer was playing? She actually laughed.

"Oh, something funny? I can assure you that nothing is," Fordyce said, suddenly serious.

Have I hit a nerve? she wondered.

She didn't have time to wonder for long as Fordyce reached in and wrenched her ring finger up, grabbed it with the pliers, and twisted. She let out a blood-curdling scream as her universe descended into a maelstrom of pain.

"Please . . . please," she called out. If she had known where Jessep was, she was afraid that she would tell them before enduring that again.

It took minutes for the intense agony to fade to an aching throbbing that kept time with her pulse. She didn't want to imagine what her hand looked like. It wasn't until she finally began to get control of her thoughts that she noticed the other jack, Derrick, had left.

"'Please?' You said 'please.' Please what?" Fordyce asked her.

"Just, please, what do you want?" she whispered, ashamed of herself.

"Oh, we'll get to that later. Now, I'm afraid you're going to have to pay for your sins," he told her.

He took the piers and put them against her lips. She clenched them tight.

"No? No teeth? OK—I don't want anyone to accuse me of being uncaring," he said, back to his facetious attitude.

He brought the pliers lower off her face and started down to her belly when he stopped, then brought them up to her right nipple. He closed the pliers, slightly squeezing the nipple, but not too hard—yet.

Michi tensed up. She knew what was coming, and she tried to fortify her will.

"You seemed to be proud to flash these around for everyone to see in your oh-so-clever camcordings. So how about it if I just yank this bad boy right off, huh?" he said, moving slightly to get a better angle.

"No!" shouted Gunter.

"Excuse me?" Fordyce said with mock incredulity.

"You said, for me helping you, I can, you know, have her."

"And so you will, but later."

"But if you take that nip off, well, I don't like that none. I want her whole when I do her," he protested.

Michi took in a deep breath. She had rather expected this as soon as she woke up in captivity. She thought she had steeled herself to the inevitable, but when faced with it, she realized that she was not the strong one to just shrug something like that off.

"Well, never say I'm a man who doesn't keep his word. Please, my dear companion, take your prize. I can always play later."

"What, here? With you looking?" Gunter asked.

"It's up to you. You can take her or not, but none of us are leaving," Fordyce told him as Chen laughed.

Michi had a moment of hope while Gunter stared at the two other men first, then at her.

That hope was dashed when Gunter shrugged and said "Well, fuck it. If you want to see me and her getting it on, be my guest."

He pulled off his shirt first, bloody from either Chen's nose or any one of her wounds. Next came his boots, then his pants. Last were his undertights. He stood there, naked and rampant with excitement. Not that there was much of a penis there. He was decidedly under-sized.

He looked like a bull moose in rut, though, almost snorting in his eagerness. Michi knew what was going to happen, and the act itself didn't upset her as much as the helplessness, the knowledge that this piece of shit was going to do to her what he wanted without regard to her as a human being.

She still had her mouth free, and that was the only way at the moment that she could strike back.

She looked at him as he panted with lust. With her best attempt at disdain, she said, "Oh come on. If you are going to use rape to try and break me, you would do better to give me a man with a big enough tool to do some damage."

"What?" he screeched! "I'll show you damage, you bitch!"

He started stepping forward, but Chen was laughing uproariously. "She's got you there. My three-year-old's got a bigger dick than that!"

Gunter stopped and glared at Chen. "Shut the fuck up! I'll show you! I'll fuck her until she begs for more!"

"Uh, maybe not," Fordyce said, pointing to Gunter's penis which had started to go flaccid as he lost focus.

With an animal grunt, Gunter rushed Michi, threw her legs open, and pushed himself between them. Except he had nothing left. He had lost it.

"See, nothing there. You might as well get back to your pliers because this little boy can't perform," she said to Fordyce, trying to inject as much of a dismissive tone as she could.

"You fucking bitch!" Gunter screamed. He scrambled off her and pulled his fist back.

As Fordyce yelled "No!" that big fist came forward with the full weight and emotion of Gunter behind it, smashing into Michi's nose and sending her mercifully into the darkness.

Chapter 34

Michi slowly came to. While still in the murky state of semi-consciousness, she wondered if she'd been raped. She tried to feel if she had what she imagined that trauma would be like, but with the rest of her pain, she couldn't tell.

It was only then that she realized someone was there, someone touching her body. With a start, she willed herself back into full consciousness.

She was still on the table, whether moments after Gunter had hit her or much later, she had no idea. A man in black utilities stood over her, running his hand across her body, manipulating her. Instinctively, Michi tried to scooch away from him, but without seeming to notice her attempts, the man kept a firm hold on her as he continued his groping.

"Add a broken clavicle," he said to another black-clad man Michi just noticed standing behind him, PA in hand.

The man reached over to Michi's right arm, which was still cuffed to the bed. He ran his hand down her arm, probing at the wound. Michi gasped at the pain, but it didn't seem as if the man was intentionally trying to hurt her.

He picked up a scanner from beside her and ran it over her upper arm. After glancing at the readout, he said, "Right arm, hypervelocity dart wound, through and through. Hairline fracture of the humerus."

"Who are you?" Michi croaked out.

The man ignored her, instead reaching out and taking the other man's PA. He read over it, then held the PA over his eye for a retinal scan, certifying whatever was there. He handed it to yet a third black-clad man who had been standing by the door of her cell. The third man took the PA, looked at it, then stepped forward to stand over Michi's naked body.

"So, Doc, you've got the dart shot in the arm, and that nicked the humerus. You've got one blown ear drum, a Class 2 concussion, a fractured and avulsed left ring finger from the middle phalanx distal, a puncture wound to the right calf, a broken nose, and assorted contusions," he said, shifting his eyes to each spot on her body as he listed them.

Michi listened in as if he was describing someone else. It didn't quite seem real. She noted that nothing was said about vaginal tearing, so she wondered if that meant that her getting Gunter to explode had stymied that.

"OK, I accept the survey," the man said, holding the PA up to his eye for the scan.

He pulled out his own PA, and tap-transferred the report from the doctor's (for that is what he had to be) PA to his. The doctor nodded, took his PA, and left, trailing his assistant.

Michi was confused. The doctor had said she had a concussion, so maybe that was an excuse. But what happened to Fordyce, and who were these people? They were military, but their utilities were black. She didn't think they were Marines. Was that what the FCDC wore? The Federation Civil Development Corps had a bad reputation, worse than the Marines, but they tended to keep in the background and did not get the same press as the Navy or Marines.

If they were FCDC, then that was a relief. Anyone was better than the jacks who had held her before. At least these people seemed to care about her injuries. Michi was under no impression that she was in a good place, though. She knew she was in big trouble. She was looking at a long term imprisonment at best, at worse, well, she didn't want to think about that.

"Henderson, get in here," the man barked and another man came in the door. "Get her cleaned up, especially that shit. I hate a dirty work place."

Michi tried to look down, mortified. She hadn't even noticed the smell, but now that the man had mentioned it, she could tell her bowels had let go at some time. She looked back up as Henderson came to stand over her, the disgust obvious on his face.

"Uh, Chief, how do I, I mean, with what?" he asked.

"St. Charles' ass, Henderson. Get a bucket and a rag and just do it. Do I have to take you by the hand?"

"OK, sure chief," Henderson said and scurried out of the room.

Michi stared at the ceiling, refusing to meet the "chief's" eyes, even if she felt them on her. Within a few minutes, Henderson had returned, lugging a bucket of water. He heaved it onto the table, and some of the water splashed out over her. He dipped a rag or towel in the water, and then after pausing as if wondering where to start, he placed the wet rag on her shoulder and began to rub. Michi just endured, not that she had much choice. She endured as he rubbed her face. She endured as he cleaned her breasts. She endured as he cleaned off her arms and legs. She endured as he got between her legs and tried to clean up her shit, sliding the rag under her butt until the chief, exasperation evident in his voice, told him to tilt her up on her side.

Utterly humiliated, she barely noticed the lances of pain that shot through her as Henderson struggled to keep her up, finally using his shoulder to hold her while he scrubbed the table and her ass. Finally, he let her back down and looked expectantly up at his boss.

"Weak effort, Henderson. But it will have to do for now. Get rid of the filthy water and clean yourself up, then get back here. We've got work to do."

Henderson grabbed the bucket and hurried out as the chief walked back up and stood over her, looking down at her face. He didn't say a word, and Michi was feeling the stress rise.

What the hell does he want? she wondered. *Just get it over with!*

Finally, Henderson came back into the room, and the chief leaned in to talk.

"Miss MacCailín, I am Chief Warrant Officer Three Virag Chopra of the United Federation Civil Development Corps. You are now under custody of the same, initially charged with disorderly conduct, but I should tell you that you will most likely be charged with more crimes under the Federation Charter. You will be questioned with regards to your participation in the attack of May 15, 335 SR, on the Marines at the refinery at coordinates 30.216355 degrees north, 52.207031 west on Kakurega. Are you in fact Michiko MacCailín, Federation ID A4793677277GB, born on May 19, 315—hmm, today your 20th birthday?"

Michi nodded.

"Please speak your response. Is this you?"

"Uh, yes, it is," she meekly said.

"And do you understand what I just told you?" he asked her, all businesslike.

"Uh, yes."

"Private First Class Antonio Henderson, United Federation Civil Development Corps, did you witness Miss MacCailín's response?"

"I did," Henderson said.

"Hold still," Chopra told her, placing the PA in front of Michi's face.

Michi didn't resist, but kept her eye open for the scan. The ready light flashed green, and Chopra took the PA over to Henderson and got his certification as well. He checked the read out, then slipped the PA into his holster.

"Now that the formalities are out of the way," he said, putting his PA back in its holster, "let me tell you what is happening. First, Miss MacCailín, I am sure you realize that you are in a world of shit. Attacking Federation Marines is bad enough, but being the person who instigated the attack will probably result in your execution."

Michi knew that, but to hear it actually being vocalized gave it a much bigger impact.

"I don't really care, though, what happens to you. My job is simple. I am here to extract information from you that can enable us to protect the Federation and Federation citizens. It is really that simple. And rest assured, Miss MacCailín, that I will get that information. I am a professional and very good at what I do.

"And don't think you will be able to withhold information from me. I am not those clowns from Propitious Interstellar's security. Yes, I have seen the tapes," he said as he saw her flinch. "Not a bad move, getting your rapist angry enough to knock you out. But nothing you say or do will change the outcome of what is about to happen to you. And I am afraid to say that after this is over, you might wish those jimmyleg[14] goons still had you."

---

[14] Jimmylegs: a somewhat derogatory nickname military personnel have for hired security.

The very calm seriousness with which he spoke struck fear deep into Michi's heart. Her treatment at the hands of the jacks had been brutal. What could be worse? She didn't want to find out.

"The jimmylegs might have succeeded over time; how quickly depending on how strong you were. But their methods are brutal and inefficient. You would end up telling them anything, whatever you thought they wanted to know, to stop them. Most of all, though, they enjoy the process, without regards to the information.

"I, Miss MacCailín, on the other hand, do not enjoy inflicting pain. I won't hesitate to do what is necessary, but that is only a means to the end. I want the information."

He picked up Michi's mangled hand, looked at it, then shook his head. "See this, Henderson? This is what I was talking about. Torture for torture's sake, the frigging amateurs. And she didn't talk, so it was all wasted effort."

He dropped her hand and said, "Bring me the I88."

Henderson pulled out a small rectangular instrument, then some wires. It was an inanimate objects, but Michi imagined she could sense the evil emanating from it. Chopra took it from Henderson, connected the wires, attaching them to Michi. One wire was placed on her right ear, the other on her left big toe. Michi trembled. The lack of knowledge of just what that thing was was tearing her apart.

"Miss MacCailín, this is an I88, which is an oldie but goodie, an intensifier. It excites nerves more than any physical stimulus. No one is actually hurting you, but you will believe they are. Your body will believe they are. I am not in love with intensifiers, but I want you to see what I have in my little toolbox. I tried it once myself, and the experience still resonates with me when I am this close to the device. And so . . ."

He reached and pressed a button, and immediately, Michi's world exploded into the bright lights of utter agony. Every nerve in her body was aflame and determined to burn up in an orgy of pain. She didn't know anything—her name, where she was, who she was—only the pain coursing through her. It was the only thing that mattered, and nothing else existed. This other dimension stretched on for days, years, maybe longer.

And then it was mercifully gone, completely gone. She lifted her head, sure her body had been burnt to a crisp. But she was untouched. She was the same battered, hurting Michi that she had been before that devil device had been turned on. Her body still hurt from her earlier abuse, but that didn't seem so impactful now that she had something much more severe than physical pain to compare it to now.

She gasped for breath as she looked up into Chopra's eyes, and he was just staring at her, expressionless.

"Fun little toy, huh?" he asked. "And I could use it, again and again until you talked. But you could tell me anything, and we could waste time finding out that you had lied to me.

"So that puts me in a quandary, right? Luckily, I have a few more tools in my toolbox. Lucky for me, that is. Maybe not for you. No, I'm being facetious. *Most certainly* not for you.

"Henderson, the Propoxinal."

Michi gulped. She'd heard of it, of course. It was a "truth serum" featured in some recent flicks. In one of them, the chemical had turned people into zombies, their minds destroyed. She realized that was fiction, but still, it was scary stuff.

"I see by your reaction that you recognize my little friend," Chopra said as Henderson gave him his dosing unit. "Don't worry, it won't turn you into a flesh-eating zombie. Although, that might be a better fate, if you ask me. A barely aware vegetable who just sits and soils herself seems a lot worse to me."

"But that's illegal, isn't it?" she asked.

Chopra and Henderson broke out laughing at that.

"You are really in no position to protest, young lady. And while Propoxinal is technically illegal, I can use whatever I want, based on my own judgment, with regards to security. You are an enemy of the Federation, and I will do what I have to in order to ensure your threat is neutralized."

"But you won! You won the battle. There is no more threat," she cried, her voice getting more panicked.

"And that is what I intend to find out. You see, Miss MacCailín, you are telling me that, but can I trust you? Can I be assured that right now, more of your friends are not massing for an attack?"

"I'm telling you the truth!"

"PFC Henderson, do you believe Miss MacCailín?" he asked his assistant.

"Sure, sir. She sounds like the honest sort," he said with a smirk on his face.

"And I believe you, too," Chopra said with mock sincerity. "But I have been wrong before, and as they say, better safe than sorry.

"Henderson, give her the prep," he said handing the man the dosing unit.

Henderson took it, entered a code, and then held the unit against Michi's arm.

"No!" she shouted, more afraid of the serum than anything the jacks had done to her.

"Oh, don't worry," Chopra said. "That's not the Propoxinal. That's just a small depressant that I've found makes the Propoxinal more effective. You've got another five minutes before you get that."

Michi jerked on the cuff locking her to the bed, ignoring the pain each jerk shot through her.

"Look at her struggle," Chopra told Henderson. "The human condition is fascinating, and you need to understand it if you are going to do well in this job. We have suicide bombers, willing to die for a cause, but when we threaten the mind, when we threaten to change the very core of a person, they all fight. I would wager that Miss MacCailín there would have been willing to die for her cause. But look at her struggle so frantically now."

Just then, the door opened, and three Marines marched in. One looked at his PA, then said, "Michiko MacCailín. She's a general in the NIP."

"I'm aware of who she is, First Sergeant" the second Marine said. "I saw the camcordings."

"Can I ask you what you are doing here, sir?" Chopra said.

"Merely checking on our prisoners, Chief," the first Marine said.

"Well, as you can see, I'm in the middle of an interrogation, so if you could come back later, I would appreciate it."

"I can see what you are doing, and no, we'll check now. The captain is a little busy to arrange his schedule around yours."

The captain came forward, and Michi could see the bars on his collar. She looked lower, and she caught the nametag: *Lysander*. Was this the man she had been attacking? He looked like the Marine she has seen on the holo.

He looked over her, then turned to Chopra and asked, "Why has she been abused?"

"Wasn't me. The jimmylegs got a little too enthusiastic. Besides, that arm wound was your boys' doing," he said, pulling out his PA and handing it to the first Marine, the one the captain had called "first sergeant."

The first sergeant looked it over, then nodded and handed it to the captain.

"He's right," he said.

Captain Lysander looked it over, then handed it back before asking, "So you didn't do that, but why hasn't she been given medical treatment?"

"There's no requirement for me to do that, sir, as you know. She's an insurgent, and a free citizen. If she was a Class Four, the company here would be required to provide the treatment, but as a Free Citizen, she needs to provide her own."

"And did you offer it? Did you contact her family? It doesn't matter. As a *prisoner of war*," the captain said, emphasizing the words, "we are required to provide full medical treatment."

"She's an insurgent, a common criminal, sir, not a prisoner of war," Chopra protested.

The captain turned towards the chief warrant officer and snarled, "She was wearing a uniform, right? She headed an army, right? She's a grubbing POW, and I *really* don't think you want to fight me on that, Chief!

"First Sergeant Samuelson, get Doc Botivic over here to check her out. I want the letter of the law followed here."

"Aye-aye, sir," the first sergeant said before speaking into a throat mic.

The drugs Henderson had given her were kicking in, and her mind was getting fuzzy. She knew what was happening, but its import was somewhat lost on her. Another doctor was coming?

"With all due respect, sir, this is an FCDC matter, not a Marine concern. I'm in charge of interrogation, and you can't be interfering in that. If you have a complaint, you can register it with my major," Chopra said.

"Do you know who I am, Chief?" the captain asked.

"Yes, of course, sir. But—"

"But nothing. I'll have your ass if you fight me on this. I'm going to get her treated, then you can interrogate her to your heart's content."

Michi's heart fell. She was not being saved, only given a short reprieve. She shouldn't have expected anything more from the infamous captain.

"Why the hell do you care? She jumped two of your Marines, brought a whole cliff down on them. She attacked your company?"

"I don't care about her, Chief. I care about us. We're on a dirty mission here, and I intend to keep us as clean as possible despite that. And it didn't do her a lot of good, did it. Not one Marine killed."

Despite the cotton closing in on her mind, that caught her attention. No Marine killed?

"I killed one of your Marines," she stammered out.

All five men in the room turned to look at her, the Marines with bemused smiles on their faces.

"I killed one of you bastards. Me!" she asserted.

"I think she means Ling," the first sergeant said.

"Oh, so you killed Sergeant Ling?" the captain asked, stepping up to stand over her.

"If that was his name," she tried to say with a snarl. "I crushed him in the Ledges."

"Yes, Sergeant Joab Ling. He's been with me quite awhile. Well, after he gets out of regen, I'm sure he would like to meet you," Captain Lysander said with a condescending laugh. "Not everyone gets to meet his killer."

She looked at him in confusion. *Regen? But he was dead! Or was he?* They hadn't stuck around to make sure, but all his readings were off.

"Oh, you messed him up but good, girl," the first sergeant said. "And he's going to have to live that down. I think half of the Corps sent him stills of that camcording you made with your foot on him like some big-game trophy. But no, he's gonna be fine. All you got was his pride."

Michi felt deflated. She couldn't believe the guy was still alive. She had failed. With the effects of the drug given to her, she almost broke down into tears.

"Um, Captain? Take a look at this," the third Marine said, speaking for the first time.

He had picked up the doser, and now he held it out for the captain. Captain Lysander looked at it, a look of anger coming over his face as he saw what the next dose was.

"Propoxinal, Chief? You know that is proscribed!"

"Not for her, sir! I can use whatever means I deem necessary. Look the frigging regulations up, if you want," Chopra said.

"For insurgents or terrorists in the course of an operation, yes. For listed groups like the SOG. But not for prisoners of war! POWs can only voluntarily offer information, not be coerced, and certainly not by proscribed drugs! You are breaking about a thousand treaties on this!" he yelled, spittle flying from his mouth.

"I'm going right to my major on this!" Chopra yelled, not backing down.

"Tell your fucking major whatever you want! I'm telling you now, Chief Warrant Officer, if you value your career and if you don't want to spend time in the brig, you will cease and desist. You will not attempt to interrogate her. I will be checking back, and if you fight me on this, your pathetic life, as you know it, is over. Do you understand?"

Michi could see the anger warring on Chopra's face, but he bit it back down and said, "I understand."

"Len, I want you to stand here until Doc arrives. Get her treated. Then I want someone in here every day to check up on her.

Sams, come with me. Let's see who else in this hellhole thinks he's above the law."

He didn't bother to look back at Michi as he and the first sergeant stormed out. Michi tried to process what had just happened. Henderson looked scared as he tried to remain unnoticed. Chopra on the other hand, was a volcano about to explode. He glared at Michi with pure hate. If not for the other Marine standing in the room with the doser in his hand, she was sure he would take out his anger on her.

They all stood like that, without moving, for at least 20 minutes before a Navy doctor and two medics, nurses, or whatever they called a medical assistant came in and began to assess her. They left her on the table, but cleaned and disinfected it before starting. They cleaned and dressed her stab wound, then moved to the arm, cleaning it up before sliding it into a portable regen unit. The doctor told her it should heal within a week. The hand, though, was more serious, and they decided to put her under for prep surgery prior to regen. They put up a medical curtain to isolate her hand as they prepped it. That gave Chopra a chance to step up and kneel, so his mouth was against her ear.

"Don't get too comfortable, there, missy. Word is that the Marines will be leaving soon, and then there won't be any Captain Lysander to protect you. Your ass will be all mine," she heard before the anesthesia pulled her under.

Chapter 35

The next week went by in a blur, or was it dragging by slowly? Michi couldn't decide. She was mostly left alone. Each morning, Chopra came by and formally asked her if she had any information she wanted to share. Each time, after Michi said no, he simply turned around and left.

A Marine came by once or twice a day, checking, but not speaking to her. The doctor and his team came by twice to check on her progress. Someone brought her meals and took away her empty plates and full honeypot. The rest of the time, she was alone.

The regen chamber on her arm was removed, and except for a tiny scar that the doctor said would fade, she would never have known she'd been shot. Her concussion would take a full regen, which was not available to her in her situation, but the effects faded, and the doctor pronounced her fully recovered. Physically, the only thing that was still wrong was her finger. Only a small portion of the finger had been lost, so after surgery, the regen should only take a little less than a month.

She'd been issued an orange jumpsuit, and she was no longer cuffed to the bed, but she still spent the hours lying on the table, albeit with a thin blanket between her and the surface of the metal. Things were much better than her first conscious hours in the cell, but mentally, she felt worse. With free time, her mind was on the 1,300 men and woman who had followed her to their deaths. She thought back to all her actions since Franz had been murdered, wondering what she could have done differently.

She realized that she had fallen into depression. It would seem natural, given her situation, but she was afraid that this was something deeper, something clinical. She knew she could fight it. In the flicks, prisoners spent solitary doing pushup or writing. She did neither. She just didn't have the energy. It was easier to lie in bed and stare at the lighting in the ceiling.

She was lying there when two Marines burst in.

"Get up," one of the Marines said.

She stared at him stupidly.

"I said, get up!"

He came over as if to help her.

"Why? What's going on?" she asked, a trickle of fear awaking in her.

She'd contemplated suicide a few times over the last week, but when something actually threatened her existence, the survival gene kicked in.

"We're moving you, so let's go," he told her.

Moving me? What the hell for?

"Why? What's wrong with here?" she asked.

Images of her being taken out into the forest and shot in the head flooded her mind. She resisted, pulling back from the Marine's grasp.

"Look, I don't give a flying fart if you come or go, rebel lady. As far as I'm concerned, the fuckdicks can have you . . ."

It took a second for Michi to realize he was referring to the FCDC officers. "FCDC." "FuCkDiCks."

". . . but the captain says everyone in this building's gotta go to the main jail. So it's up to you. We're leaving this planet in two hours, so we don't have time to sit here and convince you."

"Come on, Tse Han, let's just forget her," the other Marine said.

"You're leaving?" Michi asked.

"Yeah. The rebellion is crushed here, and things are acting up in—" he started before the other Marine cut him off.

"Opsec![15]"

"Oh, yeah. No matter, lady, we're leaving, so it's up to you. I ain't gonna be dragging you to the trucks."

The image of Chopra leaning in, telling her after the Marines left, her ass was going to be his, invaded her mind. She shuddered. There was no real decision to make. Even if it were a bullet to the head, that would be a better choice than letting that psychopath get his hands back on her.

"No, I'm coming with you," she said, jumping off the table.

---

[15] Opsec: Operational Security.

The two Marines led her out into the hallway. Other Marines and prisoners milled about. Michi recognized Max Vickery, the colonel who had led the river commandos in the attack, but she didn't have time to talk to him. Within minutes, they were pushed past several unresisting FCDC guards and out into a courtyard where a hover-truck waited. It was nighttime, which surprised Michi as she could have sworn it was noon at the latest. The Marines told them to get inside the truck, pushing those who were slow in climbing up.

A hand pushed her ass just as she was clambering over the tailgate, and she was sent sprawling into a body already in the truck.

"Sorry," she said automatically.

"Michi! It's good to see you. We thought you'd been killed," Loski Sonutta-Lyon said. He'd been one of the main planners for the attack.

"I think most of us did get killed," she said bitterly. "What the hell happened?"

"I . . . I don't know. I was back with the forward command, and without warning, we were surrounded by Marines. We could hear the fighting up forward, but there was nothing we could do."

The truck rose off the ground, and then pulled into a smooth forward motion. There were a few exclamations of fear. Evidently, Michi was not the only one who didn't totally trust the Marines.

Michi wanted to shout at Loski. She wanted to blame someone for the debacle, and it was his plan, his and Kyles, that they had tried to implement. She didn't want to blame herself for being the catalyst who got the whole thing rolling.

He looked horrible, though, and her anger faded.

"Was it bad for you?" she asked.

He shuddered. "Yes. It wasn't good. I see they got to you, too," he said, pointing at the small regen chamber over her hand.

"I was this close to getting Propoxinal," she said quietly. "I would have if Captain Lysander hadn't come in the cell."

"You're lucky. Kyle got it. They took me to see him, and his mind was gone."

Kyle was the other planner for the attack. If he was given the drug, they would have peeled back the layers, extracting all he knew. In his position, he'd known a lot.

The two sat silently in the truck as it took them to who knows where? Michi was just about to open her mouth to ask Loski a question when the truck came to a stop and lowered off hover. The two Marines who had been sitting in the back jumped out first, then shouted for everyone else to get out, too.

Michi poked her head under the tarp and was relieved to see the city jail. She would have never thought that seeing a jail and being about to be taken into it could ever be a relief, but it was much better than a ride out into the forest.

A Marine stepped out of the front entrance with another man and addressed the group. "I am Gunnery Sergeant Franco Torioko, and this is Desk Sergeant Wisuski of the Tay Station city jail. We are going to get you processed as quickly as possible. The jail is extremely overcrowded, so there'll be many of you to a cell. But for you 34 people, I think this is a better alternative than had you stayed where you were."

Michi looked around, wondering if she could slip away in the darkness. A number of Marines were in back of them, though, looking alert. She didn't know what she would do if she got away, so it made more sense to get inside the jail where she would be relatively safe—she hoped.

Chapter 36

After two days, Michi was almost missing her solitary confinement—almost, but not quite. She was crammed with 15 other women in a four-person cell. The single toilet in the corner was continually plugged, and combined with 16 sweating bodies, the smell was pretty rank.

Tempers were testy as well. When Michi stepped on one woman's foot while trying to get to the toilet, that woman had jumped up, blaming Michi for getting them into this mess. Normally, Michi might have faced down the smaller woman, but her guilt factor kicked in, and she just absorbed the abuse.

More than a couple of the women remarked on the regen chamber on her hand, saying it was proof of special treatment she was getting. Several of them had been hurt and had received treatment, but not to the extent of regen. The company was not going to fork out the cash for that for indentureds, particularly indentureds who had taken up the fight against them.

Two of the women incarcerated with her had also been in her assault force. Both had been with about fifty who had surrendered to the Marines. One of them, Tamika Dilliard-Smith, said she had seen Colonel Hannrahan go down, his head blown off of his shoulders. Michi hadn't really liked her so-called assistant, but she shed a few tears at the news.

At least the FCDC interrogators had left them alone so far. Michi thought it was because of too many witnesses. If she was taken, others would know it. If she "disappeared" or came back a vegetable, others would know it. She had no doubt that the fuckdicks—how she loved that term—would be trying to come up with a plan to isolate them, but for now, she was relatively safe.

So when the cell door clicked and swung open on the second night after her arrival, Michi looked upon that with extreme suspicion. What better way to isolate their prize prisoners than to let them go and then capture them again? If she was not taken back to their communal cell, the others could be told she had either escaped or had been killed in her recapture.

The other 15 women got up and approached the door, buzzing on what it could mean. Two women frankly said it was a trap, and they sat on one of the bunks, refusing to get up. Several other women cautiously stepped into the main corridor.

From down that corridor, Michi heard a voice call out, "Look at the guards! They're locked in!"

Despite her misgivings, Michi had to see. She pushed past several of her cellmates and out into the corridor. From each cell, both men and women were gathering outside. At the end, where the guards controlled the cells, about 20 prisoners were gathered, several pointing and laughing. Michi made her way down the corridor to see for herself.

The guard station occupied what would have been the first cell in line. However, the wall was reinforced glass, and inside were chairs and the control panel. Each cell was under 24-hour observation and could be controlled as far as locking the door, turning off the lights, and even administering knock-out gas. Only now, none of that was happening. Inside, three guards were standing, looking at the prisoners. One was holding a handwritten note that said:

Get back to your cells now!

In back of them, their control panel was off. None of the feeds worked. To make things worse for them, the red light on the door leading out into the main corridor was flashing. They were locked in.

Michi looked at the others. Was this a trap? Even if it was, she knew this could be her chance. If she left, they would still have to capture her again, and she wasn't going to let that happen. One way or the other, she was not coming back alive.

Two of the men pushed open their wing door, and it opened into the main corridor. In a rush, about forty of them poured into the main corridor. Down on the far end, there was only a set of double gates before leading to the holding room and the outside.

From other wings, people started trickling out. It looked like every cell in the place had been opened. Starting slowly, then gathering momentum and people, the tide of prisoners rushed the double gates. If they were locked, Michi figured people would get crushed in the press, but it was too late to worry about that. The mob wouldn't be stopped.

The gates were open, though, and within moments, the leading edge of the mob was out in the darkness. Several people were out and about, and they ran when confronted with the mass escape. Two jacks came around the corner, saw the mob, and turned and ran. They would report what they had seen, however, so time was a-wasting.

Michi looked around her. There had to be 200 prisoners outside the jail now, and more were still coming. Michi knew she had to get out of there, so she started running. She didn't have a destination; she just needed to get as far away from the jail as she could.

She started running out of breath within five minutes. The time she had spent as a prisoner, and her refusal to exercise, was taking its toll. She recognized the Tennyson complex and turned into it. Doug had been able to control it, so maybe others had as well, keeping surveillance out of it. She was winded, anyway, so she had to stop.

Michi crept past one of the broken-down entrances and looked around. She wasn't sure of the time, but there were a number of people going about their business. Her orange jumpsuit made her stand out, but so far, nobody seemed to take overt notice. When the word was passed, however, and a reward offered, she was sure that some of the people would suddenly recall the orange-clad figure skulking around in the night.

She knew she had to get out of sight for awhile and plan out what she wanted to do. Each complex had a small retail section, and she made her way in back of the line of stores. She thought there might be something that had been discarded she could put on to get rid of the jumpsuit.

She cautiously approached the first dumpster, looking to see if anyone was watching her. She grabbed the lid and lifted.

"Shut that thing!" an orange jumpsuited man yelled back up to her from where he was lying inside.

She dropped the lid, her heart pounding. How had he gotten there so quickly? She must have really gotten out of shape. She moved down two more, then slowly lifted up the lid. When no one yelled out, she slid inside.

There was restaurant refuse in the dumpster, so it stunk with rotten food. She didn't care much about that as she rooted around in the darkness, feeling for clothing. To her surprise, she felt something right away. Running her fingers over it, she could tell is was a shirt. It was a little difficult to get it on with only one working hand, but she managed to pull it over her jumpsuit. It had some slime on it, but it would do, she hoped. Now she just needed something for her legs, and she could get out of there and move on.

She felt something and pulled it out of the garbage, but she thought it was another shirt and discarded it. If she didn't find anything soon, she would have to bail and just hope the shirt she'd found would be enough.

She was down in the far corner of the dumpster and had put her hand into something particularly disgusting when the lid of the dumpster opened.

She wheeled around ready to attack, one-handed or not, when a voice asked, "Michi? That you?"

Doug and Tamara were standing there, concerned looks on their faces.

"Shit girl, get out of there. We've got to get you out of here and hidden," Tamara said, relief evident in her voice.

For Michi, she was not sure if she'd ever seen such a welcome sight in her life.

Chapter 37

"Get out of bed and do something," Tamara said.

"Easy for you to say," Michi grumbled. "You're not stuck in this cage."

"Look, I know it's tough, but hang in there. We'll figure out something. Doug will come by at lunchtime, and maybe we can both be here for a nice dinner. I've really got to go, though."

She kissed Michi on the forehead and then left for work.

Michi turned over and pulled her lone sheet over her head. She knew she shouldn't take it out on Tamara. She owed the two of them too much. But she had no contact with anyone else, so that left only her two friends.

It had been the two of them who had sprung her from captivity. They had scoured the lists for her name among the dead and captured. Doug had finally found reference to her on some company docs and her transfer to FCDC custody, but he couldn't pinpoint a location nor anything else. The FCDC security was just too tough for him to hack. They had been surprised and overjoyed, then when she turned up as a transfer to the city jail. It hadn't taken Doug long to pinpoint her, even hacking into the surveillance inside her cell.

Between the two of them, they had considered and rejected a number of plans, finally coming up with taking control of the jail, then locking in the guards while opening the prisoner cells. The hope was that so many people would escape that it would overwhelm the jacks, giving them time to locate and isolate Michi. Using the same technology as he had once described to Michi, he had programs scanning all surveillance cams looking for her body and gait. Michi had changed through the course of her abuse, but after several false hits, the two friends saw Michi enter the complex and walk in back of the shops. Surveillance was down in the back access, but Tamara had been sure that was her, so they had rushed to find her.

When they could not see her, they started opening dumpsters, first surprising the same other escapee, then finding her in the fourth dumpster they'd tried. They had her throw on the clothes they'd brought which added about twenty pounds with the padding, and gave her the old boots she'd worn with the gait-changing inserts. One of Doug's planned safe houses was inside Tennyson II, so within ten minutes, they had her inside and in a hot bath. Tamara had stayed with her that night, holding Michi in bed until she fell asleep.

For the next week, both of her friends tried to see her as often as they could. They brought food and more importantly, news. Michi was cut off from the outside world: no net, no vids, no holos. Doug didn't want there to be any trace of her in the city.

At first, Michi wanted to know about the attack. Doug had access to the corporate records, and the intra-company memos reported that 622 "rebels" were killed, 813 captured. Of the captured, five had died in captivity. Details of the attack were sketchy, but it seemed that Derrick, one of the first two jacks who had first awaken her after her capture, had the basics correct (other than the number of casualties). The Marines, with help from corporate security and spies within the NIP, were well aware of the coming attack. The river commando force had been captured as they entered the water. The day "patrols" that had gone out were actually assault forces, and they had quickly captured the forward command center and the gun position. Finally, the Marine assault force and supporting arms had broken up the attack and killed, captured, or scattered her fighters. Not one Marine had even been wounded.

In retrospect, to think they had a chance against prepared Marines was a ridiculous notion. Michi had thought in her heart, they could win, and in defeating that one Marine company, that would force the Federation to leave the planet.

The results sickened her, especially the knowledge that they had essentially been doing the Federation's bidding by attacking. They had been drawn out, tricked into attacking a defensible position, and then broken. With the main armed force gone, the

Marines were no longer needed, and they were taken away for their next devil's mission.

Michi wanted to know if there had been any reaction, any protesting the failed attack. There had been almost nothing, Doug and Tamara told her. If the company had expected a crushing defeat to also crush the population, then they had been correct. The people had been cowed. Even the WRP, while not disbanded, had closed shop until things had stabilized.

It looked like the company had won.

Oh, Michi and her two friends played scenarios in their minds, from simple things such as jumping another jack to fanciful plans such as enlisting the Brotherhood to invade and set thing right. Nothing was either possible or would make an impact.

Their conversations shifted from striking back to smuggling Michi off the planet and to some non-Federation world. That would be difficult, though. The jail break had been big news, and Michi was prominently displayed and declared "high importance" and with a large reward, a target for anyone wanting to cash in. Security had been tightened, and bounty hunters tracked down any trace of her.

One other aspect of the jailbreak was that the company now knew someone had a backdoor into their system. It was only a matter of time until they tracked the breach down, and Doug was getting more and more nervous. Ironically, it was Doug's own division that was part of the team trying to find the breach.

Michi turned back over to her back, holding out her right arm. Her hand itched horribly, and even though she knew that was a good sign, she was tempted to rip the chamber off and throw it away. She resisted, though: it would be hard for her to walk into a clinic for any treatment.

She finally got up out of bed and made herself some instant noodles

God, I'm getting sick of these, she thought.

She finished them, then crawled back into bed, where she still was four hours later when Doug came in the door. She caught the slight frown of disapproval from him as he saw her, but at least he didn't nag like Tamara did.

He handed her a hotpack. It was Italian! That was the best thing that had happened today. She popped the activator, waited ten seconds, then unzipped the top, letting the aromas of *amatriciana* waft through the room.

She had never realized how dependent she had been on fabricators. But with Doug vetoing any power usage in the room, fabricators were out, and she could only eat prepared food and takeout. The pasta smelled wonderful and tasted even better.

In a better mood, she started chatting with Doug. He'd been working on finding her a way off-planet, but with the heightened security, he couldn't spend much time on it yet. And that was also why he could only come over during his lunch break. No more virtual work days. He had to physically be there.

Michi peeled open the hotpack and licked the remaining sauce. "This was great! I'm getting so that I would even eat raw bases, and let my stomach fabricate them," she said with a laugh.

"Oh, I'm sure Tammy could get you some Blue-99 if you really wanted," Doug said with a laugh.

He had been calling her Tammy ever since Michi got out, but she couldn't tell if their relationship had changed,

"I think I was close enough to the damn stuff on my own," she said bitterly. "You know, even with it being a trap, if we could have just made in into the algae banks, we might have been able to win. The Marines might be the best around, but that can make people too confident. By selecting that area for us to attack," and she realized now that the company-slash-Federation had maneuvered things for just that end, "they left an Achilles heel. The company couldn't risk losing all that base, and they would have had to negotiate. Maybe we should have forgotten the attack and just snuck in and planted explosives. It couldn't have been a worse outcome."

"They've got pretty serious security around the farm. That's their most valuable base, and certainly their most vulnerable in those hydro-glass tubes," Doug said. "In order to affect them, you'd have to get them some other way. Disease, maybe. Or corruption. But then the problem would be delivery. They wouldn't let someone in a white lab coat just walk in and inject the farm with a virus, you know. A contagion is one thing, but without a vector, it would just be like all our other plans, stupid games of fantasy."

Michi checked the pack for any last traces of sauce. She was only half-listening to Doug, who, quite frankly, tended to go off on technological soliloquies that Michi had neither the background nor inclination to follow. But then she stopped. Something he had just said registered.

"We have a vector," she said.

"What vector?" Doug asked, already getting up to go back to work.

"Tamara!"

Chapter 38

"No, that wouldn't work," Doug protested.

Michi took the last piece of pizza. The three of them had been up for hours arguing, and the pizza was cold, but Italian twice in one day was a treat.

"Why not?" Tamara asked.

"The viral screens. The company is not stupid, and even without the acts of man, nature can intject a virus as it so wills. So each bank of tubes has a virus screen at the CO2 generators. Besides, what would you do? Just show up and walk down the rows? You think your little access badge is going to make them let you destroy the algae? Anyway, even if you did, all that would be is revenge, like I said before. We'd have no leverage."

"And I told you, at this stage, revenge would be good enough for me," Michi said before downing the last bit of crust.

"But that is why the programming would be a better option. We can threaten to destroy their entire strain. They would have to listen, then. And best of all, it can be injected into the matrix at the organics lab."

"I swear, I still don't understand how it could work. How can computer programming affect a growing organism?" Michi asked with Tamara nodding in agreement.

"I've tried to explain it. Let me reword it. Uh . . . OK, you know that Blue-99 is a genetically modified product, one owned by the company, right?" When both girls nodded, he went on. "So, in some ways, the algae is just a programmed matrix that sort of sits on top of the original DNA. The matrix sends signals to the DNA to do what the company wants it to do. As long as the programming functions correctly, the algae's DNA follows the instructions, making Blue-99. If that programming were modified to, let's say, activate the cells suicide switch, then all the algae would die. So all we have to do is input a worm that will change the programming."

"It sort of makes sense, but you said it might not work," Tamara told him.

“In theory, it will work. But in reality, we need the worm that will change the programming as we want it to. That’s the hard part.”

“So the simple question is, can you do it?”

“I don’t know, to be honest. I might be able to, but we wouldn’t know until we try it. And we might only have one shot at it,” he admitted.

“How long to know if you can pull this off?”

“Probably in a week or so. I would know at least if I can’t do it. I wouldn’t know for sure if I can until we send the worm on its way. Then there is the timing. Tammy would have to infect the programming while I still have my backdoor, and I don’t know how long that will be. They are closing in, and all my evasion techniques are only delaying the inevitable.”

“A week? Well, I don’t totally understand, but I’ve got to trust you, Doug. Let’s do it.”

Chapter 39

Six days later, Doug and Michi were back at Tamara's and his condo. Michi had already taken off the regen chamber from her hand and put on her costumes. Her finger was not totally healed,, but there wasn't anything to be done about that. There was nothing for her to do yet, so she had to just sit with Doug and watch.

They waited nervously, watching the time. Tamara would be at the lab at any minute, and they might have to act quickly. Doug had four disposable PAs, and one was on now, a specified AI moving his backdoor around the system at inhuman speeds. The problem was that the company AIs were rapidly closing off areas in the system, leaving fewer and fewer areas in which the backdoor could find refuge. It was only a matter of time until it was surrounded with nowhere to go. At that moment, Doug would be locked out of the system.

"Come on, Tamara, come on," Michi implored.

She was more nervous now than before the attack on the Marines. They were so close, and they might have the means to finally hit back at the company where it would hurt them.

Even if they destroyed Blue-99, however, the company would recover. It could license out another algae from a competitor while trying to rush one of their own research strains to the market. That would take time, though, and quite a bit of funds. More importantly, it was sending a message that Propitious Interstellar could not be trusted to deliver. In the galactic marketplace, that message could cost the company more than the mere destruction of the algae.

"Shit!" Doug said looking at the PA monitoring the backdoor. "That was too close!"

Michi didn't ask for an explanation. "Too close" was not "it's over," so she let it be.

"She's running out of time!" he said.

Tamara had been given the worm in a small optical drive, one like any other used throughout the planet. The lab, like all others in the company, was shielded, against transmissions, so a wireless transfer was impossible. There was no wireless inside. It would have to be an old-fashioned optical read. She would have given up her PA as always, but with her clearance and position, they hoped she would not be searched. If she was and they found the drive, she was to feign forgetfulness and just abort the mission, picking up the drive from security as she left.

Doug had given her the location of the three computers in the lab that would work for their purposes. All she had to do was to hold the drive in front of a reader, even if for a split second. Doug would have probably less than five seconds to send the worm to the three Blue-99 farms on the planet as well as the secured foundation library in the vaults. If he were too slow, the worm would get booted by the lab security AIs.

Doug wasn't sure the worm would even work. He'd cobbled it together from a number of programs, even getting one of his co-workers to complete a tricky part of the programming. He'd had to think about that, but the string was beyond him, and his co-worker didn't seem to think about what that string could be used for. He programmed the string in 30 minutes, and then was off on his next project, his curiosity un-piqued.

"I can't take this!" Michi yelled, just as Doug shouted out, "She's in!"

He pushed the "send" on his control PA just as the backdoor PA flashed red. That was the signal that his backdoor finally had been cornered and destroyed.

"What happened?" Michi shouted, pulling on Doug's arm. "Did you get it out?"

"I don't know! I think so, but I can't check now. Look, it says here it went out," he said, pointing to his PA.

"But did the worms get there, and are they working?"

"I don't know, Michi, I just don't know," he said, slumping down in his chair. "What do you want to do?"

Michi thought for a few moments. She didn't know if she could get off-planet, and she was not going to live the rest of her life hidden in an apartment. She had to trust that the worm was delivered and that it worked.

"I'm going through with it," she said with certainty.

"You sure?"

"Damn diddy well, I'm sure," she said.

"OK, you've got the code?" he asked.

Michi pointed to the side of her head. "Right here."

"It won't take long, so you'd better go. I'll leave right after you," he said.

Michi didn't know where Doug was going, nor did she ask. What she didn't know, she couldn't give up.

He picked up the disposable PA that the code Michi had memorized would reach. Depending on what message he received, he'd either have the worm extract itself or allow the suicide switches to be thrown. The switches would already be cocked, so-to-speak, so if his PA was cut off, there would be no turning back. Every Blue-99 algae cell on the planet would be destroyed and the matrix hopelessly corrupted.

Michi strapped on the pistol belt. She didn't have a weapon and wouldn't be carrying one even if she had, but they had decided that the more she looked like the Michiko MacCailín of the camcording, the better. She was not trying to hide, and she wanted attention.

Doug looked around the condo. "I'm going to miss this place," he said.

"Don't worry. You'll be back. *We'll* be back."

Michi leaned over and kissed Doug on the cheek before turning and walking to the door.

"*Gokigenyou,* Michiko, and God be with you," Doug said after her.

Michi smiled for a moment. Doug didn't speak Japanese, but he'd searched for the right thing to say, a version of "good luck." She wiped the smile from her face, walked to the elevator, and pushed the button. As the door opened, she saw that one of the ladies from the 23rd floor was already on. Michi didn't know her name, but she'd seen her out and about. The lady raised her eyebrows at Michi, but if she seemed surprised at seeing *the* Michiko MacCailín, in full regalia, she showed no sign of it.

They arrived at the lobby and walked to the front door. Michi held it open for the lady, who calmly thanked her before heading off to the right, probably to the small tea shop on the corner. Michi turned toward the left, toward the Propitious Interstellar headquarters, leaving the sidewalk and taking the middle of the street. Within moments, people spotted her and stared. A few paced her along the sidewalk, those few growing into a bigger group as more people joined. Whether they were there as some sort of honor guard or to try and cash in on the reward, Michi didn't know, nor did she care. Either would serve her purpose.

She'd gone only three blocks before two jacks showed up, running toward her.

"Stop there!" one of them shouted. "You're coming with us!"

They grabbed her, pulling her arms in back of her.

Michi didn't resist, but she shouted out, "I am giving myself up to Propitious Interstellar Fabrication. I demand a meeting with the board. If my demands are not met, the entire stock of Blue-99 will be destroyed!"

"What?" asked the jack who was about to ziptie her hands. "What are you talking about?"

"Just as I said. You want to take me in. Fine. Get your reward. But take me into company headquarters. You will still be the heroes. If you do not, and what I am saying is true, then you'll wish you'd never been born," she said quietly but with as much conviction as possible.

"Bullshit!" the jack said. "Destroy Blue-99? No blooming way."

"If I'm lying, then what do you have to lose? Present me as a prize to the CEO himself. Get noticed. If I am right," and Michi desperately hoped she was right and the worm had gotten through, "then you are still heroes. Either way you win."

"What's she saying about Blue-99?" a voice called out from the crowd.

Many, if not most of the people there probably worked for the company, and anything that damaged one of the main products would affect them all. The two jacks paused to look at each other.

"It wouldn't hurt now, would it?" one asked the other.

"I, uh, well I don't see how it would. Like she says, we still get the reward either way. Let's take her to headquarters and let them sort it all out." He turned to Michi and said, "You got your wish, but you better not try anything, you hear?"

"Lead on," Michi said.

This had been a tricky point. If they had insisted on taking her to jail, she would have had a much more difficult time, and the delay could introduce more variables. Simple and to the point was best.

Two more jacks came running up, but her two captors guarded her like dogs over a bone. They were not going to split the reward with anyone.

The crowd grew as they walked towards downtown. A vehicle came to pick her up, but by that time, there were probably over a thousand people pacing them, a good portion camming the scene. Overhead, a news drone appeared.

There were probably fifty jacks present, and after some discussion, the senior jack decided that walking was just as good.

As they entered Prosperity Square, where Michi's journey really began, five black-uniformed fuckdicks in riot gear blocked their path and demanded that Michi be turned over to them. The one on the end, not saying a word, was Chopra, and Michi thought she could feel his eyes burn into her.

The jacks were having none of it, though, and pushed past the federal officers, escorting Michi up B Street and into One Propitious Interstellar. They moved around the Cornucopia Fountain and to the front doors where a flunky, a high-ranking flunky, but a flunky none the less, awaited her.

The jacks had taken an almost festive air as they brought Michi forward.

"And what is this all about?" the flunky asked.

"I need to see someone higher on the food chain," Michi said with what she hoped was a tone of disdain. "Like the CEO."

The crowd, many who had their PA directional mics trained on her, hooted and hollered at her words.

"I'm afraid you don't have much say here, Miss MacCailín, and you are going to enjoy being our guest once again," he said, his voice dripping venom.

Oh, they picked a good one, Michi thought despite the intense situation.

"I think you had better contact your bosses. Ask them about the Blue-99 in the vault."

This was the key. If the worm hadn't made it, and if they even checked, the algae in the vault would be fine, and she would be back in the hands of the FCDC. If the worm had arrived, but didn't work, she'd be back in custody. But if the worm had functioned as designed, then the algae in the vault, the foundation batch, would be destroyed.

The flunky hesitated, and Michi could see his emotions war with one another. After several moments, he spoke into this throat mic, then came back to an easy stance, feet apart, hands clasped in front of him, the very picture of cool, collected control.

Do they have a school for that, she wondered as she tried to portray the same degree of control.

They waited, staring at each other, Michi matching the flunky's easy smile. Behind them, the crowd was getting restless. It took almost ten minutes, but the flunky put his hand over his ear to cut out the crowd noise. He nodded, said something, then looked up.

"If you will come this way, Miss MacCailín, the CEO will see you now."

The crowd erupted behind them as the people shouted. Michi couldn't tell if they supported her or they thought she was going in to be given her just desserts. She held out her bound hands to the jacks. They looked to the flunky, who nodded. Off came the zipties. Two more jacks, but jacks on steroids and in designer uniforms appeared, and the street jacks muttered, but stepped back. Michi hoped her two jacks would still get their reward.

The four of them walked to the elevator. Before getting in, one of the jacks searched her for weapons. Her bammers and top couldn't hide much, but he was still thorough. He pretty much checked everything, but with a manner that left Michi not feeling violated.

They rode up to the 50th floor, hallowed ground within the company. A woman in another tailored suit awaited them, and without saying a word walked them to the right, down a corridor, and into a conference room with a glass wall, giving a beautiful view of the city. Michi ignored it, instead, turning to the four men sitting at the end of the huge stone table. She recognized David del Solar, the CEO of Propitious Interstellar.

"Just what the hell have you done, young lady?" the man sitting next to the CEO said.

"It's not what I have done that's important; it's what you are going to do to save your precious company," she said as she armed herself for battle.

Chapter 40

Michi got out of the company hover without a word and looked up to the condo where she knew Doug was waiting. She was empty, an emotionless husk. She—no, the people—had won. They had gone up against the most powerful entity on the planet, they had challenged the very Federation, yet somehow, unlike as on Ellison or Fu Sing, they had won. Part of Michi realized that and was amazed. A bigger part of her felt like she had lost.

It hadn't been easy, but as the three roommates had known, the company had no choice. They had to give in if they wanted to survive without damage as a major Federation fabricator. The trick was to make sure whatever the company agreed to would be upheld and there would be no adverse consequences once things settled down.

There had been screaming and threats in the conference rooms. "Traitor" and "saboteur" might have been the least-inciteful names she had been called. When Mallory Yamauguchi, the company CFO had accused her of trying to destroy the company, she had bristled and attacked back.

"It's you who are trying to destroy the company, not me! The company is the lifeblood of the planet, and we need the jobs. My own family made their living servicing the company. We need you, just like you need us. We only want you to follow the charter and treat us, all of us, including Class Fours, as valued partners!" she had shouted, standing up, hands on the table as she leaned into the man, wanting to jump over the table and beat him senseless.

David del Solar had called a recess to let things calm down, telling the others to leave. Alone with Michi, he had asked her just what they wanted. Still fuming, Michi hadn't trusted the CEO's frank demeanor, but had given the brief outline that Doug, Tamara, and she had come up with. It had been based on previous demands from various opposition groups, and it gave only the basics.

He had listened and then invited her into his office. Sitting on his couch, the two of them had communicated, not merely talked.

David listened to the arguments she had prepared, but Michi had also listened to his concerns. She was holding the company hostage, a knife at its throat, but the two of them were calmly, and rationally coming to some sort of middle ground.

Michi had wanted a number of things. Strict adherence to the charter was non-negotiable. She wanted some sort of independent oversight of charter and company policies and action, and that oversight entity had to have real power to enforce adherence. She demanded that Class Four workers have the real ability to pay off their indenture. The three of them had considered demanding an end to the indentured class of worker, but that was ingrained in the Federation, so they retreated back to what they thought they might actually achieve.

David had pointed out that the Class Four program enabled people mired in poverty and hopelessness to get a fresh start, and if the company couldn't get their investment back, there would be no impetus for them to offer people that chance. He hadn't insulted her intelligence by pretending that the company didn't use shady and even illegal methods to keep the indentureds in thrall.

With the jacks so involved with day-to-day living, something had to change. Michi had demanded that the jacks be cut in strength and only have authority on company property. To fill the void, city police forces would be beefed up where they would take care of civil protection. With the company the ultimate power on the planet, Michi had known this would not make a huge difference. The city governments, even the planetary government on Dundee, were all funded by the company, so any enlarged city police force would still be beholden to PI, but at least the symbolism of such a change should be a significant step. To her surprise, David hadn't even argued against the demand.

Despite their surprisingly civilized discussion, she had known the man wouldn't hesitate to crush her as soon as the threat to Blue-99 was over. She had to protect not only herself, but all the people who had risen in protest. This was the tricky part. He had been only talking to her then because with one push of a button, the rest of his precious algae would be gone. If she and Doug followed through and incapacitated the worm, they would be vulnerable.

Michi had told David that she wanted full immunity for any person who had joined the protest as well as the survivors of the attack on the Marines. She also wanted restitution for those killed and injured. Specifically, she named Doug, Tamara, and herself. David had raised his eyes when she mentioned Doug and Tamara, but said nothing. On another personal matter, she had told him she wanted her family's property restored.

One thing she didn't request was immunity for common criminals. Without it, she could be prosecuted for Gerile Fountainhead's death. As far as she knew, though, only Tamara and Cheri knew that she was his killer.

Restitution had been a sticking point. People who were injured during a legal protest was one thing. His security was responsible for protecting the people, after all, so that could work. But attacking the Marines was a different matter, totally illegal, and not even something that the company could address. That was a matter for the Federation, not Propitious Interstellar They had gone back and forth on this for almost 30 minutes before his logic made enough of an impact that Michi had withdrawn the demand.

On his side, David had demanded full cessation of any protests, a full return of the workforce, and most of all, the destruction of the worm. Michi had readily agreed, adding the caveat of protests by people she could control. She couldn't be responsible for every person on the planet, but she had agreed to make another camcording asking for peace. As far as the worm, she had reminded him that she didn't want to destroy the algae, so when they were finished, she would give the order for its destruction. She had also left him, though, with the inference, at least, that a new worm was waiting in the wings should the need arise.

Two hours after the two had started, they had a framework to end the conflict. David had called in for some snacks and told her he would bring in his legal team to write up the agreement.

"We should get a Federation lawyer for that, don't you think?" Michi had asked innocently. "The FCDC would probably be willing to supply one."

Michi had known that David would want his own team writing up an agreement if they got that far. But it would be hard to argue against a Federation lawyer being brought in. She waited for his response. Getting an outside lawyer was probably vital to her survival.

She hadn't had to wait long. With barely a pause, David agreed, with a smile on his face that Michi had to admire as looking natural. David had made a call to the FCDC chief of operations, and a legal team was dispatched. While they waited, and with David's permission, she had called Cheri, outlined the situation, and asked that she and Su come over. To her credit, Cheri hadn't demanded a full explanation but quickly agreed.

Forty-five minutes later, the nitty-gritty had begun. David and Michi had recorded their conversation, outlining the agreement. Michi had thought that pretty clear. But with the company lawyers, Su, two other lawyers Cheri had brought along, and the city attorney there, it had been amazing how so many people could have so many different opinions on what had just been said on the recording. The FCDC lawyer, as chief facilitator, had to make several decisions when the rest of the squabbling lawyers could not come to an agreement.

One key factor, at least for Michi, Doug, and Tamara's safety, was the civil penalty should anything happen to them—and that meant anything. The company lawyers and representatives had screamed that they could not be penalized if Michi had a massive coronary, for example. But as "massive coronaries" could be easily induced by people wishing her harm, Michi was not going to back down.

"You are just going to have to hope that doesn't happen!" she had shouted. "Maybe you should put me on your health maintenance plan!"

It took David stepping in and telling his staff that he accepted the condition before they had been able to move forward.

The civil penalties had been a key to the entire agreement. The law could sometimes be bent, as the company had shown over the years. But a contract was a contract, and if there were a monetary penalty to be assessed if a specified event happened, then the contract would be honored. Huge corporation or individual, the Federation would not take sides.

With that paragraph in place, if anything happened to Doug, Tamara, or Michi once the contract was signed, the company would be hit with huge payments. That was the best Michi could do to protect the three of them.

At 4:10 in the morning, which was amazingly quick for the scope of the agreement, representatives of the union, the mayor, the senior NIP member in jail, and representatives of several other protest and civil groups, had been called in. The Federation administrator had already caught a shuttle from Dundee, and had already arrived, so the Federation was represented as well.

David and Michi had stood together as the contract was read out loud. Everyone present had a copy on their PAs, but the reading was a tradition. After it was finished, Michi had stepped forward.

She had looked down at the paper copy. It hadn't seemed like much. What had happened to her dreams of throwing the company, throwing the Federation off of Kakurega, of full independence? Had she sold out? All this really required was that Propitious Interstellar abide by the existing charter. Everything else was window dressing.

Well, it's the best that I can do, she thought as she signed her name and looked into the retinal scanning beam.

David hadn't hesitated but signed as well. Then the long string of ancillary signatories came forward. With David and Michi's signatures, the contract was in effect. However, as others outside of the company were affected, they had to sign as well to bind their organizations to the terms. The union vice-chairman had balked, saying he wanted to bring the agreement back and study it, but after a quick conference with several other people there, he changed his mind and signed.

Michi and David had shaken hands for the camcorders, and it was done despite the huge odds against them. Fu Sing, and even Ellison had been crushed, but somehow, they had averted that fate and gained some benefit, if not outright won.

Michi asked for a PA, and connecting to Doug's disposable PA, and after only a slight hesitation, she had given the code words to stand down the worm.

"Our Blue-99 is safe now?" David had asked, trying to sound calm even if Michi could hear the stressors in his voice.

"Safe and sound," she had assured him.

Michi had been rushed to a backdrop that had been erected, and with David, the mayor, and the Federation administrator standing behind her, had recorded her pleas for the protests to stop and for people to get on with their lives. She never used the word "won," but she assured people that the company had seen the righteousness of their concerns and had agreed to address them.

As soon as she was done and the recording stopped, David had actually shaken her hand.

"I can't say I'm happy that this happened, but it is what it is," he had said.

"*Arinomamade,*" Michi said quietly.

"Yes, *arinomamade,*" he had said, surprising Michi that he knew what the word meant. "But now we have to move forward. If I want to meet with you, I trust you would be willing?"

For maybe the first time during the night, Michi had been surprised. He wanted to work with her? He was the CEO of Propitious Interstellar, and she had just hurt them. She was his enemy, right? And now, he might want to work together?

What game is he playing now? she had wondered.

She had cautiously agreed to meet if needed. He had thanked her and told her he had a car for her to take her to where she wanted. Once again, she had hesitated, unsure if she could trust him. But the contract had been signed. She had agreed and was whisked to the condo.

She wasn't sure how she was going to tell Doug. She wanted to delay the inevitable, so she took the stairs instead of the elevator. She started to, at least. The emotional toll of the last day and night had affected her body, too. Michi had to stop on the fifth floor and take the elevator the rest of the way up.

She hadn't opened the door yet when Doug burst out and grabbed her in a bear hug. She clung to him, mindless of his excitement.

"We did it, Michi! I never actually thought we would win, but this is brills! I'm, I'm, I don't know what I am, but it's pretty freaking great!" he shouted, pulling her around in a circle.

She just clung to him, her tears falling unnoticed onto his shoulder.

"Tamara's going to be ready to party!" he said, drawing out the "paaarteee!"

"Doug, listen to me!"

"Michi-baby, I'll listen to anything you've got. Give me all the details! Was del Solar crushed?"

She grabbed Doug and pushed him back to arms' length. He noted something in her eyes, and he stopped hopping up and down.

"Tamara's not coming," she said somberly.

"What do you mean? She's going to be late?" he asked uncertainly.

"She's dead, Doug! She was killed by the jacks trying to get away after infecting the system."

Doug, with a look of shock on his face, slowly dropped to sit on the floor. "No," was all he said.

Just before Michi left the 50th floor of One Propitious Interstellar, Virag Chopra had approached her, saying, "Sorry about your friend, Miss Veal," his expression indicating anything other than sorrow.

"Sorry for what?" she'd asked, a feeling of dread coming over her.

"Oh, you hadn't heard? Maybe I'd better wait . . ."

She had grabbed him by the collar and yanked him forward until their faces were centimeters apart.

"If you know something, tell me now," she had hissed.

"Certainly, Miss MacCailín, if you insist. It seems as if your friend was caught inserting something into the organics control system. She tried to run, and, unfortunately, the company security shot and killed her," he had said, a smile on his face.

Michi had let go of him in shock. They had won and the company lost! How had anything happened to Tamara! As it begun to register, she had let out a primal scream and run back to the conference room.

"You killed her!" she had shouted as she rushed David.

Two office jacks stepped up and stopped her. She struggled to reach the CEO, but the two men, without hurting her, simply held her back.

"Tamara Veal is dead, and that bastard killed her! I want Propitious Interstellar crushed! I want them to pay their penalty!" she yelled at the FCDC lawyer who was still there but gathering up his belongings.

"And when did his happen, Miss?" he asked.

"At her lab. When she infected the system. They just shot her down!"

"So this was not within the last 45 minutes?" he asked without much emotion.

"I told you, it was yesterday afternoon!" Michi told him.

"Then, I'm afraid that Propitious Interstellar was not covered by the contract at the time, so there is nothing they are required to do. If you believe the company is liable for her death above and beyond this contract, I suggest you contact the city attorney," he said, picking up his briefcase and walking past her to leave.

"You knew," she accused David. "You knew the entire time we were negotiating."

"We had guessed, but until you gave me her name, no, we weren't sure. I doubt that you are going to believe me, but I am sorry about Miss Veal. I couldn't bring that up, though, while we were trying to come to a solution. I was afraid you would blow up and order your friend to destroy the rest of the strain."

Michi had glared at the man, vowing revenge. But it wasn't going to happen then and there. With an utmost display of control, she had pulled herself together and without a word, turned and left the building and got into the waiting hover.

Now, with Doug sitting in front of her, she sank to the floor as well. Both friends reached for each other as the tears broke loose, and all the stress of the last few days and the grief of their loss took over.

Her PA started ringing, but she ignored it. She had lost her fiancé, she had lost her best friend, and at the moment, she thought that cost was too high. Michi had given her all, and that was too much.

The people of Kakurega—all of them, not just the employees of the company—had won. Things would be better. But to those left behind, to those who had lost loved ones in the attack, to those who had lost property, to the family of Gerile Fountainhead, that innocent jack she had killed in that dark alley, was it all worth it?

Michi just didn't know.

Epilogue

Three years later . . .

"Congratualtions, Madame Mayor," Doug said, handing her another glass of champagne.

"Not yet, Doug. I won't be sworn in for another month, but yeah, baby, this is some night, huh? And without you managing my campaign, it never would have happened, so thanks!" she said, pulling him in for a sloppy kiss on his cheek.

"It wasn't hard, Michi. You've still got your hero status going strong, and with Lowery putting his foot up his ass so many times, it wasn't hard."

"Still, candidates just don't get elected on corporate worlds when the company is against them," she reminded him. "Hey, enough of shop talk. We've had enough of that for the last six months. Missy is over there at the punch bowl waiting for you. Go give your wife a kiss and take her home. Give Tammy a kiss for me, too."

Doug looked over to his wife who blew him a kiss. "You know, she would have been proud of you today."

"Yes, I think she would have, despite her lack of respect for authority," she agreed, knowing he was speaking of their Tamara, not the daughter he named after her.

He stood there with her a moment, a sphere of silence amidst the cacophony of her campaign headquarters' celebration.

"*Arinomamade,*" he said quietly, the word having become their private motto, something that bound them together.

"Arinomamade, Doug. Now get out of here. I don't want to see you until Friday at the earliest. Go be with your family."

Doug turned to give her a hug and kiss on the cheek. He wandered over to his wife and bent her over backwards, giving her a much different sort of kiss, one that promised much more as soon as they got home. Michi had to laugh. Her Dougie had changed so much from the geeky guy who Cheri had sent over back before this journey began. It may not have been so long on the calendar, but it was a lifetime ago.

Her PA buzzed, and Michi looked down at it curiously. Not many people had the connect code, and all of them had already called to congratulate her. She didn't recognize the code and was about to cut the connection, but curiosity overcame her. She slipped the bud in her ear and hit the connect.

"Madame Mayor-elect, I just wanted to offer you my congratulations," the voice said, the screen blank.

Without a camvid, she had to place the voice, and it took a few moments. "David del Solar?" she asked.

"The one and only," the Propitious Interstellar CEO said with a laugh.

"I didn't expect your call," Michi said with all candor.

Michi and David had met several times over the ensuing years, both in his office and at the anniversaries of the signing of the "People's Compact," as the contract had been named.

The company had twisted and turned the creation of the contract into something so far from the truth that is was awe-inspiring. The contract itself was still inviolate, but the company PR division had created a version of what happened that beggared belief. According to the new version of history, the company had instigated the reforms once their workers' unhappiness had been brought to their attention. It had been the company that had fought to get the Marines off their planet, and once that was done, they had addressed making life better for everyone, employee or not. On each anniversary of the signing, there was a memorial service for those fallen (and those numbers had been adjusted quite a bit downwards) and the names of all Class Fours who had paid off their indenture that year were posted. The company sponsored parties that were well-attended.

Michi had put aside her vow for revenge for Tamara. David hadn't had a direct hand in it. All he had done was withhold that information during the negotiations, and that probably had been smart. Michi didn't know herself what she might have done if she had found out while Doug could still destroy the remaining Blue-99.

Still, even if they weren't exactly enemies, she had just defeated the company-sponsored candidate.

"I didn't want to intrude on your celebrations, but I thought a call would be appropriate."

"A conciliatory call? I didn't know that was in you, David."

"Well, I wouldn't call this conciliatory," he said.

"Uh, David, have you been watching the newsfeeds? I just kicked your candidate's ass."

"I'm very aware of that. And I congratulate you, even if we may not have put up the best candidate."

"Oh, shite, David. Don't feed me that. You contributed to his campaign. You endorsed him. What about all your dirty tricks?"

"Michiko, you're a smart woman. Do you really think we would put up a pompous ass like Lowery if we wanted him to win. If *I* wanted him to win?"

"What are you saying?"

"Put it together. I couldn't very well put the company's support behind the woman who brought the company to its knees. So if I could put up someone unelectable, what would that do? I could show that I tried to get someone else elected. All the dirty tricks were not very effective, were they? No, because you could address each one, and no matter what else, the Federation would make sure the actual votes made would be counted. There's no tampering with the ballots allowed."

"Nice story. But why should I believe this fairy tale?" she asked, not buying it.

"Because Lowery was so bad. Because we leaked the story about his past psychological treatments. And most of all because I want you to be mayor."

"Once again, why?"

"Since you forced us into the contract, our business has never been better. You've seen our stocks. We're up almost 180% since then. Our "good for the people" persona is working. That caught me by surprise, I will admit, but the numbers are there. With increased sales and better worker relations, we're on a role. And with you as mayor of Tay Station, I think we can work together."

"I'm only going to be the mayor. I won't hold sway anywhere else."

"What about governor?" he asked.

"Don't get ahead of yourself. Let me be sworn in, first. Besides, I don't work for you."

"I didn't say work 'for' me. I said 'with' me."

"OK, let me rephrase that. I did not get elected to make things easier for the company. I will not do its bidding," she told him.

"Will you work for what is good for the city?" he asked.

"Of course."

"Then that's all I can ask for. And if what's good for the city is good for the company, then we all win. Look, I didn't plan on getting into it now. I was going to invite you to the board dining room for a dinner next week. I'm still going to do that so you can meet my team, but until then, just think about it, OK?"

"I'll think about anything that will help me do my job."

"That's all I can ask for. It's a new galaxy, and I hope we can figure out how to make it work. Take care, and one again, congratulations."

He cut off his side, and Michi stared at the blank PA.

That was one weird call, she thought.

She looked up at the room, where the die-hard revelers were still partying. They had worked hard for her. Well maybe not so much for her as for what Michi stood for: a new beginning. She was not corporate. She was an outsider.

Michi was also smart enough to know that if the company fought her, she would be stymied in whatever she tried to accomplish. Maybe getting in bed with the devil would allow her to do some good. She'd done some pretty nasty things in the past for that elusive "greater good," so why not consider David's offer?

"Madame Mayor! Come here for a drink!" one of her young volunteers, one she was ashamed to admit she didn't even recognize, called out from a group of about five very happy people.

She still had the champagne that Doug had given her, so she walked over to join them, a real smile, not a forced one on her face.

"Thank you for all your help," she said to their cheers. "It's only just begun, though. This was the easy part, and now comes the real job. *We* were elected to make a change, and by St Chuck's hairy butt, we're going to do it!"

Thank you for reading *Rebel*. If you liked it, please feel free to leave a review of the book on Amazon.

Other Books by Jonathan Brazee

Fiction

The Return of the Marines Trilogy

The Few

The Proud

The Marines

The Al Anbar Chronicles: First Marine Expeditionary Force--Iraq

Prisoner of Fallujah

Combat Corpsman

Sniper

The United Federation Marine Corps

Recruit

Sergeant

Lieutenant

Werewolf of Marines: Semper Lycanus

(Book 2: Coming February, 2015

To The Shores of Tripoli

Wererat

Darwin's Quest: The Search for the Ultimate Survivor

Venus: A Paleolithic Short Story

Nonfiction

Exercise for a Longer Life

Author Website
http://www.returnofthemarines.com

20661942R00124

Made in the USA
San Bernardino, CA
18 April 2015